TWENTY-FIVE YEARS

TWENTY-FIVE YEARS

MICHAEL BERQUIST

Michael K. Berquist

Published in the United States.

IngramSpark, LightningSource, and Ingram Content Group
are trademarks of their respective companies.

Cover design by Mary C. Esch
Author Photo by Erin Dennison

ISBN 979-8-218-07332-9 (Paperback)
ISBN 979-8-218-10787-1 (eBook)
Library of Congress Control Number 2022921722

CONTENTS

To my first, my last, Colleen.

FROM THE AUTHOR

The inspiration for writing this book stems from my simple desire to know and understand my father, Kenneth Berquist, in a more meaningful way. I am grateful for my life, and I am thankful for the lessons I have learned. I do not consider myself special in any way. I am the offspring of simple working-class parents from the "Greatest Generation."

Like millions of other children born between 1946 and 1964, I lost my father before I got to know him as more than just my dad. I never got the chance to ask Dad about the war. I never got the chance to ask Dad about his childhood, what it was like growing up in the 1920s and the 1930s. My Dad was simply the person who administered stern and swift punishment for the misdeeds of my youth.

I was blessed with a slew of family photographs. The photos held the written words of my Aunt Donna. Donna is Dad's sister. The hand-annotated photos with names, dates, and places only helped to confirm in my mind that I would be able to stitch together a story. A few of these photos only added to the mystery of my Dad, confounded and caused more research.

In an old and smelly tin about the size of a shoebox, I found a small, red leather-bound address book. It had a musty smell. As I began to read the alphabetical list of addresses within, I soon discovered I was reading Dad's war diary.

For some reason I will never know, the pages A through H had been torn haphazardly from the address book. Jagged, crispy, vintage yellowing paper edges protruded from the stitched binding of the little red book. What was written on these discarded pages? The names and addresses began on the J page with some names familiar to me. In the middle of the O page, it began, "January 29, 1944." Several pages of O and P proceeded, intermixed with addresses and a story.

The diary continued through the P section of the address book, intermixed further with names and addresses. Then, suddenly, in sections Q, R, S, T, and U—except for a few address book entries—the diary ended. One page flip further into the U section and the diary again emerged, with a twist. It was the beginning of the diary, buried deep inside the pages of the address book. Dad wrote, "I went into the Navy on July 27, 1942."

Why would Dad have started there? Again, with just a handful of addresses, the diary entries were made. It was a story that started in the middle and concluded with the beginning.

Inside the back cover—just two pages—were a couple more addresses but also, most importantly, birth dates. There were Dad's good friends: Kenny Snyder, May 11; Bob Doyle, June 24; Duds Hassell, March 14; and Thelma, August 26. My grandparents, Dad's parents, Louise and Mick, were also noted as January 17 and February 18. The address book absolutely belonged to my dad. There, on the inside front cover, in cursive, was "Kenneth E. Berquist, July 20, 1942," undeniably written in Dad's handwriting.

The discarded pages? Had Dad written something top secret? During World War II, sailors were admonished, "Don't write anything down. If you are captured, the Japs will use what you have written against you, or worse, the US." The discarded pages could have been simply notes, which maybe Dad had jotted down during navy training classes? Who was Thelma? Thelma was noteworthy enough to deserve an annotation of her birthday. We will never know Thelma, or Duds Hassell for that matter.

The hinged lid of the box initially squeaked when opened. But, over the days of opening and closing, the hinge squeak stopped. A hole in the front of the box had held a locking latch at one time that disappeared decades ago. The box was painted black on the inside and a rich orangey-yellow on the outside, undoubtedly lead-based paint from the 1920s, now chipped and rusty. The box collected and then held a trove of memorabilia from Dad's life.

I have a few memories of my dad, which are interwoven in the story. These memories help further define my dad. I am not envious of those who benefitted from having their dads around while they grew into adulthood. Consider yourself lucky. I have had a tremendously wonderful life. Dad's passing precipitated a series of events that would have not otherwise occurred. Wonderful and unpredictable changes in my life placed me in exactly the right place at the right time. Because of fate, I am now and will forever be blessed. Irony.

I strived to be historically accurate with my storytelling, but one must bear in mind, the story is fiction and it is based on real events.

I love you, Dad.

It is important you know this story about an event that occurred during Kenneth's childhood. It was an event that shaped his psychological makeup for life. This event was a contributing factor in Kenneth being held back at school to repeat fourth grade. Nineteen twenty-nine and nineteen thirty were not good years for Kenneth.

Kenneth's oldest sister, Elsie, was born on October 12, 1912. Elsie was pregnant in 1929, shortly before her high school graduation. She was not yet eighteen years old when she became pregnant. Elsie had a bit of a reputation amongst family—and others—as a "wild child."

During the Depression, had finances been different, Elsie may have been sent off to some country seclusion during the nine months. But Elsie was held a figurative hostage in her own home. In a hurry-up (shotgun-style) wedding, she married Warren Kenneth Hill on June 22, 1929. Despite Elsie's pregnancy, Warren was seldom around and was, in general, not well liked by the Berquist family. Tolerated is the best way to say it.

It was a difficult pregnancy and an even more difficult birth for Elsie. Bedridden for most of the nine months, she would never be able to get pregnant again. She delivered a healthy baby boy while sprawled on the kitchen table in front of her parents, sister Donna, and two brothers, Richard and Kenneth.

James Warren Hill was born on February 18, 1930. The scene, the sights and sounds, is easy to imagine. Kenneth was traumatized from watching and listening to his sister Elsie during labor and childbirth. This terror stuck with Kenneth throughout his life. Berquist family lore claimed the kids were forced to watch and listen to what happened as a "lesson," imposed on them by their parents. Sex before marriage was a sin in the eyes of God. Elsie's marriage to Warren only lasted long enough to legitimize James's birth. Elsie and Warren lived for a brief time out of the sphere of the Berquist household, but within a year of James's birth, Elsie was back at home with her parents, raising her son as a single parent.

Elsie's son, James, would lead a life loved by his family. Kenneth's parents, Mick and Louise, acted as parents to yet another baby in the house. They loved James. Despite the fact that James was Kenneth's nephew, the two of them grew up together in the same house as brothers. James idealized his young uncle.

Elsie was briefly married to Charles A. Stuck in the late 1930s and early 1940s. Elsie and James moved to the Los Angeles, California, area with Charles so Charles could work as a bartender in a family business there. Elsie's second marriage only lasted a few short years. Kenneth visited Elsie and James in Ventura, California, while on leave from the navy during the Christmas and New Year season in 1943–44.

James enlisted in the army in 1947 at the age of seventeen and served in the Korean War. James was making a career of the army. James's life and his relationship with family took a dramatic turn when he returned from Korea with a Japanese wife. The wounds of World War II were still fresh in 1953. James had developed terrible anger-management problems during his time in the army, and now he was an alcoholic. When James came home drunk, he was violent. Kenneth would intervene between James and his wife, Sumi, and their three children into the early 1960s. Kenneth did all he could to keep the peace until James and his family moved to Newport News, Virginia, with the army.

Elsie moved back to Burlington after James entered the army. She married Richard Mack on June 25, 1950. The third time was the trick, and Elsie's marriage to Richard endured until her death on January 11, 1979. Elsie had a massive heart attack and died while waiting in her doctor's office for her appointment to begin.

James arrived at his home in his car. He exited his car on the drive-way. He manually opened the garage door. He got back into his car. He drove his car into the garage. He exited his car again. He manually closed the garage door and, again, got back into his car. His Virginia Death Certificate states, "carbon monoxide asphyxiation complicated by alcoholism." The certificate further states that his body was "found in a running vehicle inside a closed garage." His mother Elsie is quoted in a newspaper article saying, "James died in a car crash." Leaving his grieving wife Sumi and three young children, Master Sargent James W. Hill died on May 27, 1966, at the age of thirty-six. James is interred near his mother at Aspen Grove Cemetery in Burlington.

CHAPTER 1

School Days

In 1910, Elvin Herbert (Mick) and Louise Dorothy (Lou) Berquist lived with her German-born parents, Louise A. Praetz and August H. Schmicker, at 1405 South Twelfth Street in Burlington.

1405 South 12th Street, Burlington, Iowa
Photo taken by Michael Berquist, May 7, 2019

Throughout Elvin's childhood and early school years, he was only called Elvin. It was not until he met and started courting Louise Schmicker that the nickname "Mick" evolved from mostly his Swedish friends who teased him about marrying a German. When Elvin's friends found out the name Schmicker meant "a person who makes whips or a person who whips," they were driven to call Elvin "whipped." It was not long after that the shortened nickname Mick evolved from the Schmicker last name. Louise thought it was cute. Elvin preferred being called Mick, as Elvin was such an Old World name. Mick stuck with Elvin for the rest of his life.

Within the next decade, Mick's family grew, and they had moved into their own home at 1314 South Twelfth Street. This house was Kenneth's first home.

1314 South 12th Street, Burlington, Iowa
Photo taken by Michael Berquist, May 7, 2019

Kenneth was born the youngest of four to his Swedish/German-descent parents on October 19, 1919, in Burlington.

Kenneth Elvin Berquist, circa 1920
Berquist Family Photograph

Kenneth's parents were both born in Burlington to immigrant parents. Kenneth's paternal grandparents, Matilda Jonsdotter and Per Olaf Bergqvist, from the area around Fellingsbro and Kopparberg, Sweden, barely spoke English. Both died before Kenneth was born. Maternal grandparents Louise A. Praetz and August H. Schmicker, from the area around Gardelegen and Mieste, Germany, spoke English much better and were active participants in Kenneth's early life. August died in the fall after Kenneth graduated from high school. Louise passed away while Kenneth was in the navy. Kenneth was saddened by the death of his grandmother and not being able to come to her funeral.

August H. and Louise A. Schmicker, Mick
Berquist in background by car, circa 1920
Berquist Family Photograph

This picture provides good evidence the Berquists were living at 2024 Summer Street at Christmas 1921. The photograph shows the back porch of the house on Summer Street. The exposed foundation and clapboard siding are dead giveaways this is the house on Summer Street.

Dad (Mick Berquist) with Kenneth, Elsie, and Richard standing in the backyard of 2024 Summer Street, Burlington, Iowa "First Christmas in new house" circa 1921
Photo taken by: Donna Berquist, Berquist Family Photograph

One of the significant additions to Burlington was the Southeast Iowa Regional Airport. The airport property started two blocks south of the Berquist home. The airport terminal address would be on Summer Street. The airport opened in 1929 and began commercial airline service in 1931. The airport is a source of pride for Burlington residents. Expansion and improvements have continued since its opening. The Burlington Airport offered connecting air flights to St. Louis, Kansas City, Chicago, and Moline, Illinois, starting in 1931. In the late 1930s, flying to distant places grabbed the attention of many young people in Burlington. Gradually, the thought of traveling on a global basis entered the imagination of many, and careers in the air travel industry called. Braniff Airways brought service there in 1944. The girls who fancied themselves flight attendants were dreaming of life outside Burlington.

At 1,600 square feet, the new house had four bedrooms and a kitchen Kenneth's mother loved as well as a vast living room and dining room. Upstairs, his parents had a bedroom. His sisters, Elsie and Donna, each had a bedroom. He and his brother Dick shared a bedroom. The house was spartan, but it had all the modern conveniences of the time. The house had a porch in the front and a porch on the back. And it had a full basement. Kenneth's parents were proud of their new home.

South facade of 2024 Summer Street, Burlington, Iowa showing front and back porches, box window is the dining room, circa 1921
Berquist Family Photograph

President Warren Harding died in office in August 1923. Harding's vice president, Calvin Coolidge, finished Harding's four-year presidential term and was then elected to a second term, which ran until March 1929. Ex-President Woodrow Wilson passed away in February 1924.

Perkins Elementary School at the corner of Dodge and Summer Streets opened in 1920. It would be Kenneth's first school.

Charles Elliott Perkins Elementary School, Burlington, Iowa
Modified photo from the public domain

The timing of Kenneth's birth in October meant he would be too young to start school in September 1924. Kenneth was four years old in September 1924. He would have to wait until 1925, when he was fully five years old, to start school. This delay ended up making Kenneth one of the oldest kids in his kindergarten class in 1925. Kenneth turned six just one month after the school year started. Elsie was seven years older. She was in fifth grade. Donna was five years older. She was in fourth grade. Richard (Dick) was three years older. He was in third grade. All the Berquist kids went to Perkins Elementary School for at least part of their elementary education. Elsie, Donna, and Dick started at Corse Elementary School at 711 South Leebrick Street. When Mick and Louise built the house on Summer Street, the Berquist kids all switched to Perkins after the new school opened in 1920.

Kenneth's mom, Louise, shuttled Kenneth and sometimes the Karver daughters back and forth to school for the first two years. The Karvers were friends of the Berquists and lived nearby. Carpooling responsibility fell onto Donna's shoulders and then Dick's. Kenneth was easily getting himself to and from school by the time Dick finished Perkins.

There are no records of Kenneth's kindergarten and first-grade academic progress, but when he finished second grade, the trends had formed. Kenneth was a B, C, and D student. He missed eight and a half days of school, and he struggled with reading. The Karvers moved to Gary, Indiana, during the summer of 1928. Childhood friends had moved away. Third grade was about the same for Kenneth. He was a B, C, and D student. He missed three days of school and was still struggling with reading and now arithmetic. In third grade, he was walking or riding his bike to school with his brother, Dick. And as he grew older and more comfortable with his independence, he could take the route on his own.

The events at home with his sister Elsie served to complicate Kenneth's fourth-grade year. Kenneth's teachers also taught Elsie, and they were all familiar with what Kenneth was going through at home. Gossip traveled quickly in small Burlington in those days, and Kenneth's grade-school teachers understood the difficulties he was going through.

Kenneth's grades ran the scale from A to F. He had perfect attendance. The one A came in spelling. Unfortunately, he flunked the more important arithmetic, apparently because of incomplete work. One teacher noted Kenneth's "promotion to the fifth-grade" was "in peril." Despite the teachers sympathizing with Kenneth's predicament at home, they had no choice and held him responsible for minimum levels of achievement to be promoted to fifth grade. Kenneth had to repeat fourth grade. Life events were terrible for Kenneth in 1929 and 1930.

The Berquists slipped through the 1930 federal census, but Kenneth's parents remained at 2024 Summer Street until Mick's death in 1968. The theory was, the census taker had goofed, or no one was at home on the day the census taker knocked on the door. The airport construction could have interfered. Then again, James Hill was born in February 1930, and when the census was taken in April, it was topsy-turvy in the Mick Berquist household.

President Calvin Coolidge's presidency ended in March 1929 with his vice president, Herbert Hoover, winning the nomination and election. Calvin Coolidge passed away in January 1933. Hoover served as president until March 1933.

Kenneth turned eleven in 1930, fully eighteen months older than his classmates in fifth grade. His grades stabilized, and he was a B, C, and D student. He missed six days of school and was still struggling with arithmetic. Reading had improved, but now it was geography that showed incomplete work. Nonetheless, Kenneth made it into sixth grade. He was twelve now.

The turmoil at home with a new baby in the house continued the next two years. Elsie's son James's needs superseded many decisions, and as a result, Kenneth missed several school days. In sixth grade, he continued as a B, C, and D student. He missed ten and a half days of school. There were no "notes" from his teachers, though, and with the apparent sympathy, Kenneth would be in junior high school for the next school year. Kenneth was glad to be out of grade school and looked forward to a fresh start at Horace Mann Junior High School.

Horace Mann Junior High School at 811 White Street was another half mile north of Perkins Elementary.

Horace Mann Junior High School, Burlington, Iowa
Photo courtesy of Mort Gaines Photography, Fairfield, Iowa

By the time Kenneth was in seventh grade, he was exploring a significant distance from his home on foot and on his bike. Getting back and forth to junior high was easy for him.

Kenneth loved junior high because classes would be a more hands-on type of learning, which he excelled at, plus there were now sports. Kenneth turned fourteen within a month of starting seventh grade. A lot of the kids he had gone to Perkins with also went to Horace Mann, and there were a few unfamiliar faces.

Herbert Hoover's presidency ended in March 1933. Since the end of Woodrow Wilson's presidency in 1921, a Republican president had run the country. Hoover had fallen out of favor with his home state of Iowa. With Hoover and the Republican party in general blamed for the Depression, Democrat Franklin Roosevelt easily won the presidency. Voters had had enough.

Seventh grade (1933–34) resulted in C's and D's. Kenneth missed two days of school. He struggled with math. Vocational courses, using his hands, were where he shined and received his best grades. In eighth grade (1934–35), he missed seven days of school. Grades improved ever so slightly. He raised his math grade from a D to a C during the school year. In ninth grade (1935–36), the B's, C's, and D's continued. He had much better attendance, only missing two days. The unwelcome news was, he was given D's in geography, history, and math.

Kenneth's Horace Mann Junior High School Varsity "Letters", circa
1936
Berquist Family Possession

He did not fail any classes, and he was a star athlete in junior high. Senior high school was in his sights at the end of the 1936 school year. His parents loved him, but they did take a deep sigh of relief when the report card came home.

Kenneth wrote on the front of the photo, "Taken after school. The first picture in the paper."

Back row, left to right: Bob Jamieson, Dale Stewart, Alfred Wiley, Carl Van Etten, Alvin Walters, and Coach R. H. Pemble.
Front row, left to right: Dick Fry, Dwight Malonee, Kenneth Berquist, Bob Milliman, and Paul Hyter.

Horace Mann Junior High School basketball team, Kenneth #6 middle front row, 1936
Berquist Family newspaper clipping

The Burlington newspaper ran the photo as well. Kenneth finished at Horace Mann in 1936.

Independent School District
OF THE
City of Burlington, Iowa

TO WHOM IT

MAY CONCERN

This Certifies, That _Kenneth Berquist_ has completed the course of study perscribed by the Board of Education for the Junior High Schools of the Burlington Independent School District, and is entitled to this

Certificate of Admission to the Senior High School

Principal

Burlington, Iowa, _June 5,_ 1936

Superintendent

Kenneth's junior high school diploma, June 5, 1936
Berquist Family Document

Kenneth's junior high school graduation portrait, 1936
Berquist Family Photograph

Newspaper comics, radio, movies on Saturday afternoon, and his friends would shape Kenneth's desires, feelings, and choices during his life.

Burlington senior high was yet another mile north of Horace Mann, and walking the two miles to high school was not preferable, but it was possible.

Burlington Senior High School and Junior College, Burlington, Iowa, circa 2006
Modified photo from the public domain

Kenneth could ride his bike, but the primary mode of transportation to high school was by the bus or by car. Dick and Donna were both through high school, and Elsie had moved to California by the time Kenneth graduated from high school, so he was on his own. Opened in 1864, Burlington High School served as Apollo Middle School and then an alternative high school. The building went unoccupied in 1996.

Kenneth paid no heed to the other sex through junior high school. He focused more on sports—football, for instance—and his friends. He liked girls. They were fine. He was shy, and the experience with his sister Elsie giving birth to James at home made him avoid girls. The girls, however, watched Kenneth.

He was in high school now, and the 1936–37 school year, tenth grade, had started. Burlington High School was a big school with lots of kids. Kenneth was slightly overwhelmed at first, but with the coming weeks, he would manage to fit in, finding his place among the athletes of the school. Tenth grade turned out to be a good year for Kenneth. He was a B-C student. He loved his teachers and his classes. He received the B in gym. He loved the mechanical drawing class but only earned a C for the year—he still enjoyed the hands-on learning. He had perfect attendance for the school year.

In 1937, the Berquists' household phone was upgraded to a rotary-dial type of phone, which sat on a low table in the hallway between the kitchen and the front door. It was on an exchange and still connected by a switchboard but was a considerable improvement over the previous phone. Their telephone number was 1544M.

All those years before, the Berquists had been simply a name and address in the city directory. Now there was a phone number to go along with the other information. It was terrific having a phone. They could call work. They could call a store. But it took another year, or a little longer, for all his friends to get this new type of phone in their homes. Having a phone was also a curse, as parents received phone calls the kids would prefer they had not gotten.

Kenneth could now talk to Billy Karver over in Indiana anytime he wanted. For Kenneth, talking on the phone was a whole lot easier than writing letters. It was always great talking to Billy on the phone. They caught up on a regular basis, letting each other know what plans they had made for the coming weeks. Billy had many relatives on her mother's side of the family still living in Burlington, so Billy came to Burlington many times between 1927 and 1943. She and Kenneth never missed a chance to get together.

Kenneth enjoyed the funny pages in the newspaper and liked *Abbie an' Slats*, *Dixie Dugan*, and *Li'l Abner*. Kenneth saved a few comic strips in his newspaper clippings. The cartoon girls would explain some of the reasons why Billy and then, later, Irene, Bernice, and Jane were attractive to him.

The eleventh-grade year was a mixed bag of success and not so much success. Kenneth earned B's in gym and printing classes and D's in typing, English, and biology. The good news was, he only missed one day of school. The other good news, basketball and football. Kenneth loved sports, and it showed. He was junior varsity both sophomore and junior years, and he was regularly chosen to play in senior varsity games —particularly football—during eleventh grade.

Kenneth was eighteen years old in this photo.

MAKE FIRST APPEARANCE ON HOME FIELD.

Ken. -18- Friday, September 30, 1938

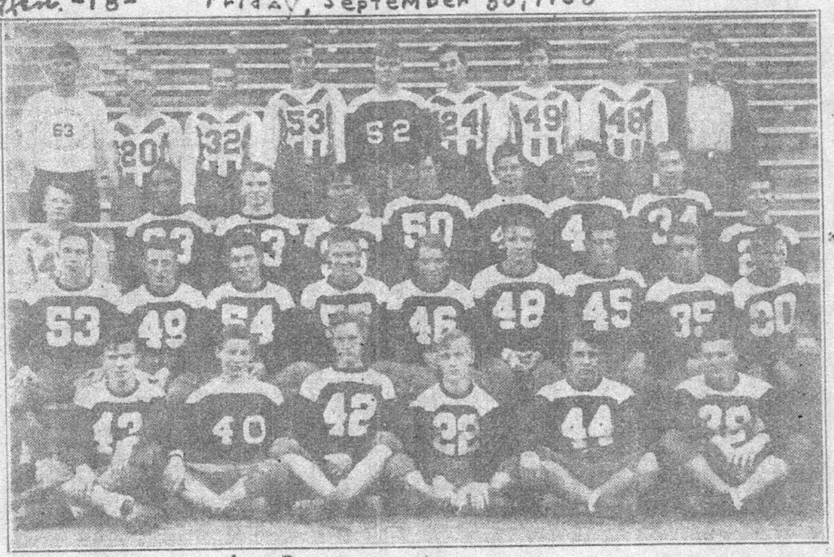

6—0

Burlington high school football team, picked from the members of the varsity squad pictured here, will play Washington, Ia., high school at the stadium here tonight. The game will be the third of the season for the Grayhounds but their first on the stadium gridiron. Squad members, as they are lined up in the picture, are:

Front row, left to right—Wayne Jeglum, Kennth Keever, Robert Welch, Howard Sisco, Don Griffith and Senn.

Second row—Ed Sessions, Paul Parry, Paul Hoschek, Capt. Carl Van Etten, Leroy Timmerman, Alvin Walters, Pierce Giffin, Paul Bloomberg and James Mennen.

Third row—Dick Fry, Sid Saunders, Harold Hogberg, Kenneth Berquist, Robert Rothlauf, Dick Glantz, Carl Brissey, Edsel Schweizer, and Norman Mauthe.

Back row—Coach Harold Tackleson, Roger Hansen, Arnold Wieman, Lawrence McColloch, George Zaiser, Dick Barnes, Albert Broeg, Warren Gerdom and William (Feather) Rundorff, student manager.

Kenneth #36 middle third row, 11th grade varsity high school football team

Burlington newspaper clipping, September 30, 1938 Berquist Family

In three more weeks, he would be nineteen. The newspaper clipping from the Burlington *Hawk Eye* newspaper speaks of the gridiron, which is Bracewell Stadium, so named for Burlington High School Superintendent R.H. Bracewell. The venue was the first high school football stadium in the nation (1929) to have lights on the field for nighttime play. Bracewell was also instrumental in getting Burlington Junior College up and running in 1919. The junior college shared space with the high school.

In 1937, Kenneth took his first job working for the National Tea Company at 420 Jefferson Street in downtown Burlington. National Tea was based in Chicago and was, for all intents, a grocery store. He was a clerk, but his duties consisted of sweeping and cleaning. During the school year, he could walk or bike to work. And occasionally in harsh weather and sometimes during summer vacation, his dad or brother, Dick, would give him a ride to work from home. The best part was, the clerk job paid twenty-five cents per hour. His pay each week went a long way, and he could stash some away for a rainy day. Saving made his mom and dad happy.

Kenneth had earned money before in the past by shoveling snow in the winter and mowing grass in the summer. He delivered the newspaper. He also did odd jobs, like painting fences for neighbors. But all this money came in sporadically. At the clerk job, the money came in regularly, like clockwork, each week. It did not take long and Kenneth was able to buy his first car—a used car, but it was a car, and even more, it meant freedom. No more bus riding, asking his brother or dad for rides. He had his car now.

The car also meant he would have the added responsibility of driving his mom around and running errands for her. It was a happy exchange for Kenneth. A vehicle would improve nights and weekends now. Going to the movies on Saturday and running around with his friends was going to be great.

Kenneth only managed to get in trouble with his dad over the car a few times—shirking house chores was the most significant infraction. It did not take long for Kenneth to understand the car was not a priority in his mom and dad's view. The car and the freedom it offered were essential, and he quickly adapted to the desires of his parents.

Like most seniors in high school, credits toward graduation were primarily earned in the two previous years, so Kenneth needed only to take a couple of tough classes: Government VIII and English VIII. For the rest of his schedule, he had two study halls, art, and chorus. It was an overall easy year. Government and English produced one C and one D. Printing and chorus were the B classes. Kenneth earned his second A—in art class. He had not gotten an A since grade school. He only missed one day of school for the year.

The highlights of the year were basketball, football, and the pep rally where he earned his senior varsity letter. All in all, it was a good school year for Kenneth.

Nineteen years old and a senior, Kenneth played basketball in the Clark Field House adjacent to Bracewell Stadium.

Burlington high school basketball squad, pictured here will go into action in the sectional tournament at Ft. Madison tonight, the Grayhounds meeting Ft. Madson high in a first round game.

Members of the squad as they appear in the picture are: Front row, left to right—Max Kemp, Russell Thomas, Dick Fray and Kenneth Berquist. Middle row—Leroy Mason, Gene Willson, Bruce Benner, Carl Van Etten and Alvin Walters. Back row—Edsel Schweizer, Lawrence McColloch, Capt. Dale Stewart (who completed his eight semesters of eligibility Jan. 20) and Coach Harold Tackleson.

Despite a lot of bad breaks in the form of illness and injuries, the Grayhounds finished third in the Little Six league and all told have won 13 out of 17 games thus far this season.

Kenneth #23 front row, high school varsity basketball team
Burlington newspaper clipping, March 3, 1939, Berquist Family

The field house was built in 1938 and made a fantastic addition to the school. The field house also hosted many dances and social events for the high school and the city. Kenneth "lettered" all three years of high school.

Kenneth's high school varsity letter set, "GO GRAYHOUNDS!"
Berquist Family Item

With his mom, dad, sister Donna, and brother Dick in attendance,
Kenneth graduated in Bracewell Stadium on June 1, 1939.

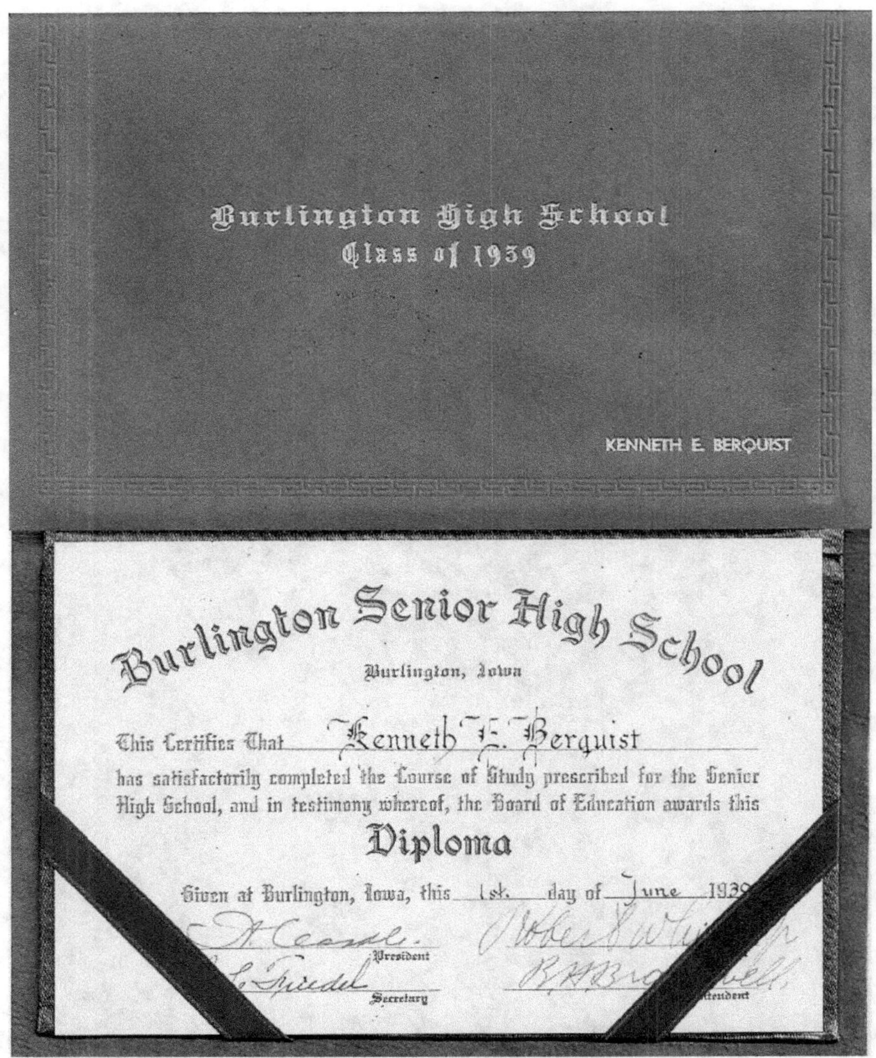

Kenneth's Burlington High School Diploma, June 1, 1939
Berquist Family Document

It would be the last time his feet would touch the turf of his beloved football field. Bracewell Stadium and Clark Field House continue to rally sports spectators today.

Kenneth graduation Cap & Gown, June 1, 1939
Berquist Family Photograph

Kenneth's high school graduation portrait 1939
Mutter's Photography, Burlington, Iowa

Kenneth had a wonderful freedom-filled summer after graduation. Freedom at last—at least for a while anyhow. The summer of 1939 was one of the hottest Iowa summers on record. All the way through mid-September, highs were regularly hitting triple digits.

There were a couple of big disappointments for Kenneth. In June, one of his favorite baseball players—Lou Gehrig—announced his retirement. Gehrig had gotten ill and could no longer play the game. Also, another favorite—Deacon White—passed away. The two professional baseball players would be a topic of conversation between Kenneth and his friends for the coming weeks.

The trick this summer was trying to find a cool place to sit and then stay for as long as they could. With only a few department stores offering air conditioning, the destinations of choice were the brand-new public pool at Crapo (pronounced "CRAY-poh") Park,

The public pool in Crapo Park, circa 1990
Photo courtesy Mort Gaines Photography, Fairfield, Iowa

one of Iowa's most historic parks, established in 1895 (and named after prominent Burlington businessman and philanthropist Philip Crapo), the movie theaters, or any place that sold cold beverages—like the soda fountains in the drug stores downtown.

There were a few of those, and Kenneth had his favorites. Sutter's was one of them. The department stores regularly shooed heat-relief-seeking teenaged shoppers from their aisles.

Sutter's Drug Store Soda Fountain downtown Burlington Iowa, circa 1939
Photo courtesy Jane Sutter Brandt

Sitting under the shade tree and sipping lemonade became boring quickly. Homemade air conditioning (a wet towel draped over a blowing fan) worked for a while. At night, they hoped for a cross breeze to blow through their bedrooms. The breeze often blew.

Billy, her sister, her brother, and her mom had come home to Burlington to visit her grandparents in August 1939. During the visit, Kenneth and Billy went to see *The Wizard of Oz* at the Capitol Theater downtown. Billy was scared, and Kenneth thought the movie was stupid.

Kenneth had other thoughts on his mind and was caught up in wondering about finding a better job and attending Burlington Junior College in the fall. He knew three months would go by fast. Kenneth did not have a clue for the course of study for college. He could always hope for an epiphany over the summer months.

First on tap, though, was the job, which would be no easy task in 1939 Burlington. He was not dissatisfied working at National Tea. He wanted to work full time and make a little more per hour. The country was on the mend. The Depression was over, although some businesses in Burlington did not recover for years. Prohibition ended in 1933, and the local brewery and distilleries were running at full capacity. The unemployment rate remained high in Burlington at seventeen percent, yet there was great excitement with everyone looking to the future. The war in Europe was helping add to the local economy regarding machinery and equipment sales increasing. In the farm-based economy, everyone locally ate fine. There were rumblings of the US Army building an ammunition plant in West Burlington, which would offer many new jobs after business started. But for now, Kenneth would rely on his dad's help looking for a job.

Full-time jobs would go to men who had responsibilities: wives, mortgages, and children to support. So the best Kenneth could hope for, look for, would be something else part time, which was okay because it was all he needed.

Kenneth enrolled in junior college, which was scheduled to start the first week of September 1939. He had a phone conversation with Billy, and she helped him decide which classes to take. His schedule would include math, English, speech, history, physical education, and engineering drawing. The plan was a full-time load with six courses. Balancing work and school would keep him busy.

World news was hardly encouraging. The week before college was to start, it was announced Germany had invaded Poland. Danzig was bombed. German soldiers were moving on the ground, into the countryside. Roosevelt came on the radio a few days later and announced the United States would continue to advocate a neutral stance on the war in Europe.

Kenneth's wish had come true, and a full-time job that his dad had intervened in arranging was available at the Iowa Biscuit Company. Kenneth could have a full-time job as a packer for thirty cents per hour if he wanted. He did.

Iowa Biscuit Company or Midwest Biscuit Company, 216-230 South 3rd Street, Burlington, Iowa, 1915-1955
National Register of Historic Places, State Inventory Number: 29-00120
burlingtoniowa.org/DocumentCenter/Home/View/248

Kenneth's dad, Mick, worked right next door at the Chittenden & Eastman Company.

Chittenden and Eastman Buildings, Burlington, Iowa
*Attribution: Ian Poellet (https://commons.wikimedia.org/wiki/
File:S_3rd_Street_industrial_bldgs_2_-_Burlington_Iowa.jpg#filehistory), „S 3rd Street industrial bldgs 2 -
Burlington Iowa", https://creativecommons.org/licenses/by-sa/3.0/legalcode*

Kenneth and his dad would carpool to and from work for the next few months. Kenneth withdrew from college before he even started.

Chittenden & Eastman had several conjoined buildings built and/or acquired between the 1870s and the 1920s. Mick worked for C&E for several years, initially as a cabinet maker, and later, as retirement drew near, he was a furniture inspector. Mick was a homeowner and raised a family of four on the salary he earned while working there.

CHAPTER 2

Billy

Julius Karver and his wife, Clara Zart Karver, lived at 1006 South Thirteenth Street in Burlington.

1006 South 13th Street, Burlington, Iowa
Photo taken by Michael Berquist, May 7, 2019

The Karvers lived a short distance north of Mick and Louise Berquist, who at the time lived at 1314 South Twelfth Street. They were neighbors and the same age. It is entirely likely they grew up as childhood friends. Mick and Julius worked together for the CB&Q

Railroad. They regularly saw each other at work. Mick would later work with Clara at Chittenden & Eastman Furniture Company.

Julius and Clara had three children. They had an older son, Walter, and two younger twin daughters, Loretta Helen and Lorraine Wilhelmina. Walter was born in 1916. The twins were born on January 8, 1920.

In 1910, neighbors were also friends and, in some cases, relatives. It was not uncommon to live across the street from in-laws or down the street from uncles, aunts, and cousins. The lines defining each became blurred, and for a good reason—in short, reliance. Let's face it—it was a different world. Those were the days when people did not lock their front doors, and kids played freely outdoors, somewhere in the neighborhood. Mothers mothered everyone. Fathers fathered everyone. The trusting, loving family relationships that developed with those living close by grew deep through the years and occasionally lasted a lifetime.

Mick and Louise initially lived with Louise's parents (the Schmickers) at 1405 South Twelfth Street. But by the time Kenneth was born at the end of 1919, the family had grown too large for all six of them to remain, so they moved up the street a bit to 1314 South Twelfth Street. The house was bursting, and within a matter of a few months, the Berquists would move again to the south rural outskirts of Burlington.

There is always going to be one, one girl who sticks in your mind for the rest of your life. She will be there in your most buried, darkest memory. She will be the one who will make you smile at a thought. She will be the one who slipped away. She will also be the one who remains nameless. For the majority, she will never be looked back upon but set aside as a dream. Men will love the women they marry and the children they bring into this world with all their hearts. The one who slipped away from Kenneth was Lorraine Wilhelmina Karver.

A generation or two before Lorraine, the middle name Wilhelmina, spelled in diverse ways, had been used in the Karver-Zart families. The girls were so identical that referring to Lorraine as Billy caught on quickly and eased confusion with family and friends when both girls were within eyeshot. Billy stuck with Lorraine throughout her life, with her grandchildren referring to her as Billy well into her late life.

Billy found a special place among Kenneth's family.

Mother (Lou Berquist) sitting on grass, Dick (Richard Berquist) standing behind, Ken (Kenneth Berquist) sitting on Lou's lap left, and Billy (Karver) sitting on Lou's lap right, circa 1921

Photo taken by Donna Berquist-Moore, Berquist Family Photo

Get-togethers often included the Karvers, with Kenneth and Billy off playing together somewhere. Billy was Kenneth's little sister, at least for now. They were like two peas in a pod, growing up together through the second grade at Perkins Elementary School in Burlington.

Summers were full of trips to the Burlington parks. Perkins Park was small, had a great playground, and was new. Crapo Park was the biggest and had the best playground equipment, with Lake Starker in the middle of the park.

The Pond—Lake Starker—Crapo Park, Burlington, Iowa
ATTRIBUTION: cardcow.com

Visitors could fish in the lake in the summer and ice skate on it in the winter. It was fun sliding on snowy hills in the winter. When kids are having fun, they're never cold, and they never want to go back home. Outside, rain or shine, was the best entertainment around. Imagination was the only limiting factor.

Sunday was "pile in the car and take a drive in the country" day. How many kids could they get in the old jalopy? The more, the merrier. Laughing and screaming and singing at the top of their lungs was the thing to do as Mick drove the car down the dusty road, somewhere—it did not matter.

Billy and Kenneth were never far apart and often would be spotted walking and holding hands when they were toddlers. Billy would be the one in the wagon, with Kenneth either pulling or pushing as Billy steered, inseparable. Kenneth's mom and Clara, Billy's mom, would put the two down together for naps in the hot, airy breeze of the summer. They often fell fast asleep together when they were babies.

When Billy moved with her parents to Indiana in 1927, she left behind cherished grandparents, aunts, uncles, and cousins from both sides of her family. Billy never knew Julius's parents, as they both had passed before 1922. Clara's parents, William Zart and Mary Elizabeth Krieger, remained in Burlington for the rest of their lives. Mary passed in 1935, and William passed in 1940. Uncles were Edward P. Zart (d: 1953), Joseph B. Zart (d: 1968), and Edward H. Karver (d: 1956). Aunts were Florence C. Zart (d: 1979) and Helen M. Zart (d: 1999). With all this family still in Burlington, Clara longed for frequent trips by car for quick visits to see them all, including close friends of the family. Billy wanted to see Kenneth, and Kenneth always knew when the Karvers were coming home for a visit.

The best part was when Billy came back to Burlington for a family visit and Kenneth would be able to take her out dancing or to see a movie. They both enjoyed a good game of pinochle as they grew up. They loved the cartoons between movies. *Tom and Jerry*, *Elmer Fudd*, and *Woody Woodpecker* caused both to scream with laughter. They both loved *Pinocchio*, and they both thought *Fantasia* was strange.

Billy loved to dance, and so did Kenneth. Kenneth was excruciatingly shy, and asking a girl to dance was hard for him. But with Billy, there was no asking—they simply went like it was a natural thing to do together. The Memorial Auditorium downtown and Clark Field House at the high school were the two places to go dancing. There were others, but these two were their favorites. Going to socials at the high school allowed Billy to catch up with old classmates from grade school. Billy was smart, pretty, and well liked, a real catch and a real go-getter.

Kenneth was anxious around girls. Kenneth was the quiet type, handsome and athletic. What Kenneth and Billy had in common was their love of music—especially the big band music of Benny Goodman. Kenneth had something at home a lot of the other guys his age did not—older sisters. Little brother Kenneth played the role of dance partner with his sisters. Of course, this was all in fun as far as Donna and Elsie were concerned. And sister dancing never happened in public. It was always inside the family home. The sister dancing frenzy was mortifying. However, sister dancing had its upside. Kenneth became a good hoofer because of sister dancing. Dancing with his sisters was not something Kenneth talked about openly with his friends or outside of the house. Kenneth often wondered if knowing how to dance before he played basketball or football helped him when he started playing sports. Kenneth knew how to dance.

Billy was cute and blonde. She could sing and dance. Billy was smart and had a cheerful smile and quick wit. She was athletic and loved to race. A floral air followed Billy wherever she walked. Kenneth did not have a clue what the fragrance was. What Kenneth knew was, it wafted behind Billy, and he liked it. Kenneth thought the fragrance was what girls should smell like.

Billy was a great catch, and the boys noticed. The attention of the other boys never bothered Kenneth, because he and Billy were friends and he liked to see her happy. It occurred to Kenneth too late. Billy could have been more than a friend. Kenneth would go to dances sponsored by school—usually at Clark Field House on the basketball court, or occasionally at the Memorial Auditorium in downtown Burlington. Kenneth would dance with Billy and all the girls. Kenneth liked the idea of girls wishing they could dance with him. Billy graduated from Emerson High School in Gary, Indiana, in 1938.

Lorraine Wilhelmina (Billy) Karver 12th Grade (1938) Emerson High School, Gary, IN, Yearbook Photo
ATTRIBUTION: Photo in the public domain

Kenneth loved dancing with Billy when she was in town visiting relatives. Kenneth thought Billy looked like Abigail Scrapple, with the floral fragrance forever present.

Abigail Scrapple with her sister and friends from the Abbie an' Slats comic strip
ATTRIBUTION: AL Capp, Raeburn Van Buren, and United Feature Syndicate

Big band music was all the rage—Benny Goodman, Artie Shaw, Cab Calloway, and Glenn Miller. Kenneth could Lindy Hop, jitterbug, and foxtrot with the best of them. Kenneth had his sisters to thank.

In July 1942, Kenneth was about to leave with the navy, and his parents threw him a big going-away party. The Karvers in Indiana, as well as all of Kenneth's aunts, uncles, cousins, and friends, were invited. It was a lot of fun for Kenneth, seeing everyone and hearing all the good wishes for a safe return.

The only sad part to the whole party was, there was an interloper—a stranger—present within the Karver family. Kenneth kept it to himself, but he was upset Billy had brought a boyfriend with her to his party. Kenneth felt slighted by this stranger muscling himself into his party— not to mention Billy. Kenneth was hurt, but when Billy later explained she had told her boyfriend, Walter, of this lifelong friendship with him, Walter insisted on coming with her to Burlington. Walter did not want Kenneth to be alone with Billy, or vice versa.

A group photo taken at the party shows and says it all.

Left-to-Right: Kenneth's friend Dick Fry, Walter Penner, Billy Karver, Kenneth, and Kenneth's friend Bob Doyle, July 1942
Berquist Family Photo

On the back, Kenneth wrote, "Billy and her boyfriend, July 1942." Kenneth was smiling, but inside he was torn. Kenneth would see Billy a few more times, but never without Walter.

CHAPTER 3

Twenty-Five Years Begin

Arriving at work each morning was a sensory explosion. Bakers had been baking in the early-morning hours, and the smell of fresh cakes, cookies, crackers, bread, and biscuits drifted through the air. The aroma was wonderful.

The Iowa Biscuit Company was assembly-line style, mind-numbing, tedious work, putting small boxes into big boxes, sealing them up, and stacking them for the shipping guys and putting cookies into metal tins, putting those into cardboard cartons, and stacking those in the corner—all day long, sometimes six days a week. Over the course of the first year, Kenneth noticed box labeling had begun to change to a more fundamental design. He learned later that these smaller, more straight-forward items were being shipped to the East Coast and would be repacked again into what was called "Type C rations" and then shipped somewhere overseas to support the war. He was not clear about the "C." Kenneth was happy for the job but still longing for something better.

The subject of war was the news discussed at work and at home every day now. European countries were either throwing themselves into the fight or staying out and declaring neutrality—like Roosevelt had done with the US.

Radio talked about Poland every day. It only took three weeks for Germany to overrun the country. They negotiated some half-and-half split with Russia. It was a little confusing as to what exactly was going on.

Norway, Finland, Sweden, Switzerland, Spain, and Ireland were the first to say they were neutral and stayed out of it. The UK, France, New Zealand, Australia, Nepal, South Africa, and India declared war on Germany. Roosevelt took a lot of dissension about the neutrality position after the Germans torpedoed a civilian ocean liner in the Atlantic, killing more than one hundred civilians. By then, even Canada had declared war on Germany.

Kenneth celebrated his twentieth birthday in October and was settling into the schedule, sharing driving responsibilities with his dad. He had an occasional thought about what would have happened had he gone through with starting college and would shudder at the thought of studying and doing homework and sitting in a classroom again. Higher learning was in the rearview mirror—he would not look back.

Toward the end of 1939, talk at work ran the gamut. The idea of the US selling weapons and equipment to Britain and France made those supportive of the war happy. It showed the world the US was at least willing to help. The sales were good for Burlington's economy.

Most people in Burlington, and this included Kenneth, were not sure what to make of this guy "Hitler" in Germany. The confusion grew more when some guy tried unsuccessfully to assassinate him. News from Europe was slow and included only the highlights, so deeper understanding was hard to find. The paper went a little more in-depth on the stories, but mostly it was a guessing game.

Hedda Hopper blabbered on and on over the radio about Hollywood, and she dropped a bombshell about a new form of communication coming, which would inevitably replace radio and newspapers in a few years, called television. Kenneth called Hedda a "bigmouth." A few weeks had gone by, and all he could do was cringe when he heard her voice. This television thing, though, caught his attention. Chicago Mobster Al Capone was released from jail because he was sick. The Jefferson Memorial was under construction in Washington, DC.

Billy came home for a visit in December at Christmas, and the two went to see *Gulliver's Travels* at the Palace Theater downtown.

Palace Movie Theater, 314 North 3rd Street,
Burlington, Iowa circa 1948
National Register of Historic Places State Inventory
Number: 29-00097 burlingtoniowa.org/
DocumentCenter/Home/View/189

They wanted to see *Gone with the Wind*, but when they heard it was four hours long, they chose to skip it. Kenneth was continually working overtime at the biscuit company in those days.

Thanksgiving, Christmas, and New Year's flew by in a flash. It was suddenly 1940. Kenneth had a new favorite cartoon now: *Bugs Bunny*. If they did not show a *Bugs* cartoon during a movie, he felt cheated. Roosevelt was sworn in for his third term on January 20, live on the radio. It was kind of a dreary winter with Charles Lindbergh popping up in the news occasionally. Kenneth longed for the baseball season to get started.

A couple of spirited conversations at work revolved around the no-hitter on opening day between the Indians and the White Sox. Everyone was behind and supporting Roosevelt. During the election for his third term in office, people did not need to vote; he was a shoe-in. Willkie was a laughingstock.

Newsreels showing the United States preparing for, but remaining out of, the war ran during all movies downtown. Patriotism—doing your part—was on everyone's lips. Everyone was getting a little annoyed with Charles Lindbergh now talking about how he thought Roosevelt should enter into a neutrality agreement with Germany. With Roosevelt's declaration of a national emergency, it was clear to everyone that the Nazi fascist ideal was going to be a dreadful thing for all concerned.

The straw that broke the camel's back for Kenneth and all Iowans was Lindbergh spouting off again—in Des Moines this time, of all places—about Roosevelt leading the United States into war at the urging of Britain and the Jews. The overtone topped it off for a lot of people.

Still annoyed with everything going on in the world, Kenneth was brought down to earth a bit when Lou Gehrig passed away. There had not been much news about Lou since his announcement to retire, and now he was gone. There were a lot of people saddened by this news. Also sad, but differently, a couple of other favorites—cowboy actor Tom Mix and baseball Hall of Famer George Davis—passed away in October.

Roosevelt signed the Selective Service Act into law on September 16, which required all men between twenty-one and thirty-five to register for the draft. Kenneth's brother, Dick, now twenty-three years old, registered for the draft during the third week in September. Kenneth had not yet turned twenty-one.

The Washington Redskins took a terrific beating from the Chicago Bears during the National Football League championship game, the Bears beating the Redskins seventy-three to zero. Kenneth was a Bears fan and took colossal delight in bragging and going on about it at work.

Kenneth's brother, Richard, enlisted in the navy on December 15, 1940. Friends and family had to tease him a little bit about it, as Dick did nothing but complain for days about the big blizzard the month before, saying he only joined so he could get to warmer weather. The proffered reason could not have been further from the truth. Dick did not want to sit around and wait for the draft to catch up with him, so he enlisted. Enlisting ensured he would have a say in which branch of the military he would be serving.

For many, the curtain rises on the horizon of adulthood at high school graduation. In Kenneth's case, this curtain call occurred in the year after high school. Many decisions about school and work took place, and then the war. It was time to drive a stake in the ground and move forward. A new life would begin. Try not to look back. The clock starts. **Twenty-five years begins.**

With the first draft lottery in October behind him, Dick Berquist knew it was a matter of time. He was reading the writing on the wall and so enlisted in the navy. Kenneth was not sure he would be drafted and opted to wait to join up. Kenneth's twenty-first birthday was Saturday, October 19, 1940. On Monday the twenty-third, he went down to the Selective Service office on his way to work and registered. Kenneth's brother, Dick, was gone.

On December 29, in a fireside chat, Roosevelt declared the United States must remain a democratic example to the world. With the Berquist household not entirely accustomed to Dick's absence, they listened around the radio into the night until all the programs had gone off the air. Kenneth was missing his older brother.

The shocking news continued to roll in from England in January 1941. Kenneth and the guys at work discussed at length what it must have been like there—in England—when the German Air Corp started bombing raids in highly populated civilian areas of London. The newspapers talked about all the people being killed and injured. Romanians were killing Jews now. The news was so incredibly hard to believe about the carnage going on over there.

Kenneth and his dad, who had nothing but praise and admiration for national hero Charles Lindbergh in 1927 and then sympathy when Lindbergh's baby son was kidnapped and murdered in 1932, were now calling him a sympathizer. Lindbergh's near-constant harping to Roosevelt about this neutrality pact with Hitler had to stop.

In February 1941, an unfamiliar word—"ghetto"—was entering Kenneth's vocabulary. It was heard on the news every night now. It seemed the Germans were herding all the Jews into big-city ghettos—to gain control over them. One of the men Kenneth worked with was a Jew. No one at work thought anything about it. He was a hard worker, and he liked baseball and football like everyone else. Kenneth could not understand why they were doing this to the Jews. German air raids continued, this time for three nights in Wales. A Churchill speech was rebroadcast on the radio toward the middle of the month. Churchill was asking for help and asked for equipment, saying England could fight the Germans better if they had the right tools. The good news was, the British had captured 130,000 Italians in Libya.

The big news in March came on the eleventh, when Roosevelt signed a law allowing Britain and China to purchase military equipment and not have to pay for it until the war was over. Roosevelt's move was a source of lunchtime discussion and was viewed as both good and bad at Kenneth's workplace. It meant the war could be over with sooner. But the interpretation was, the equipment given to Britain and China would go unpaid. While it was correct Roosevelt's plan would create jobs, the economic benefit to Burlington would be delayed or might never come. The census was split fifty-fifty at the biscuit company.

Most of the news these days from Europe was about the war in Africa. The British would win gloriously one day and then suffer a setback the next. This German general, Rommel, was a tricky guy, and the British had their hands full trying to outfox him. Germany was using a new weapon bombing the cities in England. These new bombs caused everything to burn more than to blow up. Destruction came from fires rather than explosions. The threat of fire terrorized the civilians. It had to be horrible living in England.

The United States Navy started sea patrols in the North Atlantic in early April. When shipments of military equipment swung into high gear traveling across the Atlantic, German U-boats responded with a resounding volley of torpedoes, sinking at least fifty percent of the ships that month. The US was building navy and air bases in Greenland to combat the U-boat threat. Russia signed a neutrality pact with Japan on April 13. German bombing of cities in Great Britain continued nightly. The British navy sank five German supply ships and their escort ships headed to resupply Rommel in North Africa. Greece fell to the Germans at the end of April.

May started with reports of massive German bombing—seven nights in a row—in Liverpool, Nottingham, and Belfast. The British navy captured a U-boat. The Brits captured some big-shot German official who parachuted out of his plane over Scotland.

The British Air Corps started to give it back to Germany with bombing raids over Hamburg and Berlin. On the twenty-first, Roosevelt declared a "national emergency" after a US merchant ship was torpedoed by a U-boat and sank. The British Navy sank the *Bismarck* on April 27. The news was the headline in all the papers around the world.

Kaiser Wilhelm II, formerly the German emperor, died in Holland on June 4. *The Des Moines Register* ran a story about the deportation of sixty thousand Eastern Europeans to Siberia in Russia. Militia went on a shooting spree, killing dozens of Jews on the streets, with civilian spectators cheering them on. Germans kidnapped one hundred Jewish and Polish from the area.

All German and Italian consulates in the United States were ordered closed on June 16 and their people told to leave the country by July 10. German and Italian assets were frozen two days before.

No one at Kenneth's workplace could understand why the Army Air Corps was being renamed the Army Air Force. What is the difference? Corps, Force—they all fly airplanes.

Finland, Hungry, (Czecho)Slovakia, and Albania all declared war on Russia by the twenty-seventh. At the end of the month, Germany had three hundred thousand Russian troops surrounded in Minsk.

Television became a reality. CBS and NBC started broadcasting television signals from their operations in New York City on July 1, 1941. Of course, this did not mean anything to Kenneth, or anyone he worked with at the biscuit company. It would be a while before a television would appear in the Berquist household.

News also reached Burlington: Germany had sunk to the ultimate low of mass murder of prisoners. The numbers were hard to believe, but the news said Germans had slaughtered seventy thousand Lithuanian Jews. The Germans had also killed thousands of Russian soldiers held prisoner.

Kenneth, Ken Snyder, and Bob Doyle spent the Fourth of July hanging out on the riverfront downtown. They had planned to watch the fireworks over the Mississippi from the lawn at the Memorial Auditorium. There was also dancing at the auditorium in the evening. It was Friday night.

Russian forces began the policy of burning everything as their military lines ebbed and flowed westward into Europe. Nothing was left standing. Britain had given up trying to negotiate peace with Germany by July 5. American troops relieved British and Canadian soldiers in Iceland on July 7. On July 8, Britain and Russia entered a mutual defense agreement swearing not to sign a separate peace agreement with Germany.

Joe DiMaggio's hitting streak ended during the summer—with everyone wondering if he would ever stop. He did.

Kenneth had been watching for a better job within a month of starting work with the Iowa Biscuit Company, and now, two years later, another opportunity would present itself. Hiring at the railroad shops in West Burlington began to heat up after Roosevelt signed the Lend-Lease program in March. If the United States was to become a supplier of military equipment destined for Europe, then the United States certainly needed a way to deliver this material quickly. The railroads were the movers, and the CB&Q Railroad was the biggest in the Midwest.

Kenneth went to work for the CB&Q Railroad in June 1941. When he was hired, the International Association of Machinists Union had already been operating under the rules of the Social Security and Railroad Retirement Act of 1937. Kenneth's retirement would be secured by the railroad and not the Social Security Administration. The union had voted to support the National Defense Program. There were two hundred thousand members of the union in 1941. Kenneth was paid eighty cents per hour. It was the best-paying, most-benefits job he'd ever had.

As a union member, Kenneth voted in favor of the no-strike rule in 1941. The union would not go on strike during the war. It was his first act as a union member.

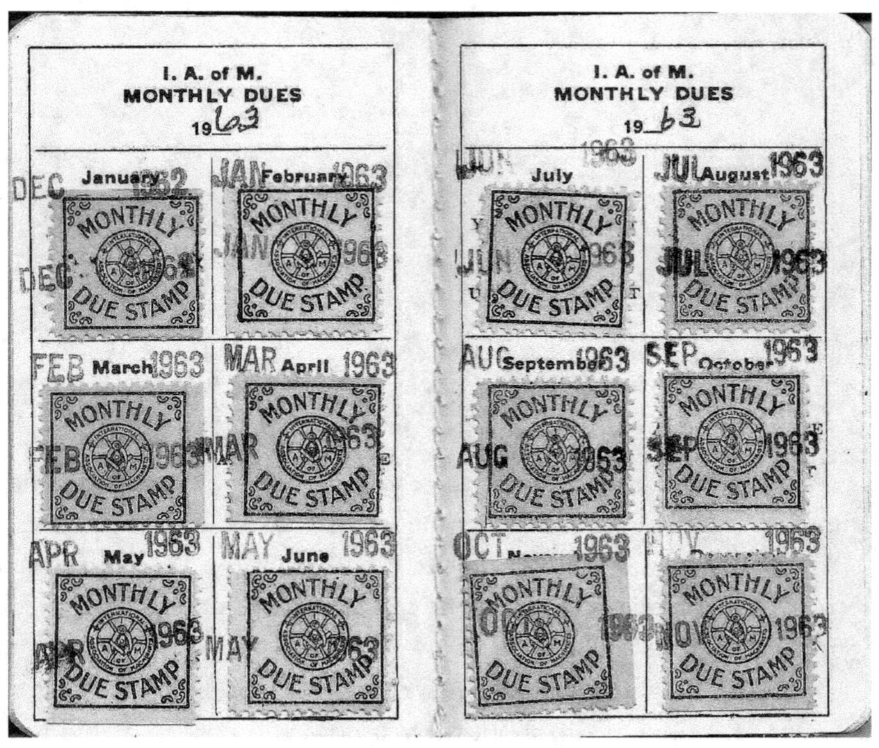

Page from Kenneth's IAM Union Dues Monthly Payment Book (1963)
Berquist Family Possession

They hired Kenneth on the spot. Kenneth was now a machinist's helper with the railroad. He would be building locomotives, proud and happy. The new job was the job he had always wanted. He could buy a better car.

The West Burlington Shops started operations in 1919.

The West Burlington Shops 1916 - 2004 1801 N.W. Burlington Ave. West Burlington, Iowa (Manufacturing and Repair) 792 feet long and 310 feet wide
Photo in the public domain

When Kenneth went to work there in 1942, the Shops were building and repairing fifty locomotives per month with about 1,500 employees. They built the last steam locomotive in 1940, and by 1946, they had reconfigured the original structure to perform repairs on diesel-powered trains.

The new job did not stop the news about the war. Kenneth did not have as much time to talk about the war now, and besides, he did not know anyone well enough to start talking yet.

Up until then, news from around the world primarily focused on Germany and the war in Europe, but this changed mid-month. The Japanese occupied French Indochina in July, so on the twenty-sixth, Roosevelt ordered the immediate seizure of all Japanese assets held in the United States. Japan had only occasionally made the nightly news radio broadcasts until then, and now Kenneth would hear something about Japan every day.

Germany continued with the murder of Jewish people and was now focusing their war efforts on the Baltic countries. The US squabbled a bit with Japan over an unfounded allegation of intrusion by the US Navy into Japanese territorial waters.

The squabble turned into a blockade by August. The US Navy was now blocking Southeast Asian oil from flowing into Japanese harbors. The barrier significantly turned up the heat between the US and Japan. When the oil resources started drying up, Japan's effectiveness of making war with China slowed. Thailand was a major supplier of oil.

The US and Britain issued a warning to Japan, on August 5, not to invade Thailand. Germany captured three hundred thousand Russian soldiers in a town less than two hundred miles south of Moscow.

Roosevelt met with Churchill in Newfoundland and Labrador, Canada, and drafted an agreement outlining post-war expectations between the Allied countries. The deal said no territorial changes without the blessing of the people. Supply convoys finally reached and relieved the British military on the Mediterranean island of Malta.

The US had known for some time Germany was murdering Russian soldiers taken captive and systematically herding Jews to confined areas throughout Eastern Europe, but what the US had not known before August 18 was, Hitler was also putting the mentally ill and the disabled to death. The German citizenry was outraged with Hitler's edict. Protestors caused a temporary halt to the killings. The protests garnered the attention of the worldwide news organizations, and by the eighteenth, everyone knew what was going on with those judged less desirable.

Spain, who had months before declared neutrality, no longer had a populace so inclined to fall in with the neutrality posture. Volunteer Spanish Fascist sympathizers started moving into Poland to begin assisting Germany with the movement of Jews to holding camps. British and Russian troops invaded Iran to save the oil fields on the twenty-ninth of August.

A decree was passed down in September from Berlin that all Jews were to wear a yellow Star of David badge—with the word "Jew" clearly written on it. Jews could not leave their towns, marry outside of the Jewish faith, or live with non-Jews. The decree was to take effect on September 19.

On October 3, 3,700 Jews in the Vilnius ghetto in Lithuania were murdered. A survivor of the slaughter provided the newspapers with a detailed account. Three days later, six thousand more were slaughtered.

Even though the US was neutral, a U-boat fired upon a navy destroyer in the North Atlantic early that month. The destroyer was not hit, but the incident caused several days of finger-pointing over who provoked whom. The tension between the US and Germany heightened over the event.

Britain bombed the hell out of Berlin on the seventh. Roosevelt issued orders to the navy a few days later to shoot on sight any ship threatened in convoy. Kenneth and the other men at work cheered and said it was about time. The papers continued to bring news from Lithuania concerning the murder of Jews. News reported the killing of three thousand during a time when they moved from one ghetto to another.

Radio broadcasts talked about the War Department building a new office in Washington, DC. The new building would consolidate the various branches of the military in one location.

In a speech at the launch of a new freight ship in Baltimore, Roosevelt quoted Patrick Henry, saying, "Give me liberty or give me death," during the christening. Roosevelt said this new class of ship would bring liberty to Europe. The liberty reference stuck with every ship of the kind from there on. The newspaper reporters started calling them "Liberty ships." The Yankees beat the Dodgers in five games to win the World Series.

The news from Washington was overshadowed by news from Europe concerning the murder of thirty thousand Jews in various locations inside Russia. The numbers were staggering.

Billy came to Burlington for a visit toward the end of October. It had been a while since Billy had been home. The Karvers arrived in time for Kenneth's birthday. Everyone went over to Kenneth's parents' house. His mom made a wonderful supper and baked Kenneth's favorite birthday cake. Kenneth's mom used a buttercream frosting instead of the chocolate frosting called for in the recipe.

CHOCOLATE CAKE

2 squares chocolate]	1 teaspoon baking soda	1 ½ cups sugar
½ cup water	1 cup sour cream	3 eggs
2 cups sifted cake flour	⅓ cup butter	1 teaspoon vanilla

Cook and stir chocolate in water over low heat until a thick, smooth paste is formed, then cool. Sift flour and soda together. With mixer on Medium speed, cream butter one minute. Add sugar gradually, continue creaming for 2 minutes. Add eggs and mix one minute. Blend in chocolate and vanilla. With mixer on Medium speed, add sifted dry ingredients alternately with sour cream, beating about 1 ½ minutes. Bake in 2 greased, 9-inch layer pans (1 ¼-inches deep) at 325° F. for 35 to 40 minutes. Use your favorite chocolate frosting.

Kenneth's favorite Chocolate Cake recipe
Clipping Kenneth had saved from a 1930s magazine

Kenneth took Billy and her sister, Loretta, to the movies downtown. They went twice. The first time, they saw a cartoon movie called *Dumbo*. Billy and Loretta loved it. A few days later, they saw a Walter Pidgeon, Maureen O'Hara picture called *How Green Was My Valley*. The Karvers went back to Indiana the next day. Kenneth wanted to call Billy his girlfriend, but the time did not seem right. The distance Billy lived from Burlington only added to Kenneth's hesitancy.

On November 6, Stalin made a global radio address declaring Germany's plan to bring England and the United States to bear against Russia was a failure. Stalin said the United States, Britain, and Russia were united in their effort to defeat the Nazis.

Newspapers reported the Senate voted in favor of a change to the Neutrality Act and allowing merchant freighters, armed by navy guards, to enter war zones. On November 11, Armistice Day, Roosevelt gave a moving address to a national radio audience from Arlington National Cemetery.

Dolph Camilli of the Brooklyn Dodgers was named the National League's Most Valuable Player. Joe DiMaggio of the Yankees was named the American League's Most Valuable Player. Kenneth thought Ted Williams was going to win over DiMaggio and lost a one-dollar bet to a coworker.

Kenneth and Dick Fry went to see the Cary Grant movie *Suspicion* on Friday night the fourteenth. Afterward, they went to the Arion Club.

Arion Club Restaurant, Main Street, Burlington, Iowa
Photo courtesy Mort Gaines Photography, Fairfield, Iowa

Radio broadcast news the following Friday reported that meetings with Japan in Washington the previous day had started and were not moving along as hoped. Japan made demands that merely would have enabled them to increase their war efforts against China. Counterproposals by the US only caused the Japanese ambassadors to stall negotiations for two weeks.

Not a day would go by when the news did not report either Russian prisoners or Jews—somewhere, Lithuania mostly—were being killed by the hundreds, sometimes thousands. Everyone thought Hitler had gone mad. Kenneth went by himself to see the Abbott and Costello movie *Keep 'em Flying*. He needed a laugh. The war in North Africa was going badly at the end of the month.

It was 1:50 Sunday afternoon when word reached Washington, DC. Pearl Harbor was under attack by the Japanese. Several more hours would pass until the news reached radio broadcasts in Burlington. The Berquist family clamored around the radio late into the evening on Sunday night, waiting to hear the story as it slowly trickled in across the airwaves. Their hearts sank with worry about Richard. Was Dick there, in Hawaii? No one knew. Everyone had to go to work the next morning; Mick and Kenneth both had jobs. Mick shut off the radio at half past ten and told everyone to go to bed—nothing could be done about it that night. All hoped for better news in the morning.

No one slept well, and it appeared Kenneth's mom was up all night with worry because, when Kenneth woke up, a huge breakfast had been prepared. Louise needed to stay busy to keep her mind off her son Richard, so she cooked. Breakfast conversation was quiet and solemn, and then Louise was home in the house alone. She could finally cry in private.

Elsie and James called home from Los Angeles the next morning and talked to Louise for a few minutes. No sooner had she put the phone down when Donna called inquiring about Dick. Had she heard from him yet? It was comforting for Lou to listen to the girls' voices, and it was a nice distraction for her talking to James and how he was doing in school in California. Lou went about her daily chores and then later began thinking about how she would arrange the furniture in the living room so she could put a Christmas tree up in a few more days.

Monday afternoon, the nation stopped what it was doing for ten minutes. Work ceased at Chittenden & Eastman downtown, and the clattering of machines ceased at the Shops in West Burlington. All gathered near radios and overhead PA speakers. All the nation listened to hear Roosevelt's speech. The war was "ON." Everyone could feel the swelling chests of pride across the United States. Mick and Kenneth came home from work later in the afternoon. It showed on their faces: they were glad the United States was not going to sit on the sidelines anymore.

Early Monday night, Dick finally called home. He was okay. Dick was at Camp Endicott in San Diego and was getting ready to be deployed again on his ship, the USS *Brooks*. Dick could not say where he was going. All hell had broken loose, and everyone on the West Coast was on high alert. Of course, everyone took a sigh of relief knowing Dick was okay, and as soon as they were off the phone, they needed to call Elsie and Donna and give them the news.

And then the inevitable happened. Four days after Pearl Harbor—on December 11, 1941—the Congress of the United States at Roosevelt's urging declared war on Germany. This declaration was not as nearly surprising as Pearl Harbor. The United States had stood on the sidelines with her desire to remain neutral when the war in Europe broke out in 1938. Much to England's chagrin, the US would provide the supplies for Britain to make war against the Axis forces but would fall short in providing men to go and fight. The United States was now fighting a war on two fronts.

While all this was happening in Washington, DC, Japan was simultaneously attacking Hong Kong, Shanghai, the Philippines, Malaysia, and Thailand. Japan and China mutually declared war. The United States Clark Air Base in the Philippines fell to the Japanese. The world was at war.

Following so closely on the heels of the "Jap" attack on Pearl Harbor a few days prior, an explosion at the Army Ammunition Plant in West Burlington set the town into a bit of a frenzy on Friday, December 12, 1941—thirteen dead, seven missing, and twenty-one injured taken to local hospitals. Causing further concern for the hospitals was dealing with the injured whose clothing had been impregnated with unexploded TNT. At the Shops, the building rattled and several of the clearstory windows shattered.

Christmas 1941 came and went. Donna and her husband, Dee, came over. Presents were exchanged. Louise made a fabulous dinner. It was not the same. Daylight shortened. It was cold, dark, and damp outside. Everyone felt out of sorts that Christmas. It was believed the New Year would brighten everyone's spirits.

Actress Carole Lombard died in a plane crash in Las Vegas on January 16. Lombard's mother and twenty-two others were among those also killed. Lombard was returning home following a tour promoting the sale of war bonds.

Elsie called from Los Angeles at the end of February to tell everyone about the nightly "blackouts" along the coast. Fear of a Japanese invasion had risen there. She said nighttime was scary with all the streetlights and building lights turned off. Elsie was considering a return to Burlington. She said the military was firing all night long at Japanese aircraft off the Pacific coast.

Kenneth's brother, Dick, who was home on leave from navy training, married Lida Blaisedale on February 26, 1942. They were married at the courthouse downtown. It was a miserable cold, snowy Thursday afternoon. Dick had been dating Lida for a few months. No one knew they were married until everyone came home for supper at Mick and Lou's. The "big" announcement method was the way Dick and Lida liked to act. Dick wanted to have a wife to come home to after his navy enlistment was completed.

Winter had taken hold in Burlington.

Historical photo of downtown Burlington, Iowa February 1942
Photo property of the late John F. Vachon, Saint Paul, Minnesota

News reported on March 18 that Roosevelt ordered all West Coast persons—of Japanese, Italian, and German descent—to report to internment facilities in various locations from Washington State to Southern California. Everyone was worried about spies and saboteurs being among the population. The internment process did not go easily. People were distraught by this announcement.

A lot of people did not believe the news reports in June about Japanese forces found on the Aleutian Islands in Alaska. People could not fathom how the Japs had gotten this close.

Kenneth received his Selective Service Physical Examination notice in the mail on July 12, 1942.

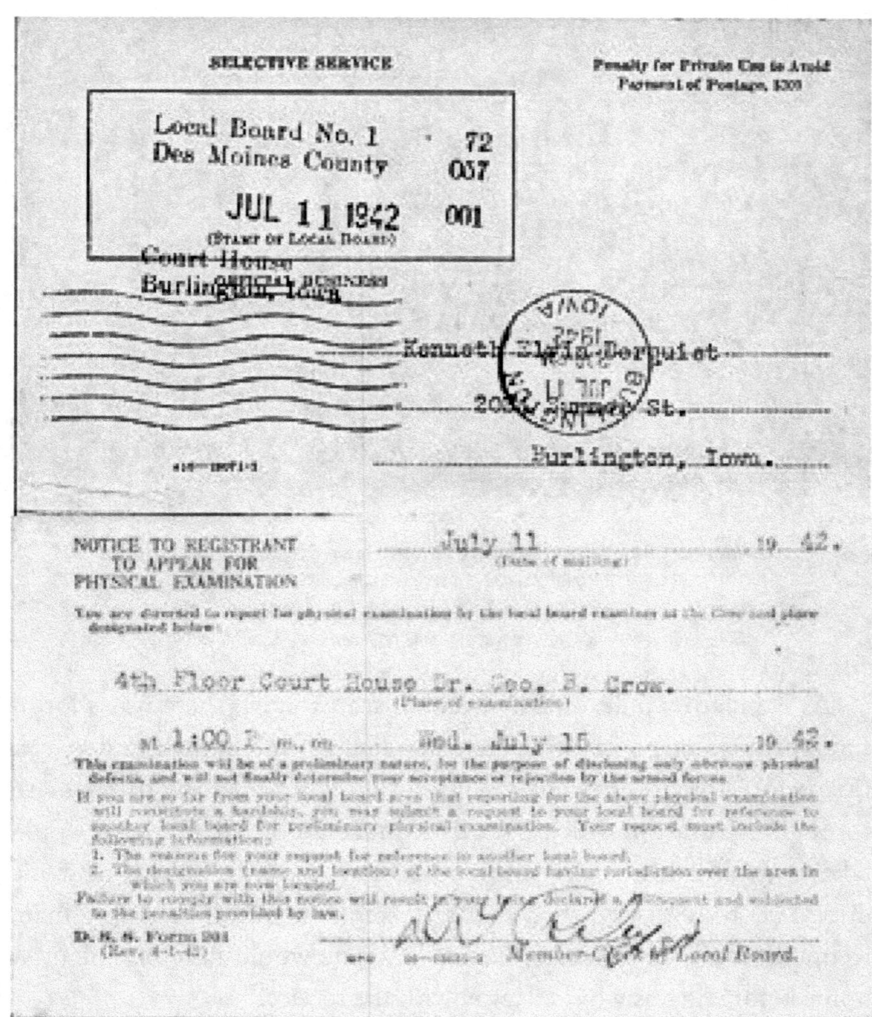

Kenneth's Selective Service Physical Exam Notification 1942
Berquist Family Photo

He reported to the Des Moines County Courthouse and took the physical as instructed.

Des Moines County Court House, 513 North Main Street, Burlington, Iowa
ATTRIBUTION: Ian Poellet (https://commons.wikimedia.org/wiki/
File:Des_Moines_County_Court_House_-_Burlington_Iowa.jpg), „Des Moines County Court House -
Burlington Iowa", https://creativecommons.org/licenses/by-sa/3.0/legalcode

As Kenneth would quickly become accustomed, there was a lot of time spent waiting with other guys standing around in their underwear. But before the government would decide what to do with Kenneth through the draft, it quickly became understood that Kenneth would take control of his destiny and enlist in the navy. It was his patriotic duty. Like his older brother, Richard, Kenneth would be a navy man. Kenneth also knew when he enlisted that he would have one night at home before he was whisked away with the service.

The navy did not let anyone have time to change their mind when they enlisted. He planned to do a few activities first with family and friends. Billy was on his mind. He was proud to serve. His mom, dad, and sisters were also proud of Kenneth. Before Kenneth's departure to the navy, he, Bob Doyle, and Kenny Snyder had one last day of sailing and golf at Geode State Park in early July 1942.

Bob Doyle (top left), Kenneth (in sunglasses) and Ken Snyder (top right), sailing on Lake Geode, Danville Iowa, July 1942
Berquist Family Photos

Golfing with Ken Snyder, July 1942
Berquist Family Photos

Kenneth had two close friends growing up. Robert (Bob) William Doyle (b: July 24, 1924; d: August 10, 1973) and Kenneth (Kenny) Paul Snyder (b: November 1924; d: 2008). Despite the four-year age difference, the three friends did all sorts of activities together. Kenny Snyder was the golfing friend. Bob Doyle was the sailing friend. Bob Doyle was also the smart-ass comedian who, on more than one occasion, made Kenneth laugh at inappropriate times. Kenneth did not see much of Doyle and Snyder during schooltime because of the grade difference, but the three of them played after school and on weekends. They went to the movies downtown during summer vacation.

Kenneth's other friend was Richard (Dick) M. Fry (b: June 25, 1920; d: July 16, 2007). Dick Fry went to high school with Kenneth. Kenneth and Dick were on the basketball and football teams. They enjoyed a competitive friendship trying to outdo each other in every sort of way. Sports was one of the situations.

Kenneth completed his last day of work at the Shops to a fanfare of good wishes. He was not the only one leaving that day. There were a few others. The attrition at work because of the war was highly visible. The crews were down to the bare minimums to keep the rail cars rolling through the building. The "old" guys—the men from the first war—remained. Kenneth's boss liked him and pulled him aside in the afternoon and told him, once he was back from the war, his job would be there waiting for him. Because of his union membership, Kenneth's job was secure and, if he desired, he could return to his job after the war with no loss of benefit or seniority.

By 1944, it was estimated 76,000 union members were active military service members. Between 1940 and 1945, union membership swelled to over 776,000.

CHAPTER 4

Enlisting

On the date of his Selective Service physical, Kenneth weighed 155 pounds and was five feet seven inches tall. Kenneth wrote in his diary, "I joined the Navy on July 27, 1942. I signed up at Burlington Iowa. Later took my physical in Des Moines." The next day, he was immediately whisked away by bus to Des Moines, Iowa.

A Navy Recruiting Poster from the Era
ATTRIBUTION: Image is in the public domain

It all worked the same way as it had with his brother, Dick, two years prior. Kenneth was the oldest of four men who traveled with him from Burlington to Des Moines. Two of the guys were from Fort Madison, and the other one was from Keokuk. The three other enlistees had recently graduated from high school in June.

The bus picked them up right in front of the Burlington Memorial Auditorium. The auditorium is where the naval recruiting substation was located.

Burlington Memorial Auditorium, 200 Front Street, Burlington Iowa
Berquist Family Photo

The bus was not full yet. It had already gotten hot, and the bus smelled of sweat. Kenneth would be there in Des Moines until the third of August—mostly waiting in line for something, like continuing enlistment activities, physicals, testing, blood samples, and shots, lots of shots.

Kenneth was not specific concerning where he was taken in Des Moines. Likely, he was bused to the armory.

Argonne Armory and World War Memorial Building, 602 Robert D.
Ray Drive, Des Moines, Iowa, Built 1934
Photo Taken by Michael Berquist: November 21, 2017

He was there from July 28 through August 3, 1942. In low-relief detail sculpted above each entry was "For the Service of the People" and "For God and Country."

**Argonne Armory and World War Memorial
Building 602 Robert D. Ray Drive, Des
Moines, Iowa, Built 1934**
*Photo Taken by Michael Berquist: November 21,
2017*

Through World War II, the building served the needs of the US Army and the US Navy.

The word in Des Moines was easy: keep to yourself. There were simple reasons for this. First, you would not find out where you were going for boot camp until the last day. Second, even an accusation of homosexuality was enough to get you a quick beating and an immediate trip home with an indelible mark on your service record. Homosexuality was illegal, and you could be fined and/or placed in jail. It was okay to chat it up with the other men, but not to get attached to anyone.

Des Moines is the capital of and largest city in Iowa. Kenneth had not seen a city this big before. It was also the farthest he had ever traveled from Burlington. It looked like Iowa, but it did not look like

Burlington. On August 2, Kenneth learned he would be going to the Great Lakes Naval Training Center north of Chicago.

ATTRIBUTION: G.M. Thatcher, Danville, Illinois

Some guys would go to San Diego and others to someplace in Virginia. On August 3, Kenneth was handed breakfast in a bag, and he boarded the bus for Chicago at 8:00 a.m. Kenneth was not looking forward to ten hours on the bus. Kenneth wrote in his diary, "From Des Moines to Chicago I went. I trained at Great Lakes five weeks. After this training, I got a nine-day leave."

The bus made stops in Iowa City and Davenport to pick up other recruits. He was given lunch—in a bag again. People had to wait in line to use a stall in the restrooms at the bus stations. It was hectic there. From there, the bus traveled to Rockford, Illinois, where more recruits would be picked up and all received another meal in a bag. In the early evening, the bus pulled into the Great Lakes Naval Training Center in North Chicago.

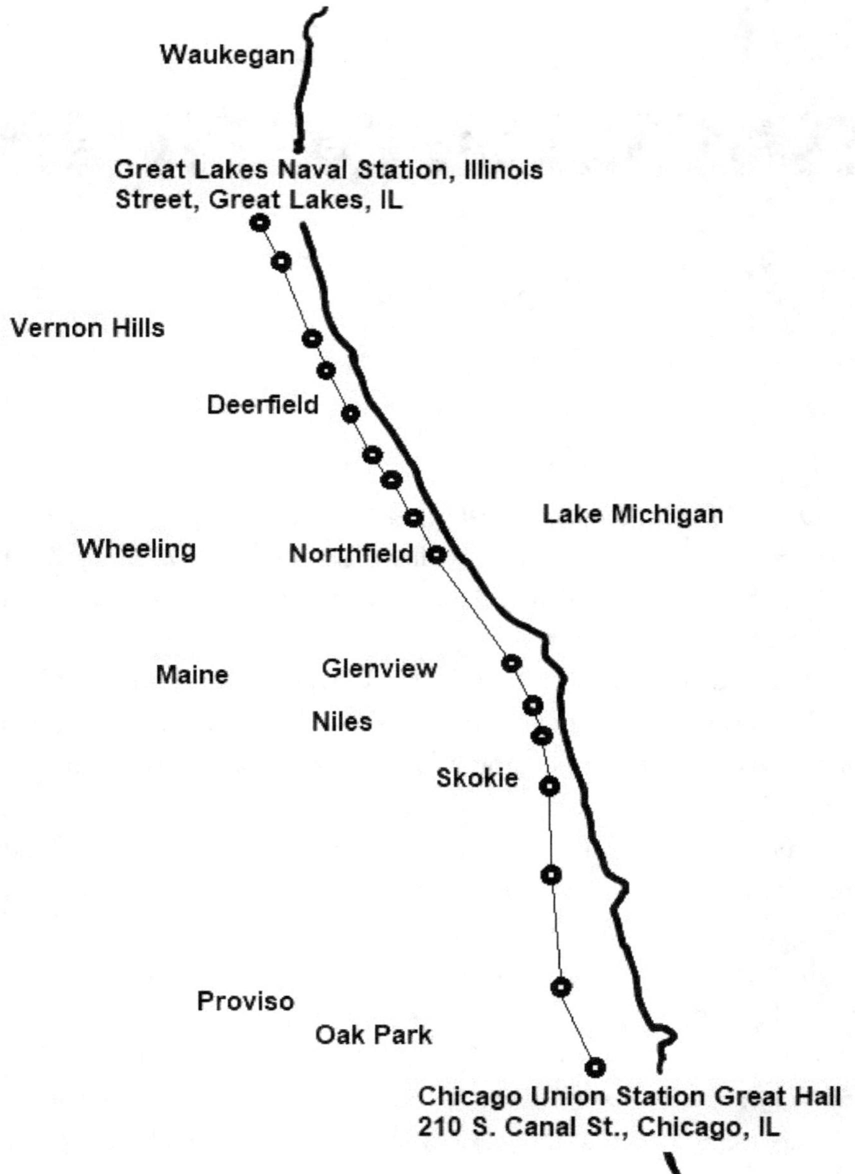

Great Lakes Naval Training Center location north of Chicago

The recruits had been warned along the way that their world would change dramatically once they arrived. The semi-freedom of the bus ride and their last few hours of civilian life was at an end.

CHAPTER 5

Boot Camp

Once Kenneth's shoes hit the deck at Great Lakes, it was a rush through every step after arrival. It all started with a lot of yelling. First up, another meal, which Kenneth had fifteen minutes to get and eat. It was a hot meal this time though. Time was also allotted for a phone call home to let his folks know he had arrived safely and would be sending his clothes home in a box in a few days. The phone call was brief. Each activity was completed in groups of about one hundred men, with someone barking orders as to what every move would be. The men were given a two-minute restroom break after eating. Next step was assembly-line haircuts. More like a head shave, the haircut took less than thirty seconds. All the hair came off except for the stubble left by the electric razor. The crew cut would be Kenneth's hairstyle for the rest of his life.

After stripping down to his undershorts, again in assembly-line fashion, each man made his way down the line as items of clothing were issued—four of these, six of those, two of these, etcetera. He would jam the pieces of clothing into a canvas bag they gave him as he went down the line. There was a sewing kit, and some other personal-hygiene items in a sack called a seabag. It was the most confusing of all the steps going in. They were expected to know what sizes they wore. Most guys had no idea what size they wore, and this only served to back up the lines.

There was lots of yelling going on between recruits and men with tape measures and men taking articles of clothing off the shelves behind them. Every item had a waiting line: socks, underwear, tee shirts, dungarees, shirts, boots, and every sort of outerwear. Uniforms would be handed out in the days to follow and would be doled out in a much more orderly fashion and at a much slower pace. Dress blues were meant to fit—exactly. Work clothes did not need to be the exact size. Make sure to have the right size of boots or be sorry.

The men Kenneth had traveled with from Burlington disappeared into the fray, and he only recognized a few of the guys from the bus ride from Des Moines. Familiar faces became a bit more of the norm after the group of one hundred he had been grouped in with were led to their barracks. Living quarters are called a ship with a deck. Restrooms are heads. The men were told to put the clothes they arrived in into the box, seal the top shut, and write the address of where they were mailing the box to on top, and then where to place the box.

Kenneth's ship was a large, long room with bunk beds down each side and a rack down the center on which to hang their seabags. With only a few minor disagreements, each man picked out a bunk. There were adjoining rooms with showers, toilets, and supplies. A quick walk-through of the area and it was time to sleep. The yelling had stopped. Tomorrow would start at 3:00 a.m. It was 9:30 p.m., and it had already been a long day.

Kenneth's company commander's name was C.B. Wilson. Kenneth thought Wilson was a swell guy—fair, honest, and concerned the men would learn the lessons taught over the next few weeks. Lives depended on it. Kenneth liked him and thought how in peacetime Wilson would have been a friend.

Kenneth did not write much in his diary about boot camp other than to say he arrived on this date and was home on leave at this time. Boot camp during World War II was quick compared to boot camp during peacetime. Kenneth's boot camp experience was five weeks long. He was busy. The time went by fast. Privacy to sit, think, and write a letter was at a premium.

The first few days at boot camp were spent filling out forms. You would not think this would have taken days to complete, but it did. There was lots of time waiting. Kenneth completed a health history, signed up for a bank account, completed forms for life insurance, and went through classroom-style learning about the benefits he would earn being a veteran.

Kenneth's Dog Tag
Berquist Family Possession

In between these paperwork activities, he and his company would march to mess hall together, back and forth. He had a dental exam, an eyesight exam, and more shots, and gave blood samples several times. He waited in all sorts of lines for additional items of clothing. Days would end with more marching. Physical training—calisthenics—started. This routine continued for a few days.

During the second week—mixed in with all the previously mentioned marching and exercise—his company went in groups to be fitted for their dress uniforms. Sizing took a long time because the navy was particular about how well this uniform fit.

Everyone stripped down to their underwear and stood around while their sizes were determined. First came bell-bottomed trousers, on and off several times until the officer in charge of the area was satisfied with how they fit. Shoes were tried at the same time as the trousers because the trousers had to touch your shoes in exactly the right way; length and how they fit around your waist were equally important. Stand straight! If you slouched, they yelled at you. If you tied your bell-bottomed trouser legs in a knot, the air trapped in the legs would act as a flotation device in an emergency.

Next was the shirt, which the navy called a short jacket. Kenneth was quickly adapting to the idea the navy had different terms for everything —for example, hats are covers. Kenneth received two of everything, one white and one navy blue. The creases in the short jacket had to match up with the creases in his trousers. Next was outerwear: a peacoat, black leather gloves, and a wool scarf. Teaching the proper way to wear these items was next. There was a particular way to don (put on or wear) your cover.

Physical training continued every day. Practice parading continued. Everything was done together with their shipmates. Kenneth knew the concept of teamwork. His football and basketball coaches had taught him well. The navy was merely reinforcing for him what he already knew. Guys who were out of shape and never played sports, etcetera, had a tough time with physical training. The importance of helping each other was stressed. They were to cheer on their compatriots. The emphasis was on teamwork.

The officers leading the physical training started talking about the confidence course.

Kenneth wrote on August 11 that his company was up at 6:00 a.m. and marched to the mess hall for breakfast. After breakfast, his group practiced parading back to their ship and dressed in their dress blue uniforms. They were told to fall in outside the building. Commander Wilson, dressed in his khakis, met them outside. It was picture day. Four high bleachers stood outside. Kenneth, Commander Wilson, and 106 of his shipmates lined up at attention and had a photograph taken. The whole thing took less than ten minutes. Kenneth was grateful because it was hot.

Photograph taken outside Drill Hall #802, CO. 642 "42" C.B. Wilson – CSP CO COM'D, August 11, 1942 U.S. Navy Training Station, Great Lakes, Illinois Kenneth second row—tenth from the right
Berquist Family Photo

It was not long and Kenneth was back in his tee shirt and shorts and off to physical training. Around the third week, courses taught included first-aid techniques, signaling with flags, procedures boarding a ship, and some basic seamanship. Kenneth, along with a smaller group from his company, rowed a boat in Lake Michigan. Teamwork was stressed. Rowing in unison as a team is what counted most. They were amazed at how fast the twenty of them could get this giant wooden boat going in the surf. Later in the week, a physical training test was given. They ran and did push-ups and sit-ups. Kenneth passed.

Small-weapons training took place at the end of the week. Kenneth had never fired a gun before. It was a bit of revelation for him. He learned how to shoot a handgun and a shotgun. He learned about ammunition, taking a gun apart and putting it back together. Each weekend, they had to march. They had to parade. They were competing for a flag. They would practice walking in step during the week, and then on the weekend, the competition would take place. Some guys plainly could not keep in step. They could not keep in rhythm to save their lives. Kenneth was a natural—thanks to "sister dancing," he thought. The flag was more a source of pride for the winning company than an actual personal reward. It was a white flag with a picture of a rooster on it. The rooster had long been a good luck charm for sailors against drowning. Kenneth's company won the pennant once in the five weeks he was there.

In the early part of September, damage-control classes started. Kenneth learned about firefighting aboard ship. He learned how to don safety equipment, how watertight doors worked, and how to operate all sorts of firefighting equipment. At the time, he learned to strap on a gas mask in a highly stressful situation. The dreaded gas chamber they had been told of came and went. It turned out to be not as bad as Kenneth had imagined. Only a handful of the guys suffered any ill effects. He was happy when the doors opened and he could run outside.

All training during the last week led up to the final test, called battle stations. The trial took all day. Trainers threw every scenario they had been taught about over the past five weeks at the recruits. It was a crazy day. General quarters was called—the sirens screamed—starting at 0300 hours. Kenneth was exhausted, hungry, and soaking wet when it was over, but the company passed, and the cheers rang out. They could eat supper in peace that night. Kenneth was promoted to apprentice seaman (AS) on September 4, 1942.

September 6 was a graduation of sorts. All it meant was a march in a parade called Pass-in-Review. Everything he learned in drill and ceremony would be on display. After Pass-in-Review, Kenneth went back to his ship and packed his seabag, navy style. Kenneth wrote in his diary, "I got a nine-day leave. After my leave expired, I returned to G. Lakes the 17th day of Sept."

He had his orders, which included travel documents for his next duty station, where training would continue. Kenneth did not waste any time getting to the train. He and a friend he had made—Jesse Bates—would travel together to Chicago and then split up from there.

Jesse had the same orders and would be meeting Kenneth back at Great Lakes in nine days. Kenneth was going home.

Kenneth, September 1942 between Boot Camp in Chicago and Gunnery School in Little Creek Virginia At home, on leave, tying his shoe on the bumper of his 1941 Chevy Special Deluxe Coupe automobile
Berquist Family Photo

Donna and Mick had driven Kenneth's car a few times while he was away. Kenneth had purchased this vehicle new shortly after he started working for the CB&Q. It was his transportation out to West Burlington. The car was his pride and joy. He had been taking the city bus and carpooling. Owning the car gave him the sense of freedom every young man wanted. Kenneth was happy he had the car, but he dreamed of the day he would be able to buy a convertible. He was a top-down kind of guy.

On leave, Kenneth ate his mom's home cooking, he slept as late as he wanted, and he went to the movies. Rest and relaxation were the plan. He saw everyone in his family, and he spent time together with his friends a couple of nights. Kenneth took the train back to Great Lakes on September 17. He and Jesse Bates met up back on base. The next morning—September 18—they had breakfast and boarded the train headed for the East Coast. Kenneth wrote, "I went to Little Creek, Virginia."

CHAPTER 6

Gunnery School

Kenneth wrote in his diary, "There I was for two months at gunnery school. I went on liberty exactly three times in 2 months. I hated Virginia very much. It was a lousy town." Kenneth turned twenty-three on October 19, 1942. There was no celebration.

When asked why he thought Little Creek was lousy, he would say, "Norfolk was a long way away. The roads were pure mud. It was hot. Sweat came out of me like I just got out of the shower. And it stank." Virginia Beach, in 1942, was a small town. Only twenty thousand people lived there. Norfolk was heavily industrialized. Military bases springing up out of nowhere only served to make the population swell during the war.

In a bean field, the base, dotted with swamps, was constructed in July 1942. Native Americans called the area the "Great Marsh." When Kenneth arrived in September 1942, the station was still under construction. Living conditions were bleak. When it rained, areas flooded with ankle-deep water. It rained most of the time. They were using latrines in some areas of the base. Latrines would flood, thus the smell. Going on liberty meant a three-day weekend pass, not enough time to travel anywhere and get back on time. So leave time was spent in either Norfolk or some beachfront area south of Virginia Beach along the coast.

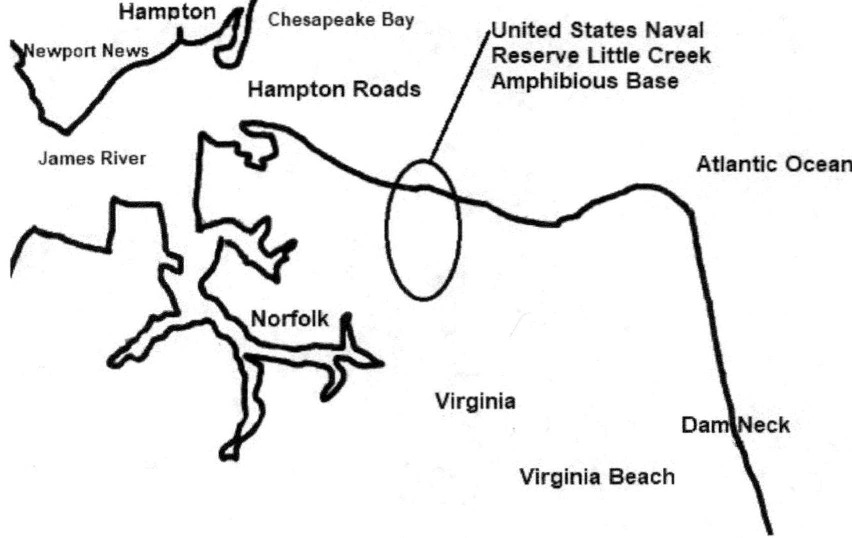

Norfolk, Little Creek, Dam Neck, Virginia--Gunnery School, 1942

The anti-aircraft (AA) firing range located in Dam Neck was only a few miles away. Sailors were bused back and forth every day. Kenneth learned about (Oerlikon) 20mm and (Bofors) 40mm AA guns.

20mm twin-barreled Anti-Aircraft Gun
Photo taken with permission by Michael Berquist
Aboard the USS Kidd DD-661 Floating Museum
Baton Rouge, Louisiana, February 2017

40mm twin-barreled Anti-Aircraft Gun
Photo taken with permission by Michael Berquist Aboard the USS Kidd DD-661 Floating Museum Baton Rouge, Louisiana, February 2017

The guns came in several varieties: single, twin, and quad-barreled. Kenneth learned how aiming worked, how to shoot them, how to load them. He learned how to disassemble and reassemble all the guns. He learned about all the parts and assemblies of the weapons. He learned how to quickly change out gun barrels—without getting his hands burned. Kenneth also learned how much destruction could occur with a squeeze of the trigger.

Sailors shot at these big wooden targets floating out in the ocean. They shot the floaters up so bad they would merely sink in the water. They also shot at sand dunes, but it was not as fun.

The 40mm guns were on a geared turret, which could be driven either manually with hand cranks or automatically with hydraulics and an electrical motor allowing two, or more, forties to be controlled by a ship's gun director. It could be operated hands-free if desired, except for loading. Loading was still done by hand. Ammunition for the guns was supplied in two ways. The rounds came loaded in belts, which were several feet long. Or the rounds came in these preloaded magazines. Each magazine held several rounds. The magazines and the cartridges could be reloaded. The shell casings for the smaller-caliber guns were typically thrown away.

All the guns were loud. The 20mm gun was like a machine gun that could fire continuously for several seconds at a time. You could hold the trigger down and empty a belt of ammo in a matter of seconds. The 40mm twin-barrel guns fired in succession, back and forth, first the right barrel and then the left barrel. They were undoubtedly slower firing than the 20mm guns but packed a punch. The forties made more of a pound-pound-pound sound at 120 rounds per minute. The twenties sounded like angry bees—making a continual buzzing sound at 320 rounds per minute.

The 20mm gun could be operated by two or three guys, a shooter and one or two loaders. The 40mm gun required at least six men to run: the man with his finger on the trigger; right seat and left seat gun trainers; and two loaders. The trainers cranked the hand cranks to move the gun right and left and up and down.

The 20mm and 40mm gun training was not as complicated as learning about five-inch/.38-caliber guns. There were many sizes of these big guns, but Kenneth remembered most about this size gun, as it would be the gun he would be in charge of in a few months.

The five-inch guns required lots of practice to shoot. Everyone in Kenneth's class learned how to do all the steps of the five-inch. Kenneth learned the five-inch so well he could operate the gun in his sleep. The operation—when performed correctly—ran like a well-orchestrated ballet. Each sailor had a job, and all of them relied heavily on the others doing their jobs correctly. Operating the five-inch gun started on the lowest deck of the ship.

A five-inch/.38-caliber gun had a crew of fifteen to twenty-seven men located throughout the gun house, upper handling room, projectile storage, and powder magazines.

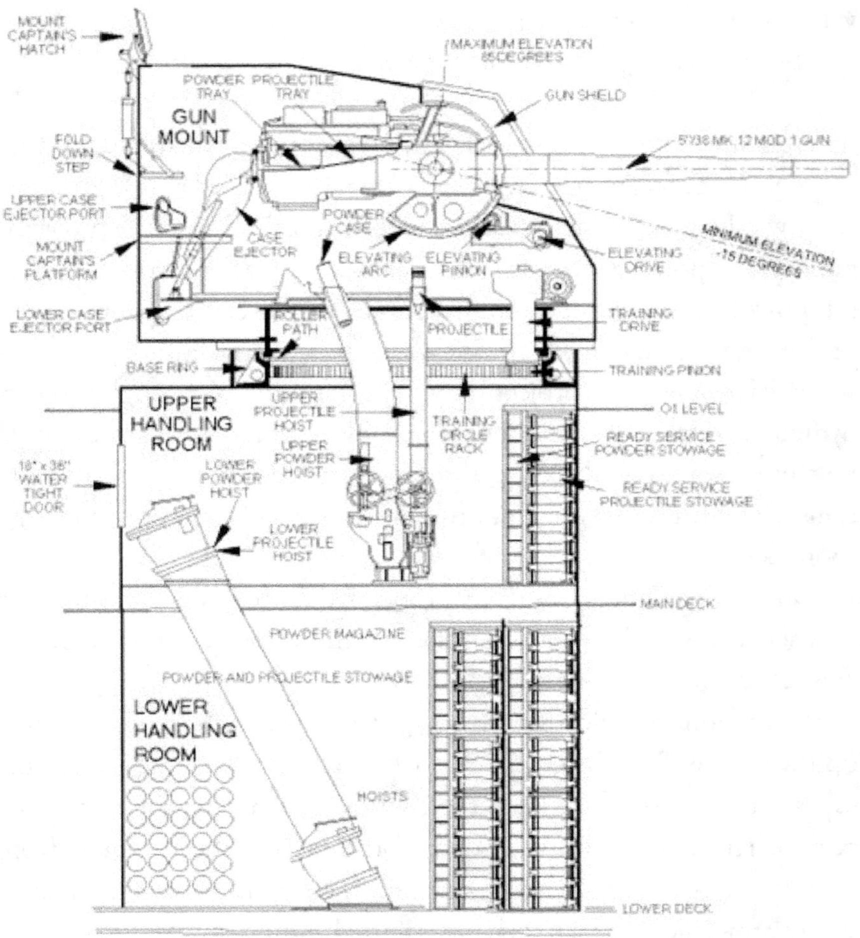

Cut-away of Five-Inch/.38 caliber turret mounted gun illustrating
major mechanisms as they pass through two decks
Illustration by Michael Berquist

There were two modes of operation. The crew was trained and was expected to know both. The primary method was automatic control, where the mount, controlled by the fire-control system, was fired remotely. If the fire-control system became dysfunctional for any reason, the gun could continue operating under local control.

There were five to seven men at each station. Starting at the bottom was the projectile room and the powder magazine. Projectiles came in a variety of types, everything from a substantial chunk of metal, in a kind that blew up on impact, to other types that blew up before or after landing, sending small pieces of metal flying in every direction. There were different incendiary types as well. The powder magazine stored the gunpowder. Gunpowder tightly packed in what was called a powder case is what would get ignited in the breech of the gun and send the projectile sailing. The powder magazine was a hazardous place to work. Flashless gunpowder or smokeless gunpowder were used interchangeably—night or day—depending on which task was being undertaken.

Powder cases and projectiles would get fed up through electric-hydraulic hoists to the handling room above. Projectiles and cases would be stored, sorted, and fed up through two more hoists into the gun house. The ready service ammunition was kept in the upper handling room below the mount.

Once in the gun house—in proper sequence—the projectile and powder case would be loaded in the breech of the gun and the breech closed, one man for each job.

The mount captain stood on an interior platform located halfway up the back wall of the gun house, where a hatch opening allowed the captain to peer out and see if the rounds were hitting the designated targets. The hatch had a steel hood protecting the mount captain from the muzzle blasts of adjacent weapons. The mount captain watched where projectiles were landing and adjusted aiming.

The gun captain was responsible for maintaining the mount. The gun captain knew every mechanical, electrical, and hydraulic mechanism in the mount. He watched the actions of the powder man, projectile man, breech block, and rammer. He knew every job and can take over when necessary. The gun captain floated between the gun house and the lower decks, ensuring all was running smoothly.

The pointer controlled the mount's elevation and firing. He sat in the left front corner of the mount. The trainer controlled the mount's angle and sat in the right front of the mount. The sight setter operated the aiming equipment; he stood behind the trainer. The fuse setter operated the apparatus that set the fuse on projectiles with mechanical timers. On a single enclosed mount, he sat below and outboard of the pointer's seat. The powder man slid the primer protector off the powder case and then lifted the case from the powder hoist to the rammer tray. The projectile man moved the projectile from a different lift to the rammer tray. He then pulled the rammer lever to load the projectile and powder case into the breech. The hot case man caught the ejected powder case and threw it out of the mount.

The check sight man verified the mount was aiming at the target.

The last man in the gun crew was the man in the fire-control room. He had his finger on the trigger. When executing rapid continuous fire, firing keys (triggers) would be held closed, and the gun would fire as soon as the breech closed. The fire-control man could choose to pull the trigger, causing the gun to fire intermittently. It all depended on orders he received.

When all steps ran as planned, a five-inch gun could be fired fifteen to eighteen times per minute. The crew could move between thirty and forty-four projectiles and powder cases per minute. The men in Kenneth's mount crew practiced every day. Practice would continue even while at sea. Kenneth never knew when general quarters sounded if it was a drill or not. He had to move as if it were a real action every time. The crew at each duty station would be timed and observed by an officer. The results of a drill would be written down in a book. Each time an exercise ended, the officer would tell the crew if they did better or worse. It often became a source of pride (or embarrassment) when announcements were made after drills were over.

Kenneth also learned about depth charges and torpedoes at Little Creek, but this training was specialized—like the guns. Men would get in-depth training on one or the other, but not both. The AA guns were fun, and he knew what to do while working with them, but his preference—what he liked best—was working on the five-inch gun.

The two months at Little Creek dragged on, and Kenneth could not wait to get out of there. Kenneth wrote, "I hated VA. It was a lousy town."

On November 17, 1942, word came down to Little Creek that Kenneth would be promoted to gunner's mate third class (GM3c) after completing one overseas trip. It was like dangling a carrot on a string.

CHAPTER 7

Armed Guard Center

Kenneth wrote in his diary,

From Virginia. I went to New York 19 Nov. I was very crazy about it too. Anybody in service clothes sure did rate. I got in shows for twenty-eight cents. Sometimes for free. I took in a lot of movies! I also went skating too. I enjoyed myself very much. Learned to skate a little better too! I met a swell girl named Irene Batlin from Brooklyn. I had numerous dates with her. Later I met another girl. She was nice, only had one date with her. I mess cooked for six weeks. I did not mind it very much. We sure had nice Christmas and Thanksgiving dinners.

When recruits chosen for armed guard duty completed their training, they would go to one of the three armed guard centers located in different areas of the US. Kenneth was assigned to the base in Brooklyn, New York, and would be aboard ship in the Atlantic. The train pulled out of Newport Depot in the evening of November 18, 1942. Kenneth slept on the train overnight. The train pulled into Penn Station in New York on Thursday morning November 19. Kenneth wished he had been awake for the overnight trip because when he arrived in New York, he was in another world. New York City was like no place he had ever seen or dreamt of before. People and cars were everywhere. His group was quickly shuffled to a waiting bus, and off they went again across the river—gazing out the window in amazement.

At first, it looked like boot camp all over again.

U.S. Naval Armed Guard Center (AGC), circa December 1943 1st Avenue and 52nd Street, Brooklyn, NY
ATTRIBUTION: http://www.armed-guard.com/bag2.html

They were waiting in line to be handed something. Each man was issued three pairs of heavy socks, two sets of woolen underwear, two types of winter helmets, waterproof mittens, winter mittens, a face mask, sea artic wear, rubber boots, oilskins, goggles, a winter jacket and trousers, and a parka rain jacket and pants. Kenneth walked away with an armful of clothing. His seabag was stuffed full. He slung his seabag over his shoulder, and off he went.

Kenneth's ship was the old armory building at the armed guard center. Kenneth climbed into the middle rack in a triple-decker bunk bed. This bunk was one rack in a sea of five thousand. It was his rack in the affectionately named "jungle."

Bunks AGC Main Deck, Brooklyn, circa July 1943
ATTRIBUTION: http://www.armed-guard.com/bag1.html

The quarterdeck served as the drill deck during the day. Kenneth never had to sleep in the USS *Newton*. Kenneth was grateful for this, as the *Newton* was an old wooden firetrap.

USS Newton, AGC Brooklyn, circa 1944 Served as both Barracks and Brig
ATTRIBUTION: http://www.armed-guard.com/bag3.html

The Brooklyn AGC would be his base for the next eleven months. Kenneth mess cooked from the day of his arrival through New Year's Day 1943. The commissary served five thousand meals per day.

Brooklyn AGC Main Deck Mess Hall Looking to front of building
ATTRIBUTION: http://www.armed-guard.com/bag2.html

It was okay work—he did not mind. He ate well during the time. There were no waiting lines for meals for men working in the commissary. Cooks and people who worked in the kitchens ate when they could as they were working. Plus, they could select the best of the food prepared. Sailors ate in shifts all throughout the day. Meals were continually being prepared.

The cooks were extremely proud of the Thanksgiving and Christmas meals they prepared for the holidays in 1942.

Merry Christmas!

TO THE OFFICERS AND MEN OF THE ARMED GUARD:

This Christmas time we are closer to the conclusion of the task to which we are committed—the successful end of this war. As your Commanding Officer, I wish you and your families the best of the season's happiness, health, and good cheer.

After the war, we will remember today—for this Christmas in the service will be unique, —and it will stand out in our memory. That is why we here at the Armed Guard Center have tried to make this a Christmas vibrant with the comradeship that comes more fully to men when united in danger and driven by zeal to hold for the good in life.

We, the officers and men of the Armed Guard, have the satisfaction that we have tried to the best of our ability to accomplish the task for which we have been especially selected and trained. We have further satisfaction in the fact that our efforts and deeds have been given recognition by our superiors, and are appreciated by the people of our great country.

We are dedicated to a particularly important, little known, and unadvertised duty, sparkling with excitement and the unusual, such as few men experience. The Armed Guard is charged with a mission to get through to our comrades of other services and to our allies the equipment to conquer. Thus, the Armed Guard unites both foreign and home fronts. By this union we are today all brought into closer relationship as Americans and fighters in the middle of the fight, confirming our beliefs in right and God.

May He permit us to carry on in the way in which we have begun!

WILLIAM J. COAKLEY, Commander. USNR.

Program--Christmas Eve

MUSIC ....Station Orchestra
CANDLELIGHT SUPPER
CHRISTMAS MESSAGE FROM THE SECRETARY OF THE NAVY
ORGAN PRELUDE ....Organist
CHURCH CALL...Non-Sectarian Services
SELECTIONS...All Male Choir
Church of the Blessed Sacrament
Warren Foley, Director
CHRISTMAS PLAY...Station Players
TREE PARTY...Gift Distribution
MOVIES..."Talk of the Town"
with Jean Arthur and Cary Grant
Cartoon, Screen Songs,
Hollywood Snapshots

MIDNIGHT MASS

Christmas Day

CHURCH CALL

DINNER

M E N U
Tomato Juice Cocktail
Mixed Olives   Celery   Pickles

★

Combination Salad

★

Stuffed Young Turkey   Raisin Dressing
Giblet Gravy   Baked Spiced Ham

★

Cranberry Sauce

★

Mashed Potatoes   Asparagus Tips

★

Mince Pie   Fruit Cake
Ice Cream   Mixed Nuts
Coffee   Candy   Cigarettes

VERNON J. JOHNTRY
Lieut. (SC) USNR
Supply Officer

W. E. BIMBIE
Chief Commissary Std.
USN (RET)

GAMES

PRESENTATION..Touch Football Championship Award
to Armed Guard Yeomen Team

ENTERTAINMENT

SUPPER

LUCKY LETTER AWARDS

CHOW CONCERT

"MOST USELESS GIFT" CONTEST

MOVIES.."Somewhere I'll Find You"
with Lana Turner and Clark Gable

TAPS

Christmas Program, AGC Brooklyn, 1942 Dinner and a Movie
Berquist Family Document

Officers were pleased and complimentary of the cooks. Sailors were a little bit harder to satisfy. A sailor who spent the day stevedoring could eat a lot.

Mess cooking also afforded Kenneth a regular work schedule, which allowed him to make actual plans for what he would do with his friends when they were off work. Besides, this was his first holiday season away from home. Cooking kept his mind off what he was missing back home.

With the beginning of the New Year—January 1943—mess cooking ended and training of a different sort began. Even though Kenneth never knew what each new day would bring, he could tell something was afoot. His navy life was about to change. There were lots of practice drills, classroom time, and review from gunnery school. Kenneth's work as an armed guard was about to start.

It was winter, so most activities were conducted indoors. Dancing at the clubs moved back indoors. Kenneth was a great dancer and loved music. He had a swell time off base. When he wore his uniform, it guaranteed him special privileges in the civilian world. Seeing movies for free or at least cheap, eating at restaurants for next to nothing, and getting into the hot spots was easy. New Yorkers sure knew how to treat those in the service. Brooklyn and the navy by day. Manhattan and fun by night.

Kenneth and a couple of his friends were lucky enough to get into the Astor Hotel one night in December 1942 when the Harry James Orchestra was playing in the bandshell on the roof of the hotel. Kenneth remembered vividly listening to Helen Forrest sing "I Had the Craziest Dream" and "I Don't Want to Walk Without You."

Helen Forrest and The Harry James Orchestra, circa 1942 Time, Date, Place, Photographer Unknown
ATTRIBUTION: http://indianapublicmedia.org/afterglow/voice-big-bands-helen-forrest

He danced until midnight.

CHAPTER 8

Irene and Bernice

Kenneth wrote, "I met a swell girl named Irene Batlin from Brooklyn. I had numerous dates with her." They met the week after Kenneth arrived at the AGC one night when he was out ice skating at Prospect Park with a couple of his friends.

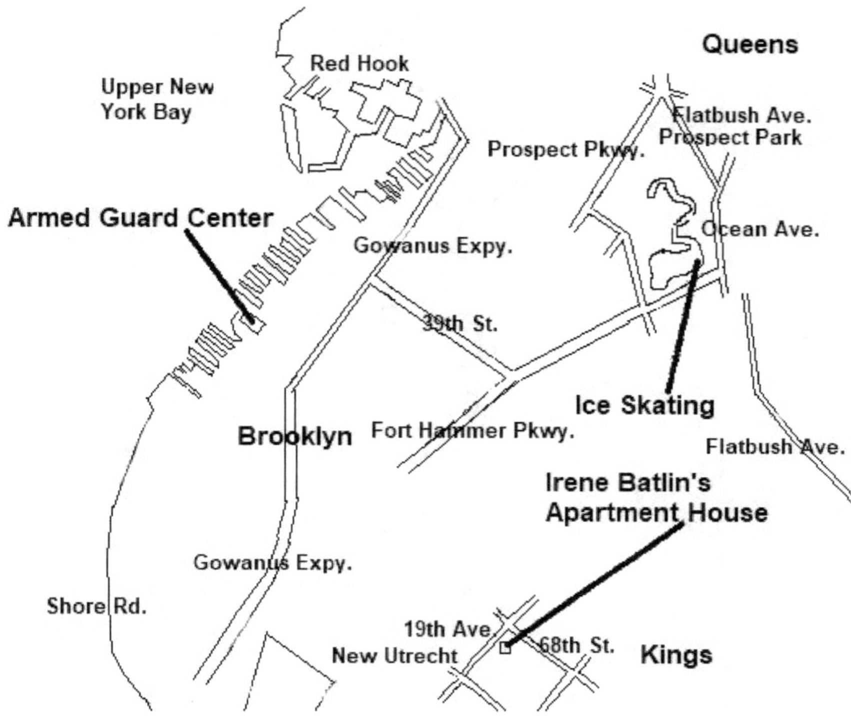

Irene lived with her parents and brothers in an apartment building at 6801 Nineteenth Avenue in Brooklyn. She was nineteen years old and had graduated from New Utrecht High School six months before. Irene was out ice skating with a couple of her girlfriends from her neighborhood. Kenneth was an excellent ice skater and could perform trick skating moves on the ice. He looked impressive skating. This caught Irene's eye. Irene complimented Kenneth and then asked for some pointers. And the rest, as they say, is history. Irene liked the idea that Kenneth was a sailor stationed within walking distance. Kenneth thought Irene looked like Daisy Mae Scragg. Irene was pretty.

Daisy Mae Scragg
Al Capp, Li'l Abner, Comic Strip Character 1934-1977

Kenneth went on dates with Irene as often as he could in November and December. It was more haphazard with date planning. But still, he and Irene managed to see each other—for a movie, a meal, dancing, or more ice skating. After Thanksgiving Day in 1942, Kenneth and Irene went on what could be considered their first date—even though they had been with each other before—with friends. Kenneth and Irene went to see *The Road to Morocco* with Bob Hope and Bing Crosby. They also saw the John Wayne movie *Reunion in France*.

After mess cooking duty had stopped, days were spent waiting, for the most part. Drills and drills and drills and loading ships took up the days. Days started at 6:00 a.m. Work would take the day—until dark. It was winter, so darkness came early, around 5:00 p.m. Once they had the hang of it, transportation around New York was easy. There were buses and cabs galore. The subway and trains went everywhere, it seemed. Kenneth would meet up with Irene at a predetermined location, and off from there they would go for the night. Kenneth was always a gentleman, and polite with Irene, opening doors and assisting with stepping up and down from the bus, the way his mother, grandmother, and sisters had taught him. It had stuck with him from an early age. This old-fashioned chivalry appealed to Irene. She was appreciative of Kenneth's gentlemanly ways.

During those first fifty days at the AGC, Kenneth went out on a date with Irene a total of six times. Neither he nor Irene had much experience with the other sex and were shy, but Kenneth held Irene's hand, at first reluctantly and then later with more confidence. He had put his arm around her as they walked. It was Irene who kissed Kenneth for the first time—nearly knocking Kenneth's feet out from under him. Irene led, and Kenneth followed. It was sweet, innocent, and pure. Irene worked at a bank. She was a bit of an arithmetic wizard. Kenneth admired this, as mathematics had always been a problem for him in school.

Kenneth wrote, "I left the base on January 3, 1943. I went to Wilmington, North Carolina," by train. He was only able to get a cable off to Irene, letting her know he would have to leave for a few days. Kenneth was again waiting in lines. He did not like Wilmington at all, writing, "It was a junk of a town," and spent his time waiting by going "to several shows." On January 6, Kenneth wrote, "We went aboard ship. From there we went to Norfolk, Virginia." Norfolk was one more of those backwater towns, which Kenneth did not appreciate, calling it, "one of the worst towns on the east coast." He longed for New York, and he missed Irene. Norfolk time was spent drilling and training in classrooms and out in the swampy marshes that seemed to surround everywhere he looked.

Finally getting to leave, he boarded the SS *James J. Pettigrew* (0874) and steamed for New York, arriving on the fifth of February. He wrote, "I saw Irene for about 15 minutes. I had to leave so I could get back to the ship." Kenneth steamed for Africa on February 7, 1943.

Kenneth and Irene went to see the Bogart movie *Casablanca* during a five-day leave in New York between May 4 and May 22, 1943. He would not see Irene again. The next time Kenneth returned to the States, in July 1943, he could not find Irene anywhere. As Kenneth had been away to sea for three months, it was apparent Irene had moved on during the time. And since Kenneth knew he would be leaving again soon, it was for the better.

Kenneth wrote in his diary, "Later, I met another girl. She was nice. Only had one date with her." Her name was Bernice Victoroff.

Bernice Victoroff, Teaneck New Jersey High School
1940 Yearbook "The Hi-Way" Sophomore Photo—Photograph in the public domain

He met Bernice at the Hurricane Club in New York City. They danced and had a wonderful time. So Kenneth asked her out. Going out with Bernice was going to be difficult, as she lived in an apartment building with her mother and brother at 50 East 191st Street in the Bronx, eighteen miles away.

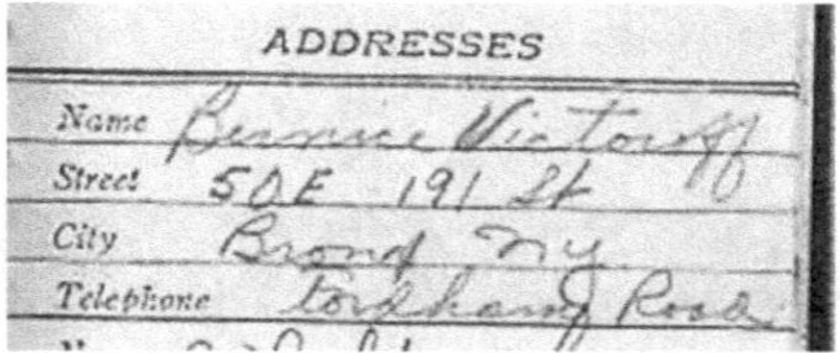

**Bernice's Address in the Bronx, from
Kenneth's Address Book**
Berquist Family Document

Kenneth cut their date short when he learned she was only eighteen years old and had lied to get into the dance club where they met. Bernice was also a little fast, and Kenneth did not like it either. It made him think of his sister Elsie. Kenneth was disappointed, though, because he thought Bernice looked like Dixie Dugan. Bernice was cute.

Dixie Dugan, Comic Strip Character Dixie Dugan, 1929 to 1966
ATTRIBUTION: J.P. McEvoy & John H. Striebel

The Atlantic 1943

The typical armed guard detachment was twenty-four gunners and one officer, plus as many as three communications guys.

Kenneth's AGC Armband--apparently never worn, circa 1943
Berquist Family Possession

Ships carrying troops had more armed guard detachments because there were more guns on troop ships. Experienced armed guard sailors were reassigned from duty aboard merchant vessels to serve as gunners on ships in the Pacific, where their training and experience made them particularly valuable. This switch would be Kenneth's fate in another year.

Kenneth wrote, "We left the states the 7th day of February."

Liberty Ship (EC2 Designation) S.S. James J. Pettigrew 0874, Hudson River mooring date unknown, Note Lipton's Tea sign on the rooftop of the building in the left background
Photograph in the public domain

The SS *James J. Pettigrew* left Brooklyn, steaming south toward Virginia, where she would join Convoy UGS.5 outside Hampton Roads. Forty-nine merchants and twelve escorts had converged at this location and were now making a beeline for the Moroccan Coast of Africa. It was February 8.

The convoy traveling east leveraged cover from the air corps and the safety, which eyes high overhead would provide for as long as they could.

Kenneth's Axis Submarine Identification Manual
Berquist Family Possession

Kenneth's "Frontline" Magazine, Issued by the Ministry of Home
Security by the Ministry of Information, 1942, His Majesty's
Stationary Office, The Official Story of the Civil Defence of Britian
Berquist Family Possession

There were two or three incidents during the crossing. The SS Pan
Royal, SS George Davis, and Norwegian Merchant M/T Evita were
involved in a mid-ocean collision two days out.

SS Pan Royal, circa 1920
Public Domain Photograph

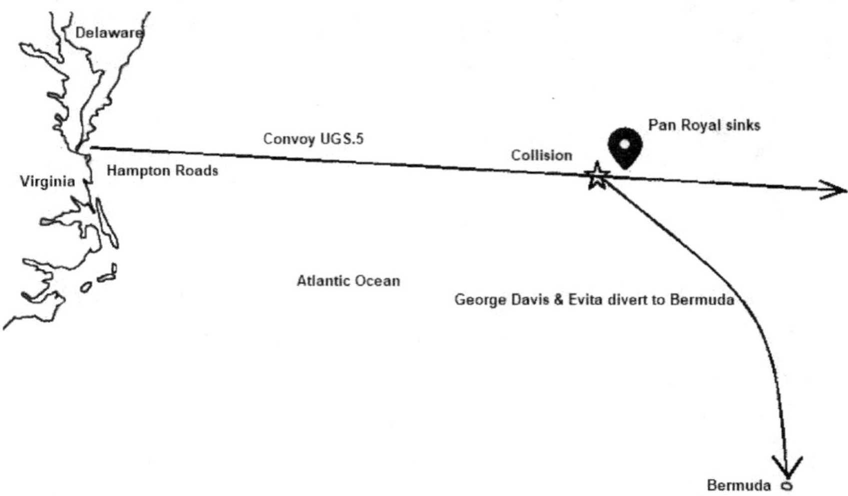

British motor tanker M/T *Seminole* in formation with Convoy UGS.5 broke ranks with the group west of the African Coast and headed for Oran, Algeria.

M/T Seminole
Photo Courtesy http://uboat.net/allies/merchants/ships/2693.html

On February 27, halfway between Gibraltar and Oran, she was torpedoed, twice. One man died. Fifty men abandoned ship and were rescued by the ship *Merchant Prince*. *Seminole* remained afloat and was towed to port only to go back into service the following year.

There were so many U-boats on patrol in the North Atlantic it was difficult for convoys to evade detection. Being detected resulted in a series of vicious battles. *Pan Royal* was an old ship and had been on duty off and on since 1919. She previously sailed under two other names before *Pan Royal*. Both *Evita* and *George Davis* accidentally rammed *Pan Royal*. *Pan Royal* sank with the loss of eight men. Her fifty-four rescued survivors were picked up by US Navy destroyer *Boyle* (DD-600).

The SS *George Davis* (876), a new ship laid down in 1942, went to the scrapyard in 1960. *Evita* was loaded with diesel oil and was able to put in at Bermuda on February 10. Kenneth knew nothing of the mishaps with the four ships or the sailors who lost their lives in the crossing.

UGS.5 was one of the last few convoys to be considered part of Operation Torch, more specifically the Tunisian campaign, which lasted until May 13, 1943. The amphibious assault on North Africa was the largest to date. Rommel squashed the Allied forces in French North Africa. The battle at Kasserine Pass in Tunisia was a blow to Americans and British alike. A lull in fighting occurred in mid-February, with opposing forces taking stock of their situations.

Kenneth wrote, "Arrived in Casablanca, Morocco February 25, 1943. Pettigrew took 19 days to make the Atlantic crossing." The ship delivered its medical load for the Sixth General Hospital. Kenneth did not stray far from his ship.

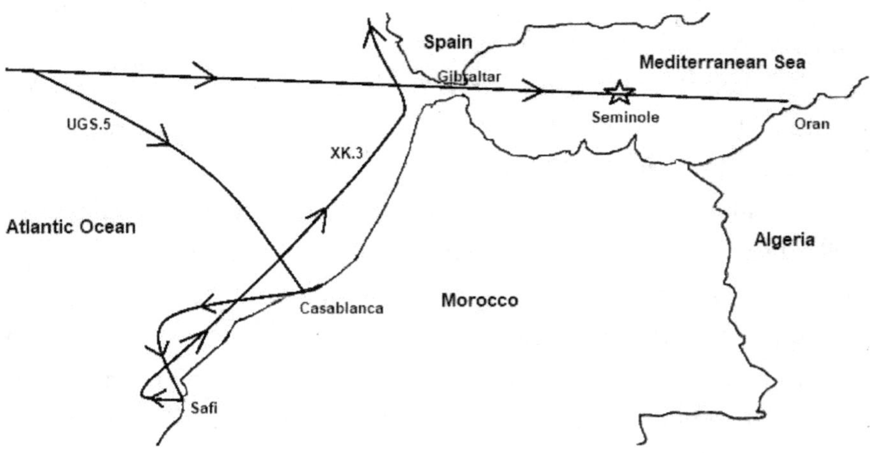

On March 6, 1943, command of the US II Corps in North Africa passed to Patton, with Bradley as assistant corps commander. Fighting in North Africa would continue until the surrender of the Axis powers on May 13, 1943. Taken were 230,000 enemy prisoners. The loss at Kasserine a few days before would prove to be, in hindsight, a fateful twist to what now would become a major victory for the Allies.

Pettigrew left Casablanca on March 7, steaming south to Safi, Morocco, and arriving there the following day, March 8.

Safi would be a different story, and Kenneth would be a bit more of a tourist at this port. Feeling much more confident with his surroundings, venturing off ship into town felt comfortable this time. It was time to have some fun. The bazaar in Safi proved he was in a different world, with so many unidentifiable foods to eat and people everywhere. It was loud and dirty-dusty. The bazaar was also colorful and exciting. Sellers bartered with the shoppers—sometimes loudly. Children ran loose in the streets as their parents scurried along gathering items needed for meals. Music echoed down the streets and drifted through the alleys. It would not be wise to travel alone through town.

Kenneth was grateful to be with a group of sailors who were all destined for the same adventure—eating from the local cuisine. They quickly learned they did not need to speak French. Simply pointing and motioning was enough to get anything they wanted to eat or drink. Sweets were abundant, as were fruits and vegetables. All were unidentifiable. Kenneth had not realized there were so many unusual species of fish. The fish market smelled bad. The meat market was not much different, looking unsterile with flies clinging to every piece of meat. Eviscerated poultry hung by their feet from overhead.

The sailors managed to get rice and cooked meat and bread and ate well on several occasions. The men would eat while sitting on the steps of a building or in a central square area, watching the passersby. It was difficult to tell what the girls looked like, as they were dressed head to toe in loose-fitting robes. Girls were never alone. Kenneth was in Safi for a week and, during this time, ventured out so often with his friends they soon found restaurants that became their favorite places to go. Either the food was excellent or the sights were agreeable, or both.

One day on an outing, one of Kenneth's friends—Tom Aitkens—got hurt riding a horse. Or rather, the horse stepped on Tom. Tom had been horseback riding on the beach with a couple of other guys. When they returned to the stable, Tom dismounted, and the horse spooked and came down hard on Tom's foot. At first, everyone thought Tom was only joking around—they had been drinking. Everyone was laughing, but Tom was not kidding. The horse's hoof had cut Tom's leg from the knee to the top of his foot. The horse had broken Tom's foot. An ambulance from the Sixth General Hospital took Tom, who was in some degree of agony, back to Casablanca. Tom was out of the action and not seen again. With their armed guard crew down one man now, a new kid by the name of Red Coury joined the group on the same day they steamed out of port at Safi. Red was from Providence, Rhode Island, and recently out of high school. It was March 13, 1943. Two days later and now part of thirty-seven ship Convoy XK.3, *Pettigrew* passed the Straits of Gibraltar.

**Convoy XK.3, Safi, Morocco to Bangor Island (Belfast Harbor),
Northern Ireland**

Pettigrew was carrying phosphates this time—used for making explosives. Kenneth thought Gibraltar "was a beautiful town located on hills."

Land and ocean battles went back and forth, both losing and gaining ground, from March through April. Both sides suffered a tremendous loss of life. But then in May, the tide changed, and the Allies had licked the Axis naval forces.

Facing what would have been an unmitigated disaster, "Black May" as it became known left 34 U-boats at the bottom of the Atlantic – "a frightful total, which came as a hard and unexpected blow," Dönitz wrote. These were losses he could not sustain. "We had lost the Battle of the Atlantic." Donitz ordered his boats to abandon the ocean – for now. They would return with renewed technology, but too late to affect the course of the battle.[1]

Pettigrew with Convoy XK.3 arrived in Belfast Harbor, Bangor, Ireland, on Saturday, March 27. It was an uneventful voyage up the coast of Portugal and into the Irish Sea. The convoy had air cover for most of the trip.

After a less-than-one-day stop in Bangor, Ireland, on March 27, 1943, *Pettigrew* steamed for Avonmouth, England, arriving there on March 29.

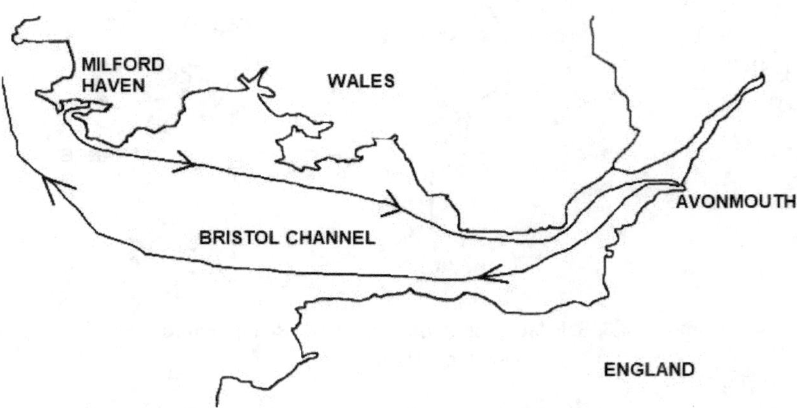

Milford Haven to Avonmouth and back

The ship unloaded about half of the phosphate cargo in Avonmouth, and then they hurried independently to Milford Haven, Wales, around the fourth of April and emptied the other half of the shipment. Then came one more trip back to Avonmouth to wait. April 9–15 was spent sightseeing in Bristol. *Pettigrew* departed Bristol, England, on April 16, 1943, with ballast in her hold and her US Navy Armed Guard crew ready to take on New York City.

A brief stop in Liverpool, England, to pick up Convoy ON.178 and out into the open Atlantic they would go.

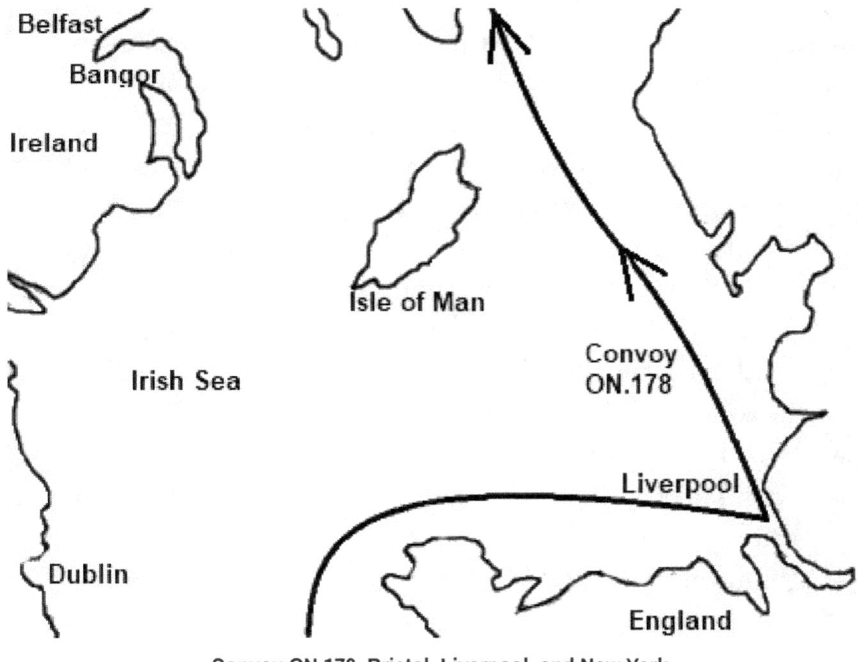

Convoy ON.178, Bristol, Liverpool, and New York

Departing the North Channel, taking an arcing shot toward the southern tip of Greenland, provided the best air cover course for the convoys—at least on bright days. And then came a further arc southwest along the coast of Canada. It would be a straight shot into Brooklyn from there heading home.

By the spring of 1943, the British had developed a useful sea-scanning radar small enough to be carried in patrol aircraft armed with airborne depth charges. Centimetric radar significantly improved interception.

During 1943 U-boat losses amounted to 258 to all causes. Long-range B-24 Liberators closed the mid-Atlantic gap, which had been unreachable by aircraft.[2]

It snowed, off and on, over the next few days. Snow only served further to slap Kenneth's face in the below-freezing temperatures. *Pettigrew* was among a group of seventy-eight vessels in Convoy ON.178 bound for New York, but as the convoy moved out into the Atlantic, two ships turned around and went back to Liverpool, one ship diverted to Iceland, and two others fell behind and were picked up by another convoy. It was an unusual mix of destinations this time. Of the seventy-eight ships, only fifty-three of them were going to New York. Others would end their voyage in Halifax, Nova Scotia. Two would turn in at St. John's, Newfoundland and Labrador. Still one other would turn in at Boston. ON.178 steamed ever cautiously westward home.

April 21, 1943, started out like any other day freezing ass in the North Atlantic. He thought about seeing Irene in New York. He thought about his older brother, Richard, and wondered where the navy had taken his brother that day. He thought about his mom, dad, and sisters. He thought about being able to see Billy again. He did his job—these days shoveling snow overboard—while scanning the horizon and fighting off the doldrums, which another day at sea would bring.

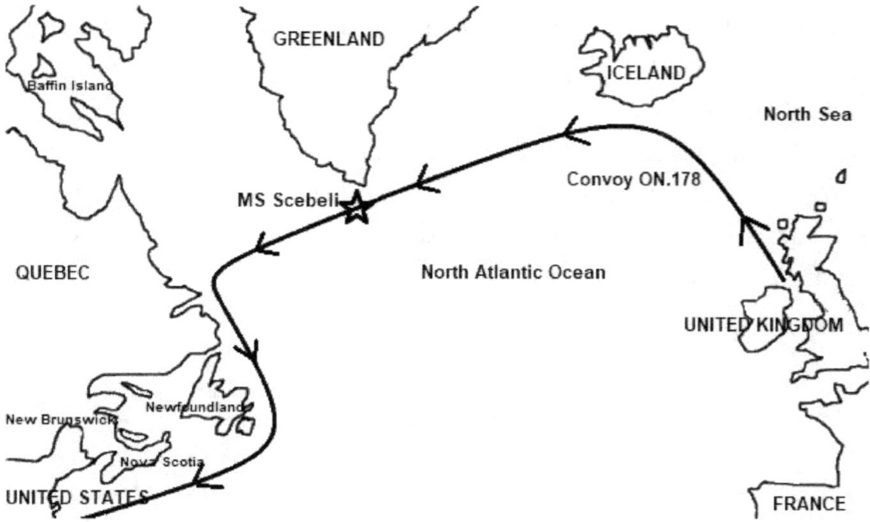

The German Kriegsmarine had their work for the day also laid out. The work did not include shoveling snow—they were hunting. At 6:30 in the evening on April 21, U-191 torpedoed Norwegian (Motor Steamship) M/S *Scebeli*.

M/S Scebeli
Source: Historical Department, MAN B&W Diesel, Copenhagen

The roll of the ocean obscured the view, but the explosion could be felt—whacking Kenneth in the chest. At general quarters, the alarms screamed. Two torpedoes were sent, and one connected on her port side, sending *Scebeli* tipping toward the surface, slowly sinking. The crew abandoned ship, going into lifeboats only after some men trod the freezing North Atlantic. Two men lost their lives. Kenneth wondered if *Pettigrew* was next. HMS *Hurricane* and HMS *Kale* plucked thirty-nine souls from the sea. Survivors were deposited at St. Johns, Newfoundland and Labrador, on April 26.

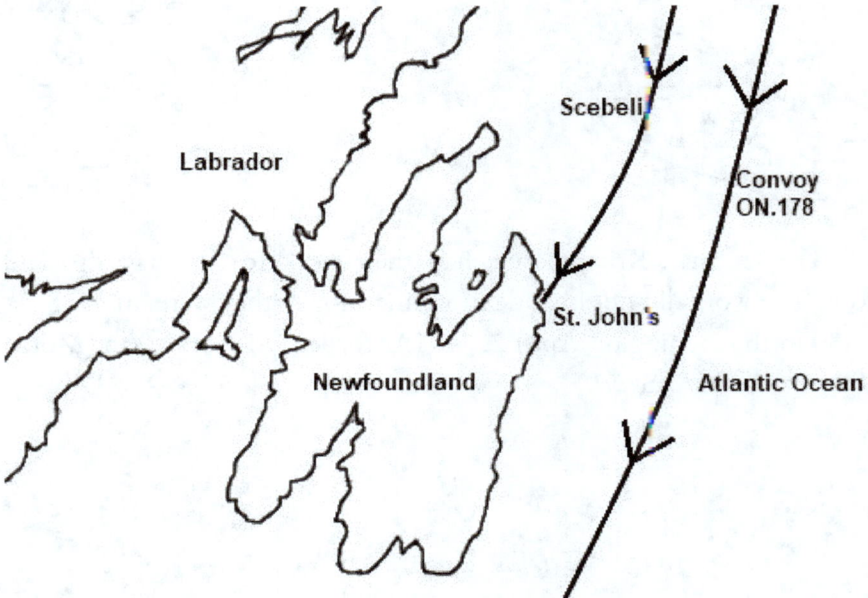

A lot of correspondence heading to the States from Europe went to the ocean floor that evening. The torpedo attack changed the whole itinerary for the convoy, and *Pettigrew* put in at Halifax, Nova Scotia, on April 29.

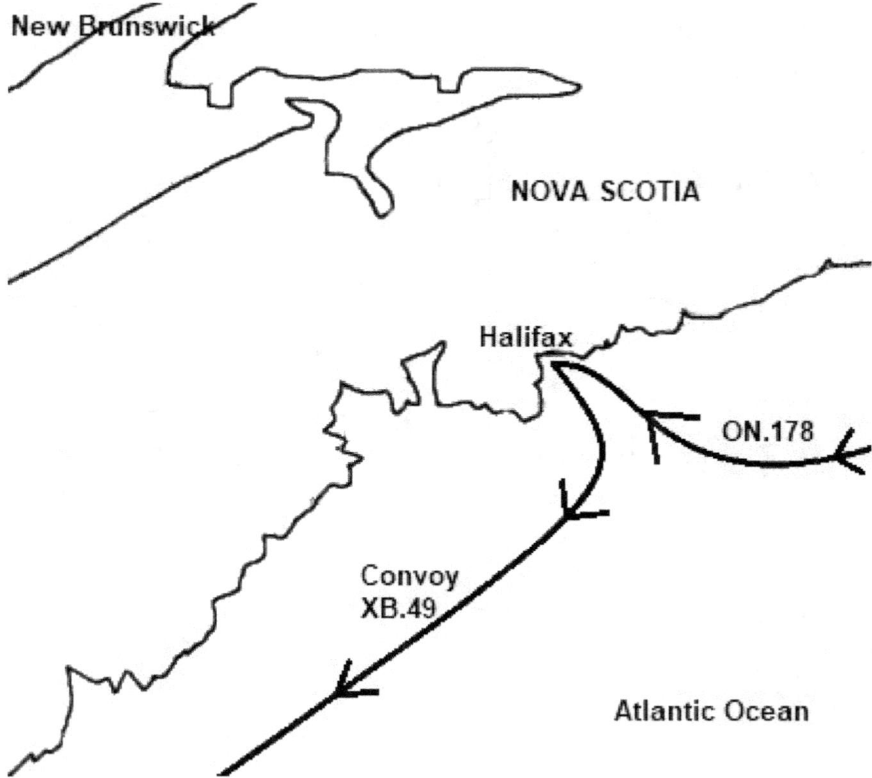

Pettigrew departed Halifax on May 2, 1943, bound for Boston and part of the twelve-ship Convoy XB.49. Kenneth wrote in his diary, "Landed in America 4th May Boston. I was in Boston 22 days. I had five days leave. Went to New York."

Kenneth saw Irene. They went to see the Bogart movie *Casablanca*, which was ironic to Kenneth, as he had recently been there. They also caught a baseball game. On Tuesday, May 18, they watched the Brooklyn Dodgers lose to the St. Louis Cardinals, seven to one. Even though the Dodgers were first in the league at the time, with the Cards trailing by five games, he was thrilled watching his Cards beat the pants off the Dodgers. As they walked out of the stadium, Kenneth was quietly chuckling to himself. He did not dare laugh aloud with all the Dodger fans around.

Pettigrew departed Boston on May 26, 1943, bound for Halifax, part of Convoy BX.54.

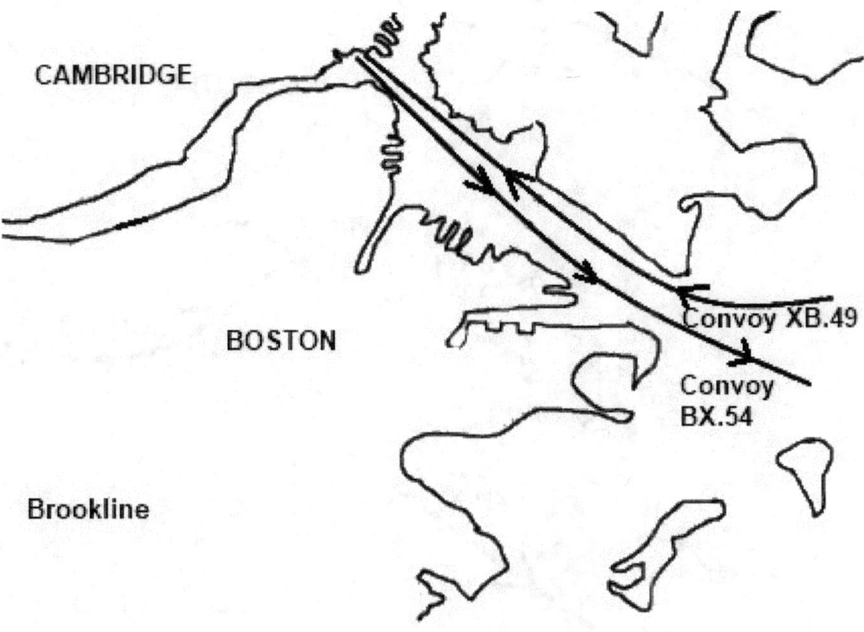

Kenneth wrote, "We left Boston May 26th on Wednesday afternoon. We arrived in Halifax, Canada, 28 May. We were there for five days." As promised, his promotion to gunner's mate third class (GM3c) took place on May 26, 1943.

June 2, 1943, found *Pettigrew* now part of Convoy HX.242 leaving Halifax, steaming for Ireland.

There were ninety-three ships in convoy. Except for two, which hit icebergs, neither severely damaged, the crossing was uneventful. Pettigrew arrived in Belfast on June 15, 1943.

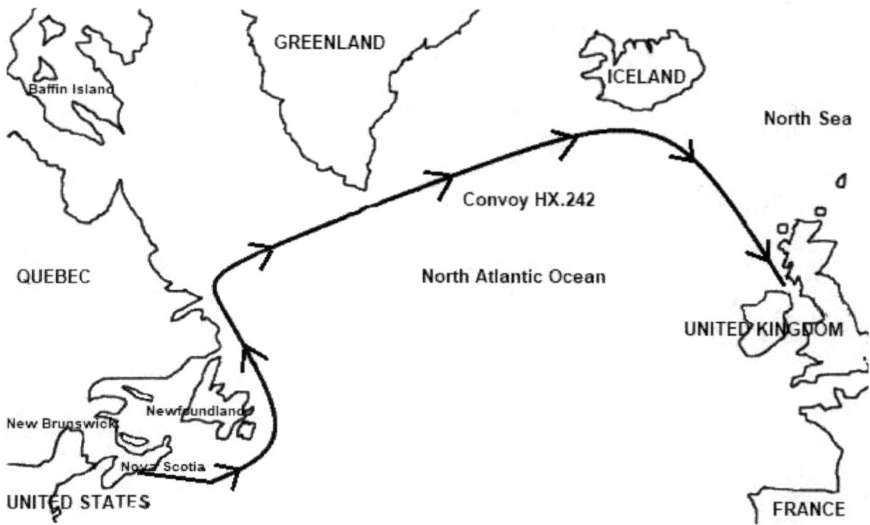

The cargo, in its entirety, was discharged. The load was a little bit of everything—called General Halifax Exports. *Pettigrew* spent one day at the dock in Belfast. The next day, as part of a twenty-ship Convoy BB.300, made way for a one-day trip to Newport, Wales.

Pettigrew steamed independently to Milford Haven, Wales, and then to Barry Roads, Wales.

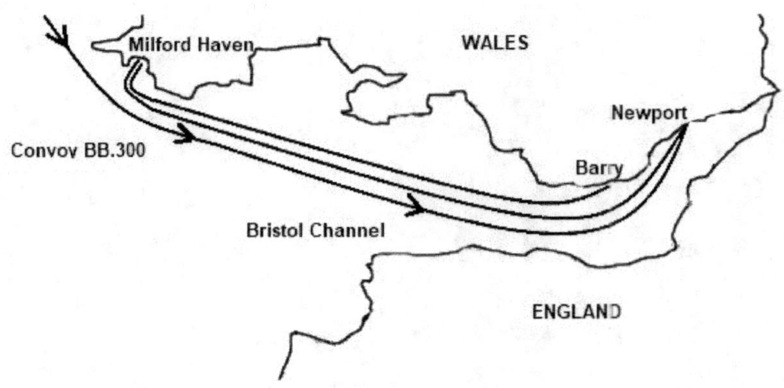

Kenneth wrote in his diary, "We left there June 2nd. We arrived in Newport Wales 16 of June. We were there 12 days. I went to Cardiff, Wales. Sure, saw a lot of things. We went to dances too." Kenneth would be a tourist this time.

Apparently, joining the Red Cross gets you into all the best service clubs in the UK.

AMERICAN RED CROSS
SERVICE CLUB
9. BERKELEY SQUARE, CLIFTON, BRISTOL
Membership Card
CARDS HONORED IN ALL A.R.C. SERVICE CLUBS
NAME Bergquist K   A.O.P. No. USN
SERIAL No. 6207544

Kenneth's tourist belongings included the photogravure, which holds six postcard-sized photos of various points of interest in Cardiff, and a two-hundred-page guidebook.

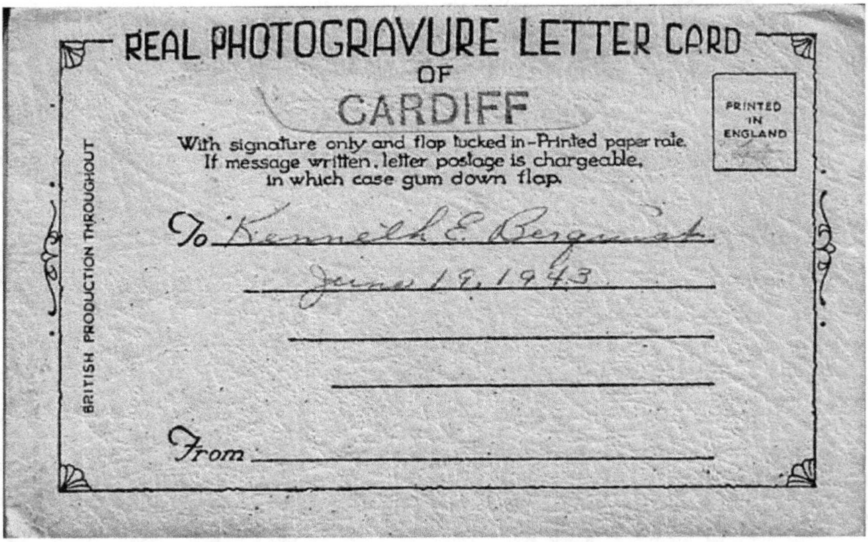

REAL PHOTOGRAVURE LETTER CARD
OF
CARDIFF

PRINTED IN ENGLAND

With signature only and flap tucked in—Printed paper rate.
If message written, letter postage is chargeable,
in which case gum down flap.

BRITISH PRODUCTION THROUGHOUT

To _Kenneth E. Berquist_
June 19, 1943.

From _______________

The guidebook also included forty pages of advertisements for various travel services. Kenneth ended up with twenty-five sixpence coins in his pocket before he returned to the US from his last trip to Europe.

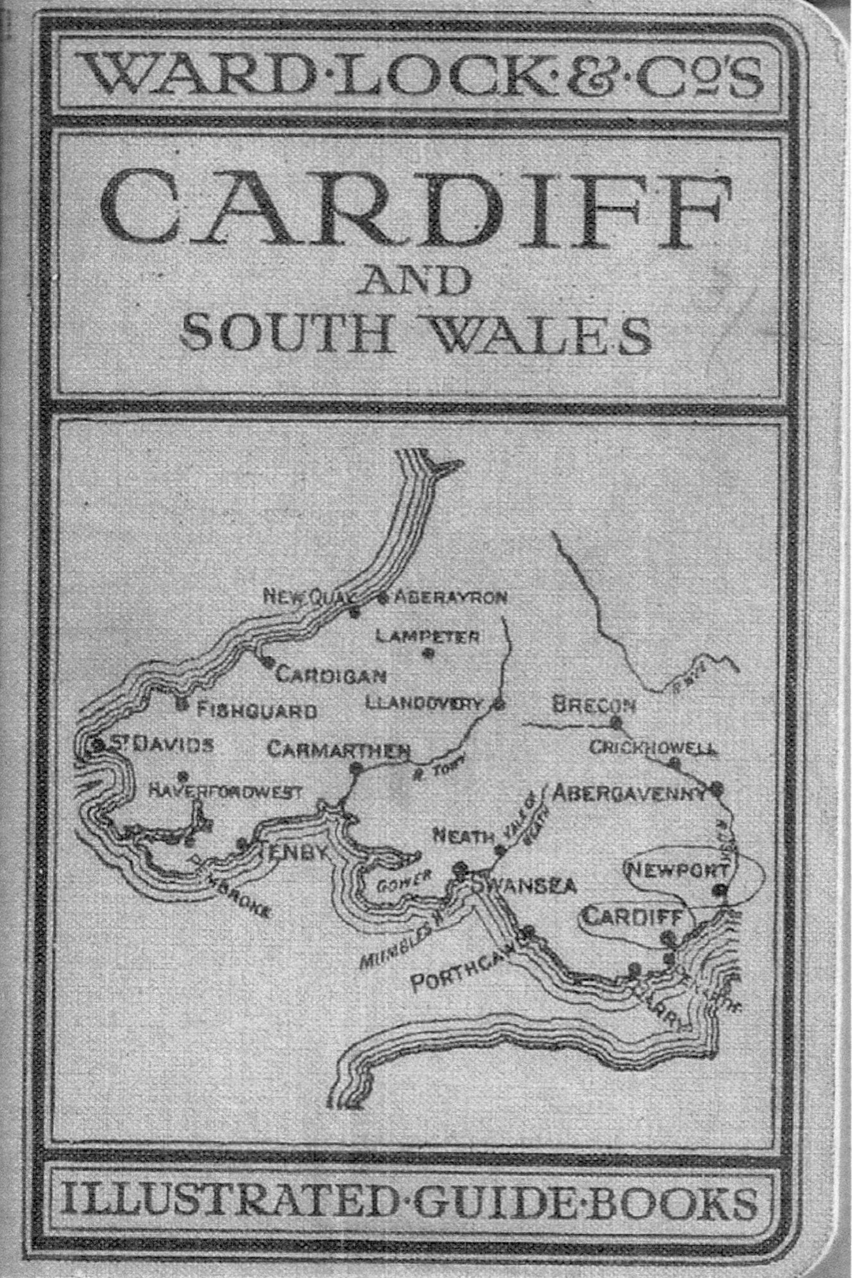
WARD·LOCK·&·C.'S
CARDIFF
AND
SOUTH WALES
NEW QUAY
ABERAYRON
LAMPETER
CARDIGAN
FISHGUARD
LLANDOVERY
BRECON
ST DAVIDS
CARMARTHEN
CRICKHOWELL
HAVERFORDWEST
R. TOWY
ABERGAVENNY
NEATH
VALE OF NEATH
TENBY
PEMBROKE
GOWER
SWANSEA
NEWPORT
CARDIFF
MUMBLES H.
PORTHCAWL
ILLUSTRATED·GUIDE·BOOKS

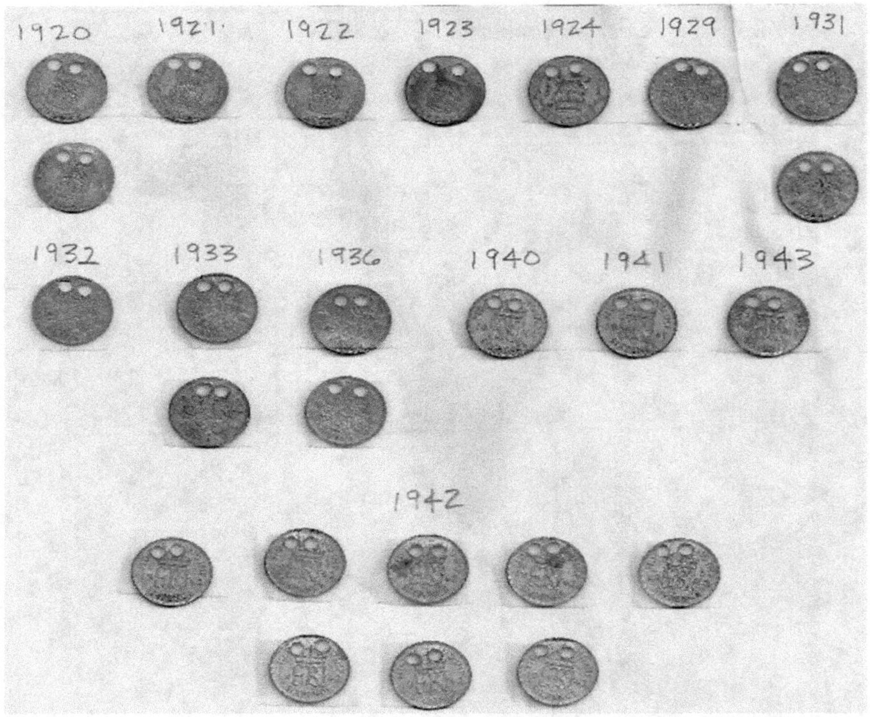

Kenneth came home with a pocket full of six pence
Berquist Family Possession

"Something old, something new, something borrowed, something blue, and a sixpence in her shoe for good luck."[3]

Kenneth wrote in his diary, "We left Newport around 30th of June. We arrived in States around the middle of July 15."

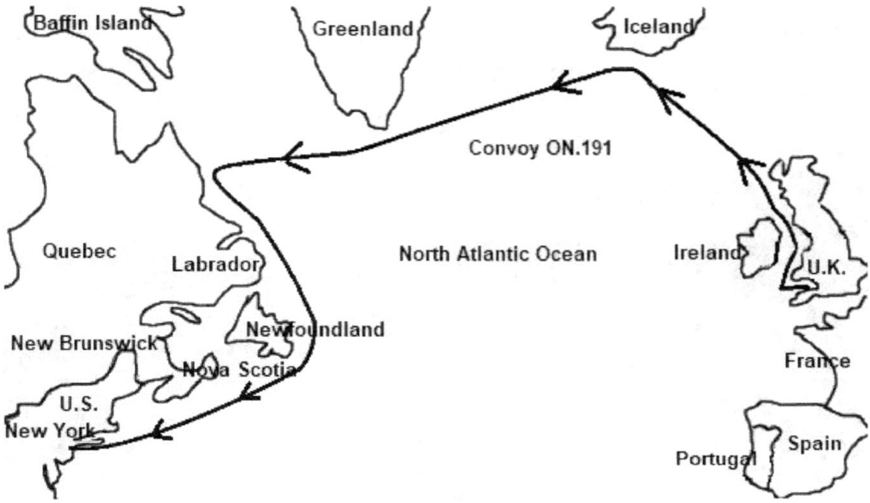

This time, with eighty ships in Convoy ON.191, *Pettigrew* steamed to New York on July 15, 1943. It was an uneventful crossing. Kenneth disembarked in Brooklyn, New York.

Kenneth aboard the James J. Pettigrew, circa July 1943
Berquist Family Photo

Pettigrew continued to Philadelphia a week later, staying at the dock until August 3, 1943. She had completed her mission. When Kenneth returned from Europe, he was moved to the new building, Barracks B, which was built behind the armory.

New "B" Barracks AGC Brooklyn circa 1943
ATTRIBUTION: http://www.armed-guard.com/bag1.html

This move resulted in more space and came as a bit of a reward for surviving duty in the Atlantic, no small feat. The benefit lasted only a short month before he was shipped out to Washington, DC, for some advanced training.

Washington, DC

After Kenneth returned from England on July 15, 1943, he wrote, "I got leave 21st July, 16 days." Kenneth was able to catch a quick train ride home and saw his friends and his parents. The visit was brief, but it was nice to be home for a few days. Kenneth did not realize it, but this was going to be the last time he would see Billy.

Billy Karver and Kenny Snyder, at cousin Clifford Martin's home in West Burlington, Iowa, July 1943, NOTE: C, B & Q Railroad Shops buildings in the background—Kenneth worked there.
Berquist Family Photo

Kenneth on Leave July 1943, (L-R) Kenny Snyder, assumed Billy Karver's boyfriend—Walter Penner, Kenneth, Cousin Clifford Martin. Picture taken at the Martin home, 602 West Mount Pleasant Street, Trailer #5, West Burlington

Berquist Family Photo

Kenneth on leave July 1943, Kenneth (right) with Kenny Snyder.
Kenneth had time to put his civilian clothes on for a few days.
Berquist Family Photo

Kenneth on Leave July 1943, man wearing light colored trousers is Kenneth's Dad—Mick Berquist. Pictures taken in front of 2024 Summer Street, Burlington—Kenneth's home. Kenneth's car 1941 Chevrolet Special Deluxe
Berquist Family Photos

Kenneth on leave July 1943 with his buddy Dick Fry
Berquist Family Photo

Kenneth on leave July 1943 with his buddy Dick Fry
Berquist Family Photo

Kenneth on leave July 1943 with his buddy Dick Fry
Berquist Family Photo

Kenneth wrote, "Came back to New York after leave then went to Washington, DC. I liked it very much. I met a couple of girls there. They did not mean a thing to me anyhow. I was there two months. Went to school."

Gyro School, August–October 1943, Bainbridge, Maryland

When Kenneth returned to the East Coast, he had gotten his orders. He would deploy to the Pacific after completing naval training school, fire control advanced, in Washington, DC. Finally, Kenneth thought he would have a chance to see Washington.

Located in Bainbridge, Maryland, Service School Port Deposit was about seventy-five miles northeast of Washington. The school graduated thousands of sailors during World War II, providing them with unique technical skills, such as gunnery, fire control, radio, and telemetry. These were not recruit sailors. Sailors who attended this school were already experienced sailors. Kenneth trained in gyrocompass repair and operation at Port Deposit. Gyrocompass played an integral role in fire control.

The Lionel Corporation of New York, famous for model railroad trains, ceased toy production in 1942 to build gyrocompasses for the US Navy. Lionel returned to toy manufacturing after 1945.

Lionel Gyrocompass
Photo taken by Michael Berquist with permission aboard the USS Kidd DD-661 Floating Museum, Baton Rouge, Louisiana, February 2017

Gyro school must have been something for Kenneth. Not only did he get chosen to go, which made him feel special, but it offered him the opportunity to tour Washington. The year prior, when traveling between gunnery school in Virginia and Brooklyn, New York, he passed through DC and longed to stop and take it all in. He hoped for a chance to go there someday. Now the opportunity to see the nation's capital presented itself.

Not only was Kenneth a gunner's mate who knew the workings of all types of guns and artillery aboard ship. He was a gunner's mate with specialized training in the operation of a gyrocompass. Gyro school improved Kenneth's arithmetic skills, which had always been a challenge for him when he was a kid.

While attending what Kenneth described as "a big army show," he and three friends from gyro school toured Washington, DC, on September 26, 1943.

Tom Mecca, (assume school classmate) (assume Thomas L. Mecca, GM2c, Connecticut) (assume USS Barton DD-722) at "Big Army Show", Washington, D.C. September 26, 1943
Berquist Family Photos

Kenneth with V. Costello, assumed school classmate (unknown rank or ship association) at "Big Army Show" Washington, D.C. September 26, 1943
Berquist Family Photo

James Climp, Classmate, Denver, in front of the Capital Building. Kenneth wrote on the back of the photo that, "James would remain with him for the remainder of the war."
Berquist Family Photo

Kenneth in front of U.S. Capital Building, September 26, 1943
Berquist Family Photo

Kenneth in front of the U.S. Capital Building, September 26, 1943, on the back he wrote, "I got caught winking."
Berquist Family Photo

Kenneth on the lawn in front of the U.S. Capital Building, September 26, 1943
Berquist Family Photo

The U.S. Capital Building steps, September 26, 1943
Berquist Family Photo

The Lincoln Memorial, September 26, 1943
Berquist Family Photo

Waiting in line at the Washington Monument, September 26, 1943
Berquist Family Photo

Reflecting Pool - Washington Monument, September 26, 1943
Berquist Family Photo

Kenneth finished gyro school and, within a few days, returned to the armed guard center in Brooklyn. He would quickly be on his way via train again, this time to San Francisco, California. Kenneth did take a brief layover in Burlington for a few days in October 1943.

Kenneth arriving for brief stop in Burlington on his cross country trip
to San Francisco; previous photo; Kenneth's sister, Donna Berquist
Moore, whispers something to Kenneth at the train depot, October
1943
Berquist Family Photos

CHAPTER 11

The Pacific 1944

Kenneth wrote, "Then I came to S. Frisco. I've been here for three weeks Wednesday 10th Nov." Kenneth arrived on October 25, 1943. Treasure Island was the destination.

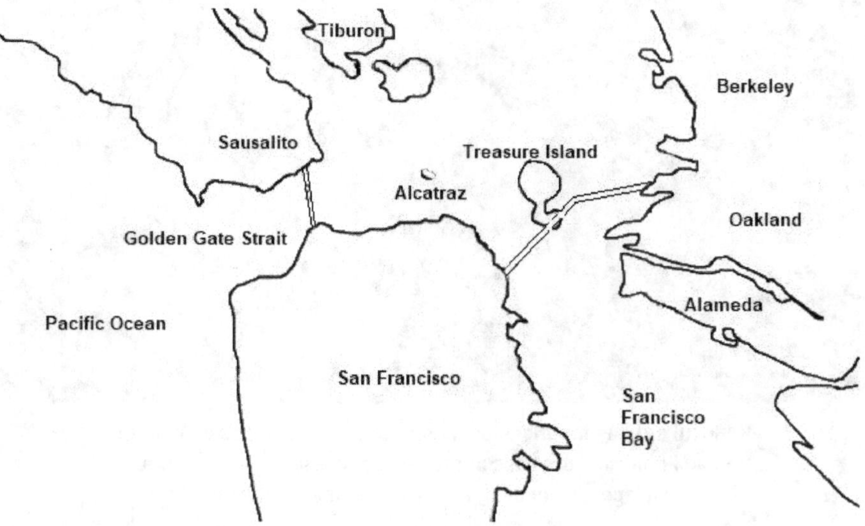

San Francisco, California (Treasure Island), October 1943

The trip had been an incredibly long train ride, first on the Pennsylvania Railroad from Penn Station in New York City to Union Station in downtown Chicago. The usual 950-mile train ride would take twenty-five hours, but with winter setting in, the route was plagued with weather delays. The train arrived ten hours late in Chicago. Thirty-five hours on the train and he was not even to Burlington yet. He hopped on the old reliable CB&Q in Chicago and luckily arrived in Burlington in a typical eight-hour trip. After forty-three hours on the train, he spent the next five days in Burlington with his mom, dad, and sister Donna.

They celebrated Kenneth's twenty-fourth birthday early because he had to get to San Francisco before the end of the month. Kenneth's mom, Louise, was thrilled her son was home—at least for a little while. She made him his favorite cake with the buttercream frosting. Kenneth could have eaten the whole cake by himself.

October 10 arrived, and it was time to leave. Everyone went to the train depot in Burlington to wish him well as he boarded the Zephyr back to Chicago. Another eight hours and 350 miles on the train. The next day, after a restless overnight stay in a nearby hotel in Chicago, he boarded a Union Pacific train in the morning. San Francisco, here I come, he thought.

He was happy knowing he would get to see more of the United States but was not pleased it was going to take several days to get there. Winter weather and equipment failure in the worst of places hindered the usual 2,400-mile, ninety-six-hour train ride. The dining cars ran out of food on the fifth day. Running out of food meant food would have to be loaded on the train each time at several different depots as it traveled west. Freezing temperatures in the Rockies caused the plumbing to freeze. Drinking water stopped flowing. But worse yet, they could not use the toilets. When the train pulled into the depot in Cheyenne, Wyoming, a riot nearly broke out with people rushing inside to use the restrooms.

Similar tempers flared in Salt Lake City and Reno, Nevada. The thing that topped it all off, though, was when the train broke down outside North Platte, Nebraska—in the middle of nowhere and miles from the depot. A blizzard blew through, burying the train tracks in three feet of snow. They stayed right there for three nights, waiting for another locomotive to be dispatched and pull them along into North

Platte, where they could swap the two engines out in the switchyard and get them going again.

Kenneth arrived in San Francisco 4,050 miles and fourteen days later. It was the worst experience in his military life until this point. It was like he was held captive by the railroad system for two weeks. It was October 25. He was late getting to Treasure Island.

Kenneth had gotten his orders in New York that he was to be transferred to the USS *Feland* (APA-11), an attack transport.

USS Feland APA-11
ATTRIBUTION: Photograph in the Public Domain U.S. Navy photo from Navsource.org

However, by the time Kenneth had finally gotten to Treasure Island, *Feland* had deployed and was making runs between Pearl Harbor, New Zealand, the Marshall Islands, the Gilbert Islands, and the Cook Islands. Kenneth was again waiting.

In hindsight, it was a blessing Kenneth's ship was not there when he arrived, as he had developed an issue during his trip from Chicago that, by the end of October, had grown into a painful problem. Kenneth wrote, "I'm in the hospital now, cyst operation. I hope to get leave after I leave the hospital." He had developed a pilonidal cyst on his tailbone, which required surgical intervention. Kenneth had gotten what would coldly be called "Jeep disease" during his long train trip across the country. Living in unhygienic conditions, sitting for extended periods of time, and not bathing was at the root of the problem. Kenneth had surgery on November 10, 1943. He spent the next five weeks in the hospital, waiting for an open wound on his tailbone to heal. Medical treatment required the surgical wound to remain open and drain. Bodily fluids and dressings needed frequent changing and cleaning. Infection was a constant concern. Kenneth learned how to sleep on his stomach. He ate lots of ice cream. And he took a tremendous amount of ribbing. The taste of the cold ice cream trickling down his throat helped take the sting of the jokes away.

Kenneth faced the real aftermath of war during his time in the hospital. There were men from the South Pacific in the hospital with Kenneth who had suffered genuinely horrifying injuries.

Among all the other smells of various bodily excretions, the smell of burnt flesh was truly horrendous. The pain many of the men were forced to endure in unimaginable agony was heart-wrenching. Every day, Kenneth watched as another stretcher with another dead sailor was quickly whisked away to avoid attention. The various wings of the hospital stored the bodies of broken men who had lost arms, legs, and some even their eyesight. Being held at the mercy of the doctors and nurses at the hospital over such a small thing on his ass was embarrassing. He ached to get out of the infirmary.

After surgery and five weeks of convalescence in the hospital, Kenneth got a three-week leave. He wrote, "I got 21 days leave." He was off to Ventura, California, to see his sister Elsie and nephew James.

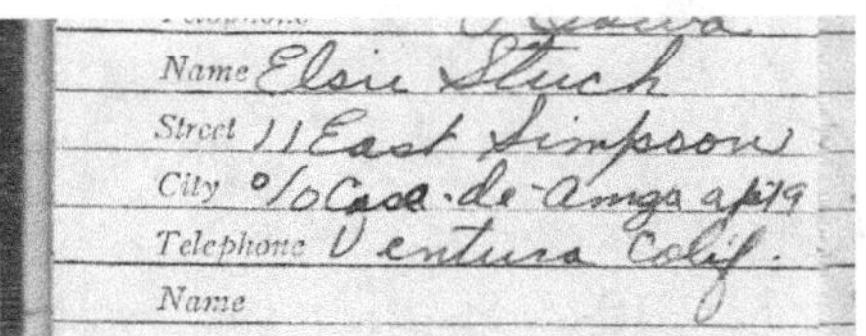

From Kenneth's address book, his sister's
address in Ventura California, Elsie
Berquist-Stuck, 11 East Simpson, c/o Casa de
Anza Apts, Apt #9
Berquist Family Possession

Leave was a blessing for Kenneth, as he wrote in his diary, "I didn't care much for San Francisco." Did this dislike come from being in the hospital from the day he arrived there or because it was winter and it was bone-chilling cold? We will never know. It was a wet, damp weather, which cut right through. Kenneth had not experienced this before.

Kenneth was on leave from December 22, 1943, through January 12, 1944, spending Christmas and the New Year holiday with his sister Elsie and nephew James.

The "Casa de Anza Apts" 11 East Simpson Street, Ventura, CA
Photo taken by a Berquist family friend in 2019

Kenneth with his nephew James Hill, James 13-years old, Christmas/New Year's 1943/ 1944, at his sister Elsie's apartment house in Ventura, CA
Berquist Family Photo

Kenneth on leave—at sister Elsie's
Apartment, Ventura, California Elsie mailed
the photos to their parents in Burlington.
Elsie wrote on the back, "Picture taken of
Kenneth when he was here. All taken in front
of our apartment. You can have these."
Berquist Family Photos

Kenneth on leave—at sister Elsie's Apartment, Ventura, California. Elsie wrote on the back, "Ken. Taken right where we live. Notice the high hill in back?"
Berquist Family Photo

Kenneth wrote he "had a swell time" on leave. Ventura sure beat San Francisco in the winter. He loved the milder weather of Southern California. Kenneth wrote, "Returned the 12th day of Jan. 1944," to San Francisco after leave and, "Left hospital 29 Jan 44. I went on S.P. Duty. I'm waiting to be shipped out now."

Kenneth was put on shore patrol duty for four weeks, writing, "I was on S.P. Duty for a month at Treasure Island." Shore patrol consisted primarily of running back and forth between Treasure Island and the various civilian police stations and court buildings throughout the Bay Area. He worked days and was not faced with dealing with drunk, belligerent, angry sailors, whom night SP contended with regularly. The detained individuals Kenneth transported typically spent the night in jail, sleeping it off. Some were absent without leave from their ships and faced desertion charges. Some had been brought up on charges of homosexuality. Still others were arrested for various simple infractions: traffic laws, public intoxication, assault, disorderly conduct, public urination, or having too much fun on liberty.

Getting into the Fight

Feland arrived back in the States on February 23, 1944. Three days later—February 26—Kenneth was aboard as a casual navy passenger headed for Pearl Harbor. Kenneth wrote in his diary, "I left the States 26th of Feb arrived at Pearl Harbor 3 March."

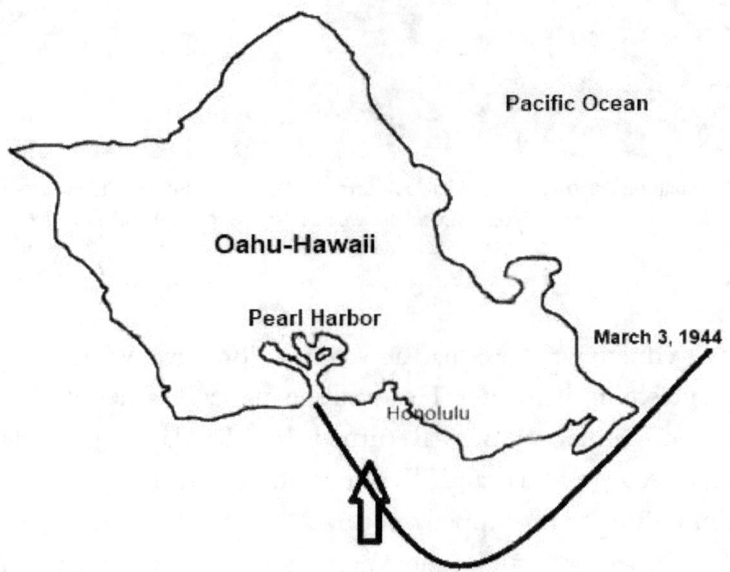

Feland returned to San Francisco after the run to Pearl. Kenneth was in catch-up mode now, waiting. He had a new ship assignment. Kenneth was at Pearl Harbor for twenty-eight days. He wrote, "I was there four weeks, sure liked it there."

Kenneth was frequently given liberty while he waited in Honolulu for his deployment to the South Pacific. While strolling along the street by Waikiki Beach, taking in the sights, the sounds, and the smells of the tropical flowers always in bloom, Kenneth's thoughts were never far from home. Sightseeing and going to Kapiʻolani Park were all part of the touristy places to see when not on duty. There was breeze at the botanical garden, and the zoo was adrift with hibiscus. It was at this point Kenneth understood the fragrance Billy wore. It was the same fragrance wafting through the park. Hibiscus! The flower Billy had pinned to hold hair back behind her ear was hibiscus. He stopped for a moment by himself in the park and stood there breathing the air in through his nose. Billy.

The man walking on the sidewalk in this photograph is wearing a swimsuit.

Kenneth (left)—with Unknown Sailor—Waikiki Beach March 1944
Berquist Family Photo

Also, in the background is the N. AOKI Groceries Meats sign. The Waikiki Beach Resort & Spa replaced the old grocery store at the corner of Kalakaua Avenue and Oahu Avenue in Honolulu. Nearby is the Prince Kuhio statue. Kenneth, his buddy on the park bench, and the buddy who took the photo were out sightseeing. On Waikiki Beach, it is easy to imagine what "sights" they were "seeing."

Kenneth left Pearl, again as a casual navy passenger, aboard the USS *Nehenta Bay* (CVE-74). *Nehenta* was an aircraft carrier escort. She was delivering mail, men, and planes to the Marshall Islands.

USS Neheta Bay CVE-74
ATTRIBUTION: Photograph in the Public Domain U.S. Navy photo from Navsource.org

Kenneth wrote, "Left Pearl H. April 1, 1944. Arrived at Majuro Marsh group April 7th." On the way to Majuro, Kenneth was promoted to gunner's mate second class, GM2c(T), on April 7, 1944. A spit of an island surrounding a large lagoon, Majuro was one of many atolls in the Marshall Islands group.

The destroyer USS *Laws* (DD-558) had returned to Majuro on April 5, 1944.

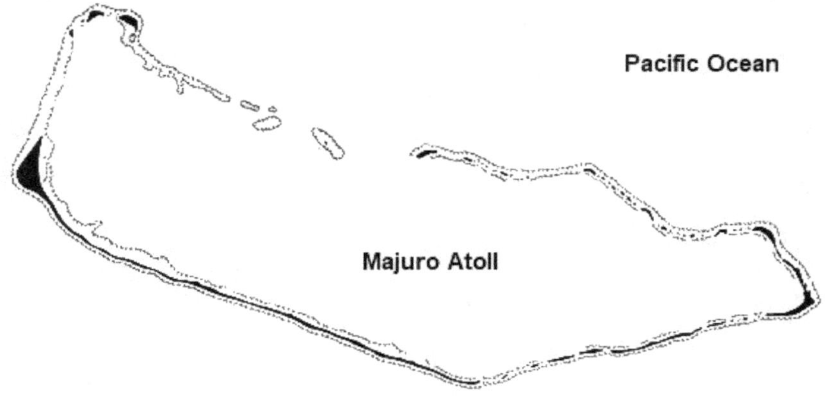

Upon Kenneth's arrival at Majuro, he went immediately aboard *Laws*.

USS Laws DD-588, in post-war configuration, circa 1954
ATTRIBUTION: Photograph in the Public Domain U.S. Navy photo from Navsource.org

Laws would be his new home for the next twenty months. *Laws* left Majuro on April 12, 1944, heading for tanker escort duty in Manus—part of the Admiralty Islands group.

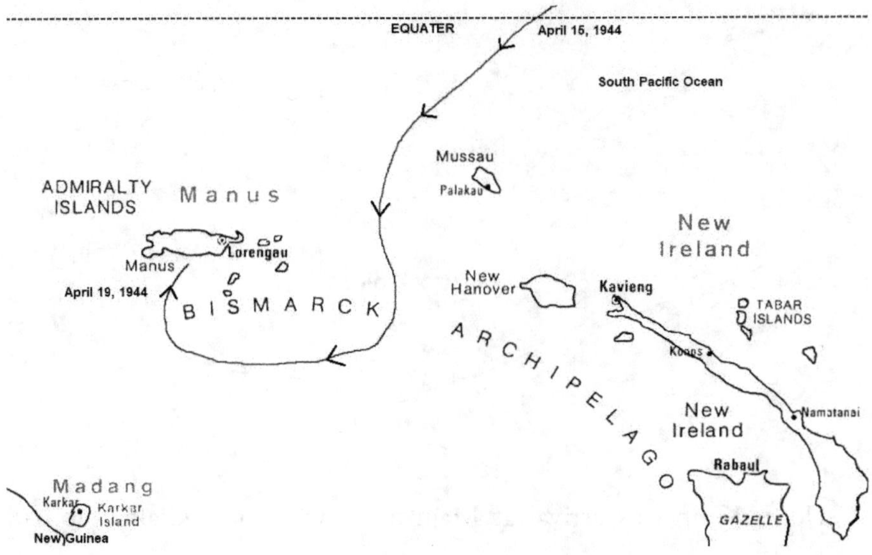

On the way to Manus, *Laws* crossed the equator on April 15, 1944. In the ceremony, Kenneth would become a "Trusty Shellback," joining the Ancient Order of the Deep sworn to silence to its Solemn Mysteries.

**Kenneth's "Imperium Neptuni Regis" Solemn Mysteries of the
Ancient Order of the Deep certificate**
Berquist Family Possession

The two-day event was a ritual in which previously inducted crew members were organized into the "Court of Neptune" to induct "Pollywogs" into "the Mysteries of the Deep." Physical hardship, in keeping with the spirit of the initiation, was tolerated, and each Pollywog was expected to endure a standard initiation rite to become a Shellback. The eve of the equatorial crossing was called "Wog Day" and, as with many other night-before rituals, was a mild type of reversal of the day to come. All the uninitiated could capture and interrogate—for example, tie them up, crack eggs, or pour aftershave lotion on their heads—any Shellbacks they could find. The Wogs were made acutely aware of the fact it would be much harder on them if they did anything like this.

After crossing the line, Pollywogs received subpoenas to appear before King Neptune and his court who officiated at the ceremony, which was often preceded by a beauty contest of men dressing up as women, each department of the ship being required to introduce one contestant in swimsuit drag. Afterward, some may be "interrogated" by King Neptune and his entourage with the use of "truth serum" and whole uncooked eggs put in the mouth. During the ceremony, the Pollywogs underwent some increasingly embarrassing ordeals—for instance, wearing clothing inside out and backward, crawling on hands and knees on nonskid-coated decks, being swatted with short lengths of firehose, or being locked in stocks and pillories and pelted with mushy fruit. Locked in a water coffin of salt water and bright-green sea dye (fluorescent sodium salt) was the worst. Wogs crawled through chutes or large tubs of rotting garbage. And there was the general humiliation of kissing the "Royal Baby's" belly coated with axle grease or having hair chopped off. All was done for the entertainment of the Shellbacks.

Neptune's Royal Court, USS Petrof Bay CVE-80 (Carrier Escort)
ATTRIBUTION: http://www.navsource.org/archives/03/080.htm

Laws arrived at Manus (Admiralty Islands) on April 19, 1944. Kenneth was acting turret captain on the #51 Gun. The five-inch guns were numbered one through five from stem to stern. Thus, #51 was the forwardmost five-inch gun. *Laws* earned her Battle Star and Kenneth his first ribbon for the Hollandia landing—New Guinea Operation, April 18–29, 1944. Kenneth wrote, "Then we were on tanker escort duty. Submarine contact on May 2 dropped depth charges."

Kenneth wrote in his diary, "After passing a month at this (escort duty) we went to P.H. May 9th. Arrived at P.H. In four days, out five days, in five days."

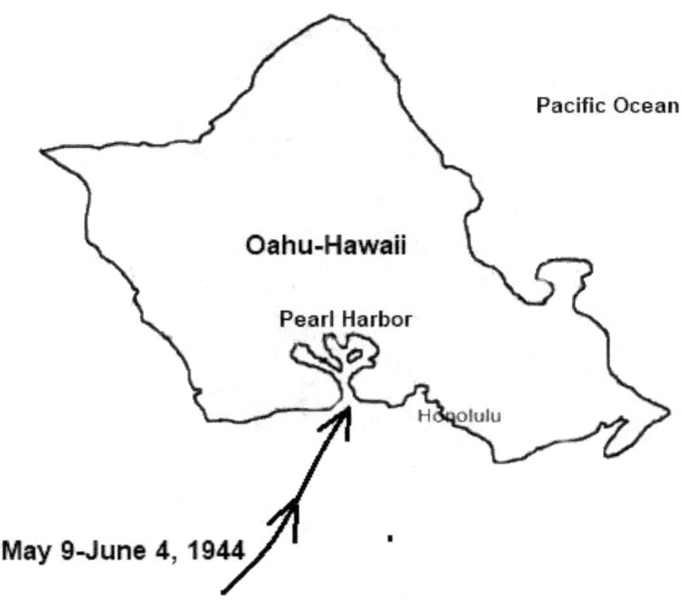

Laws received twenty-two new men at Pearl on May 9.

TOP LEFT: Kenneth squatting in front of a grass hut. TOP RIGHT: Sailor identified as B.J. Rung—Michigan. MIDDLE: Kenneth in outrigger canoe. BOTTOM: Kenneth and B.J. in outrigger canoe. All photos dated May 1944
Berquist Family Photos

B.J. Rung was later identified as GM3c Bernard Joseph Rung. At three in the afternoon on May 21, 1944, *Laws* was steaming out of Pearl on another four-day escort mission. As she passed the 1010 dock, an enormous explosion, followed immediately by a massive fireball sent skyward over the West Loch, was both seen and felt. Believing a second Jap attack was underway, they called GQ—all-hands battle stations. Within minutes, all clear was sounded. Still, more explosions and fireworks. An LST had accidentally blown up. It was confusing to all aboard.

Kenneth wrote, "Then to Roi in Marshalls moving on to Saipan & Tinian & Guam."

After the breather in Pearl, *Laws* arrived at Roi-Namur on June 8, 1944, and joined a carrier group. Kenneth wrote, "We escorted CVL at this time," on the way to Saipan.

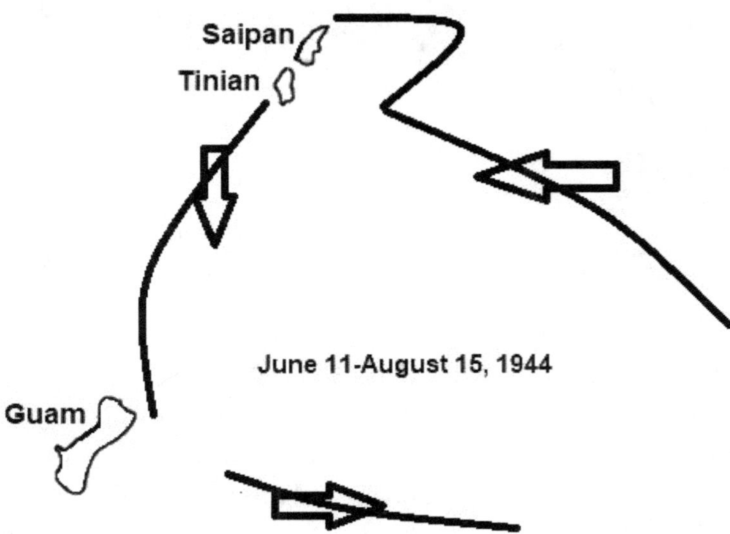

Word of the invasion by Allied forces on Germany reached *Laws* on June 7. Eisenhower had led the D-Day troops onto the beaches of Normandy the day before. In the Pacific, Operation Forager was underway.

Kenneth wrote in his diary, "Two attacks, two planes. Both planes shot down. June 18 & 19." Downing one of the Betties earned Kenneth's gun crew a Silver Star.

A Betty could reach high altitudes for bombing raids, but in this case, they had been used by the Japanese as low-flying torpedo planes, such as the one shown in the photograph.

Japanese G4M2e bomber, "Betty"
ATTRIBUTION: http://senri.warbirds.jp/19english/izoku/17/izoku17.html

In this first air attack were forty Jap planes. Another air raid occurred on June 19, with another Jap plane downed and its pilot recovered. In the evening of June 22, three torpedoes passed through the formation. All missed. Same thing again on June 28, with another projectile launched through the group. General quarters had been sounded in the middle of the night. Some firing occurred, but nothing was hit.

Laws entered the harbor at Saipan to refuel in the afternoon of July 16. There were several sunken ships in the port and dead bodies floating in the water. The ship was assigned to Task Force 58 now. USS *Laws* returned to the same harbor again on the twenty-sixth and transferred ammunition to light cruiser Cleveland on the twenty-seventh. On the way to Enewetak, *Laws* plucked a fighter pilot out of the water.

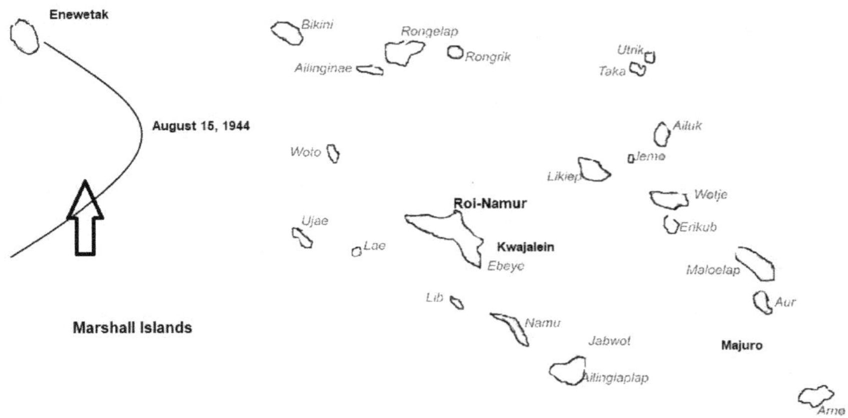

The pilot had bailed out of his crippled plane, trying to make it to the airstrip at Kwajalein. He was grateful to be out of the shark-filled ocean.

Laws earned another Battle Star and Kenneth another ribbon for the capture and occupation of Saipan, Tinian, and Guam (Northern Mariana Islands) June 11–August 15, 1944.

Kenneth wrote, "August 13th we pulled into Enewetak (an atoll in the Marshalls) until the 29th of Aug. then to Palau and the Philippines."

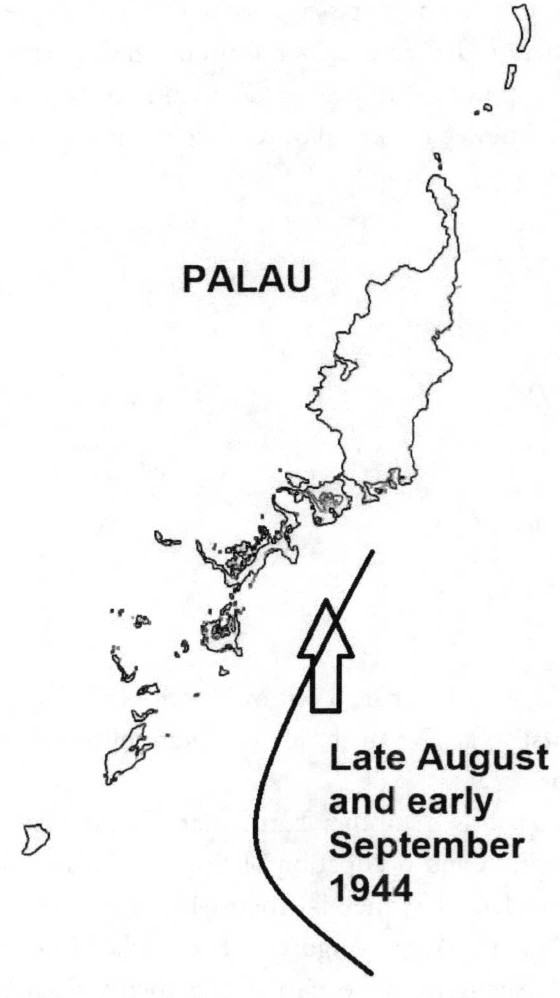

Located about seven degrees north of the Equator and east of the
Philippines

Laws refueled from battleship *Iowa* at Enewetak. The ship pulled in next to destroyer tender USS *Markab* (AD-21) on August 19 and then went into floating dry dock—scraping bottom—for repairs on the twenty-fifth and out of dry dock on the twenty-seventh. The two weeks was a welcome rest.

On September 1, *Laws* crossed the equator again with thirty-five Pollywogs aboard this time and Kenneth on the other side of the equation as an Honorable Shellback. This time, he would be doling out the initiation.

On September 6, planes from the carriers in the task group hit Palau hard. *Laws* picked up a three-man crew from a ditched Grumman TBF Avenger torpedo bomber.

To a small extent, *Laws* participated in Operation Stalemate II at Palau and was diverted to the Philippines within the first week of September 1944.

Kenneth wrote in his diary, "We were the first ship to approach the Philip. And the second ship to fire on her. We sank three sampans." *Laws* was part of Destroyer Division 110 in Task Force 58. On September 9, 1944, the six-ship division was sent by reports from overhead aircraft to Sanco Point on the east coast on Mindanao to destroy a flotilla of forty sampans. All forty of the "sitting ducks" were sunk or left burning. *Laws* received credit for sinking three boats. She picked up two Jap survivors.

Laws earned another Battle Star and Kenneth another ribbon for the capture and occupation of the southern Palau Islands (Micronesia) and assaults on Philippine Islands September 6–October 14, 1944 (September 9–24, 1944). Kenneth's gun crew was awarded three Gold Stars, taking recognition for sinking three Japanese sampans. *Laws* slowed off Palau to pluck a Jap out of the water, but right before he was taken captive, he shot himself in the head. The shot nearly removed the opposite side of his head from where the round went in. The crew had seen kamikaze attacks before and realized they were suicide, but this was the first time they were exposed face-to-face with Japanese fanaticism.

Rather than be taken prisoner, he would prefer to be dead. Blood and brains sprayed into the ocean as one of the *Laws* crew grabbed him.

In the Philippines and throughout Southeast Asia, civilian sampans were commandeered by the Japanese and used surreptitiously to transport Japanese military and supplies.

Asian Sampan
ATTRIBUTION: http://mandragore2.net/dico/lexique2/navires2/sampan-2-gd.jpg

Dropping a sampan was the same as sinking a cargo ship or a troop transport. Sampans were wooden boats not used in the open ocean. Sampans were propelled by rowing, pushing with long poles, using a small outboard gasoline engine, sailing, or any combination of the four.

Kenneth wrote, "After some boring patrolling duty (September 25–October 8) in Palau, we proceeded to a small island off the coast of Japan, 250 miles to be exact."

Photo simply titled, "Alfred", apparently drawn by a bored sailor on a
five-inch/.38 caliber gun house
Berquist Family Photo

Admiral Halsey's Third Fleet began a series of vicious battles, starting with Okinawa on October 10, 1944, and moving south from there, passing Formosa and into the Western Philippine Sea.

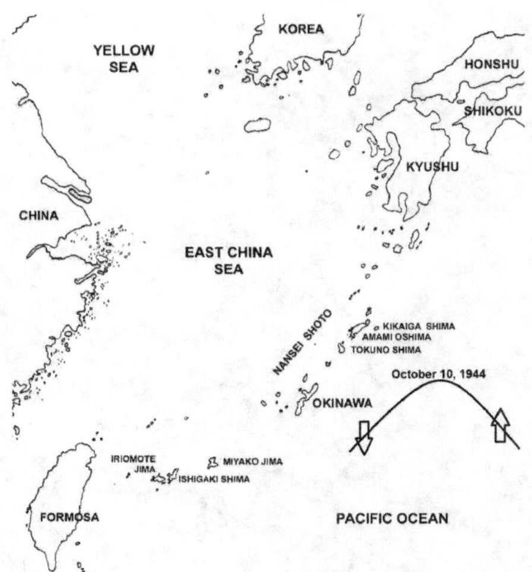

**Japanese Ryukyu (Southern) Island Chain
Estimate the Strait between Tokuno and
Okinoerabu Islands to be 250 miles from the
Japanese Mainland**

On October 12, *Laws* had a frustrating GQ with a lot of bogies and rough water. Japs dropped flares over the formation. The formation replied with smoke. There were casualties on other ships from friendly fire.

Kenneth wrote in his diary, "Then to Formosa. Three raids (October) 13-14-15 all at night.

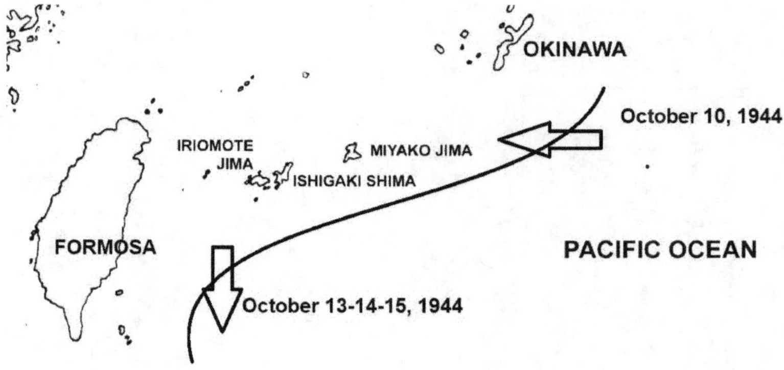

"13th GQ 06:30 to 14:00," heavy cruiser USS *Canberra* (CA-70) hit by a torpedo but did not sink. Under tow, she went to Ulithi.

"14th GQ 18:30 to 20:30 p.m. then again at 01:00," light cruisers *Reno* (CL-96) and *Houston* (CL-81) were both torpedoed during an evening attack. Neither ship sank. Both towed to Ulithi for repairs.

"15th GQ at 06:00 to 16:45 p.m. again at 18:30 until 20:45 at night." *Laws* was patrolling for the Jap fleet around Formosa, and the disabled *Houston* received her second torpedo.

By October 17, the Jap fleet was nowhere to be found. Kenneth's twenty-fifth birthday went by unnoticed on October 19, 1944.

Kenneth wrote in his diary, "Japs sank Princeton CVL. The sinking was something to see. They took a terrific beating." The light aircraft carrier *Princeton* (CVL-23) sustained a dive-bomber hit amidships. The bomb pierced the wooden top and then blew up in the lower decks. Exploding gasoline below started everything above on fire. From miles away, they could see the smoke of the fire. Several other explosions followed. *Princeton*'s powder magazines blew up. Casualties were worse in the vessels that came to *Princeton*'s aid. Losses were heavy all around.

At GQ, all day on the twenty-fourth, over 1,300 were rescued from *Princeton*'s crew. The USS *Irwin* (DD-794) and USS *Reno* (CL-96) scuttled *Princeton*, and she sank shortly before 1800 hours on October 24.

Besides the *Princeton*, the task force lost two CVEs (*Kitkun* and *Gambier Bay*), three destroyers, one destroyer escort, and some PT boats in the second attack on the Philippines between October 25 and 27, 1944. With the count of ships sunk not yet complete, one third of the Jap fleet would be destroyed or severely damaged in the days after.

Kenneth wrote, "Then to Ulithi," in the Carolines. *Laws* was there only long enough to refuel, resupply, and take one long, deep breath before she returned to Luzon.

Untitled Crew Photo-no date, no location, in front of the #51 Gun—USS Laws docked somewhere
Berquist Family Photo

Attacks continued along the eastern shores of the Philippines from Luzon on November 5 and 6 to the Visayas on the eleventh. Roosevelt was elected to his fourth term as president on November 7.

Kenneth wrote, "The Japs interrupted again—this is Nov. 12, 1944." He also noted the kamikaze attack on the *Lexington*, saying, "Last week (November 5, 1944) a plane dove into the Lexington, killed 15, and wounded many." She took a deadly hit near her island. Flames were under control and flight operations resumed within twenty minutes. She put in at Ulithi on November 9 for repairs. The USS *Lexington* (CV-16), nicknamed "The Blue Ghost," was an Essex-class aircraft carrier and one of the most decorated vessels of World War II. She rests at anchor in Corpus Christi Bay, Texas, as a floating museum. The "Blue Ghost" nickname came because the Japanese Empire reported her sunken or destroyed on several occasions.

USS Lexington (CV-16)
ATTRIBUTION: M. Hansen, U.S. Navy photo 80-G-268028 from the U.S. Naval History and Heritage Command—Photo in the Public Domain

Laws patrolled and escorted north and south along the eastern coast of the Philippines and participated in attacks on Luzon on November 13 and 14 and plucked another fighter pilot from the sea on November 14.

Laws put into Ulithi on November 20, 1944. During the night, two Jap mini subs managed to get through the harbor nets and succeeded in torpedoing two tankers. The two oilers burned all through the next day. The two subs were depth charged by a couple of escorts and PT boats that had gone out looking for them at sunrise. *Laws* returned to screening carriers.

Laws hit Manila Bay area hard on November 25. Jap aircraft that had gotten through the fighter screens were ineffectual by the time they reached ships off the coast. One crashed the Essex but did insignificant damage.

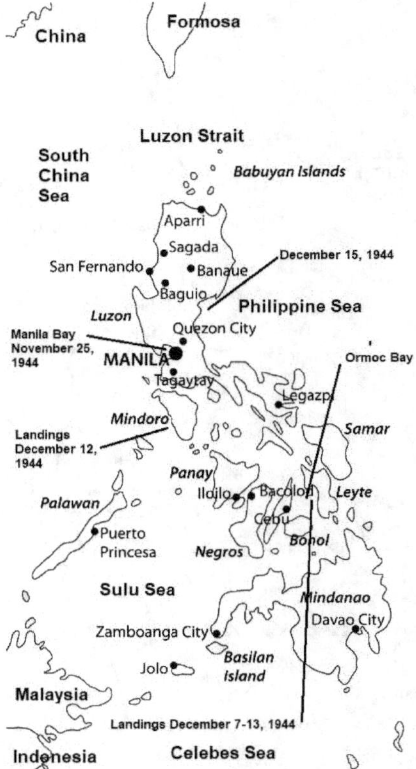

Laws escorted landing craft during the Mindoro landings on December 12 and was then redirected to Leyte to support landings there. *Laws* supported the Ormoc Bay landings the seventh through thirteenth of December, picking up another fighter pilot on the fourteenth of December and then participating with further strikes on Luzon until the fifteenth, when fighting of a different type started.

Typhoon Cobra, also known as Halsey's Typhoon, was a tropical cyclone which struck the Pacific Fleet on December 15th. Task Force 38 had been operating about three hundred miles east of Luzon and was conducting air raids against Japanese airfields. The fleet was attempting to refuel its ships. As the weather worsened, it became increasingly challenging to refuel, and the attempts discontinued. Despite warning signs of deteriorating conditions, the vessels remained in their stations. Information given to Halsey about the location and direction of the typhoon was inaccurate. On December 17th, Halsey unwittingly sailed Third Fleet into the heart of the cyclone. Because of 100 mph winds, high seas, and torrential rain, three destroyers; USS Hull *(DD-350), USS* Spence *(DD-512), and USS* Monaghan *(DD-354), capsized and sank. 790 lives were lost. Nine other warships were damaged, and over one hundred aircraft were wrecked or washed overboard.*[5]

The light aircraft carrier USS *Monterey* (CVL-26) was forced to battle a severe fire, which was caused by a plane hitting a bulkhead as it fell overboard. Kenneth wrote, "I never will forget those three awful nights we took spray over the forecastle something terrible. I had to change clothes three and four times a day no kidding."

CHAPTER 12

The Pacific 1945

When the typhoon eventually moved, *Laws* made way for Ulithi on December 18, 1944.

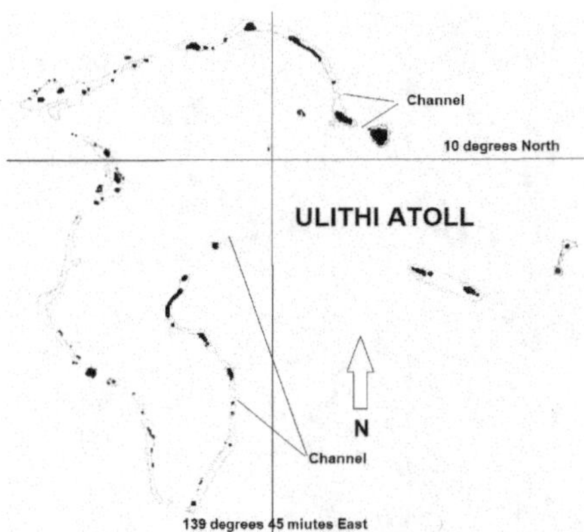

**Ulithi westernmost atoll in the Caroline Island
Chain 22 miles long and 15 miles wide**

The refueling operations started again on the nineteenth. *Laws* stopped briefly to pick up two sailors who had been swept overboard from a different ship during the storm. The two had spent thirty-six hours in a flotation net and were grateful to be aboard and dry. *Laws* spent Christmas in Ulithi.

All enjoyed a buffet dinner in the combat information center aboard ship.

Combat Information Center (C-I-C) USS Kidd DD-661 Floating Museum Baton Rouge, Louisiana
Photo taken by Michael Berquist with permission February 2017

Kenneth did not actually eat in the C-I-C. He passed through in line to get his plate filled and then move into the crew's mess to sit down and eat his Christmas dinner.

Crew's Mess Aboard the USS Kidd DD-661 Floating Museum Baton Rouge, Louisiana
Photo taken by Michael Berquist with permission February 2017

"The Paint Crew" Laws Docked Somewhere 1945 L-R: Kaine, Richardson, Smith, Rassmussen Note: Twin 40mm AA Gun Mount behind
Berquist Family Photo

Sailors in the above photo were later identified from USS Laws Muster Logs as; GM1c Francis Bernard Kaine, GM2c William Herbert Richardson, GM3c Glenn William Smith, and GM2c Vernon Rasmussen.

Entrance to the Crew's Mess past the Chow Line aboard the USS Kidd DD-661 Floating Museum Baton Rouge, Louisiana
Photo taken by Michael Berquist with permission February 2017

The problem with the port screw that went out during the storm could not be found—it miraculously fixed itself. The guys on the tender all thought the *Laws'* engine crew was crazy. There was lots of teasing and name calling. It was all funny. While still at anchor in the harbor, other ships in the fleet took to practice firing and accidentally lobbed a shell toward *Laws*, landing about fifty feet from her stern. The narrow escape was not funny. On December 30, *Laws* put back to sea.

At sea on January 1, 1945, *Laws* headed to Formosa, arriving there on January 2 and immediately joining the strike force shelling the island from every direction.

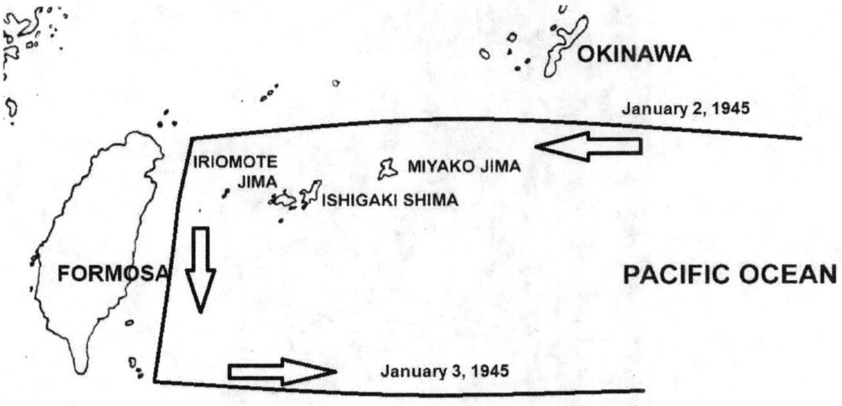

Shelling continued to the third, until *Laws* received orders to move on Lingayen in the Philippines to cover landings there. *Laws* stayed at Lingayen until the fifth and was then directed to join the group attacking Luzon.

Strikes at Luzon went on from January 6–7. It was stormy on the sixth with high seas.

As *Laws* maneuvered to pick up a floundering pilot, the ocean swell grew so high the sea delivered the aviator to the ship's deck without the need to stop. The swell simply sat the pilot down without a scratch. The amphibious assault was such a success the war moved one step closer to Tokyo. *Laws* moved back to Lingayen Gulf on the eighth to provide cover for marine landing craft.

China
Formosa
Luzon Strait
Jan. 8, 1945
South
China
Sea
Babuyan Islands
Jan. 4-5, 1945
Aparri
Jan. 6-7, 1945
Sagada
San Fernando
Banaue
Baguio
Lingayen Gulf
Luzon
Philippine Sea
Jan. 9, 1945
Quezon City
MANILA
Tagaytay
Legazpi
Mindoro
Samar
Panay
Iloilo
Bacolod
Leyte
Palawan
Cebu
Puerto
Princesa
Bohol
Negros
Sulu Sea
Mindanao
Zamboanga City
Davao City
Basilan
Island
Jolo
Malaysia
Indonesia
Celebes Sea

Kenneth wrote on the back of the photo, "Tor-pedo Gang", naming;
Balta, Swanson, Steinhu, Crum, Beabat in the photo, location
unknown 1945
Berquist Family Photo

Sailors in the above photo were later identified from USS Laws Muster Logs as; Balta was identified as William Gregory Baltas, TM3c, Clearance Arthur Swanson, TM3c, Steinhu was identified as William Wilburn Steinke, TM3c, Daniel James Crum, TM2c, and Beabat was identified as Donald Richard Bebout TM2c. Other sailors are not named.

Then it was back again to Formosa on the ninth for more shelling on the island as well as the Chinese coastline. On the eastern side of the Philippines, the invasion of Luzon had begun.

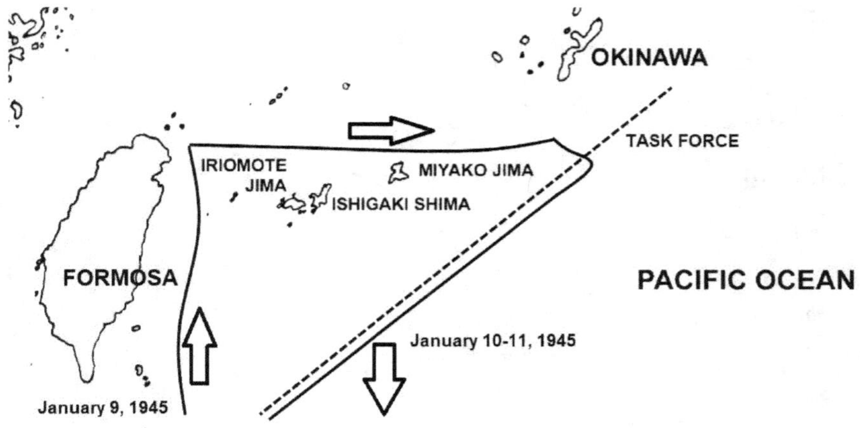

Laws joined the task force piercing the Luzon Strait and prowled the South China Sea on January10–11, providing cover for landings in Lingayen Gulf.

January 12 found *Laws* off the southeast coast of French Indochina (Vietnam) at Cam Ranh Bay striking land-based convoys from twenty-one miles.

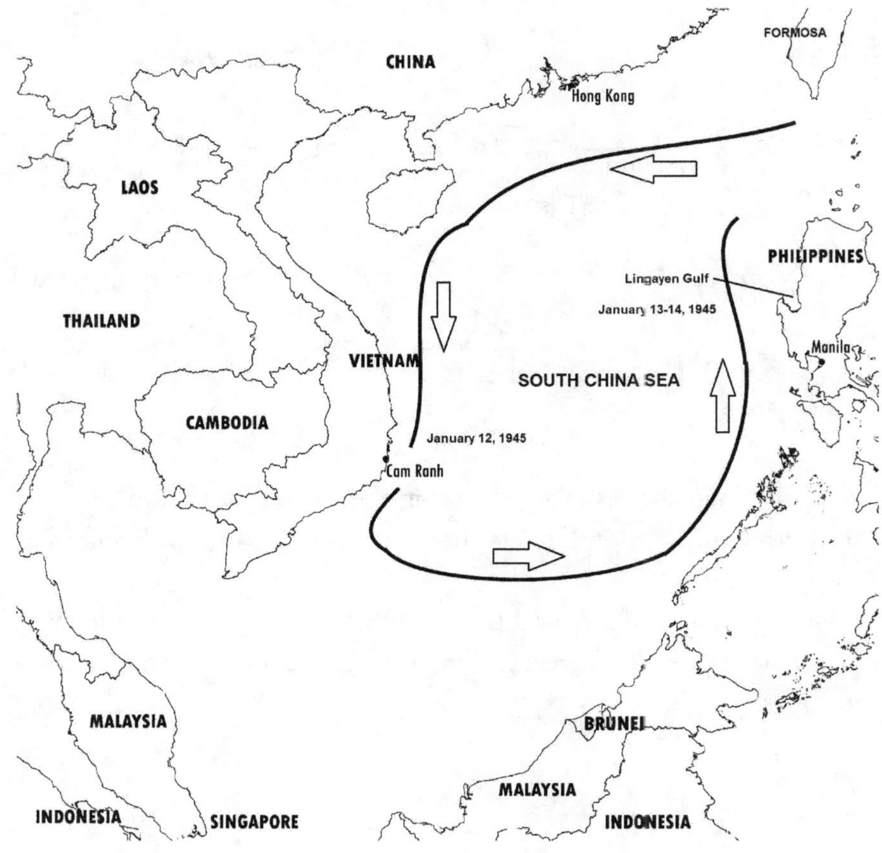

On January 13–14, *Laws* returned to Lingayen Gulf for continued coverage of the army and marine landings.

On January 15, *Laws* began strikes at Hong Kong, Amoy, and Swatow on the Chinese coast.

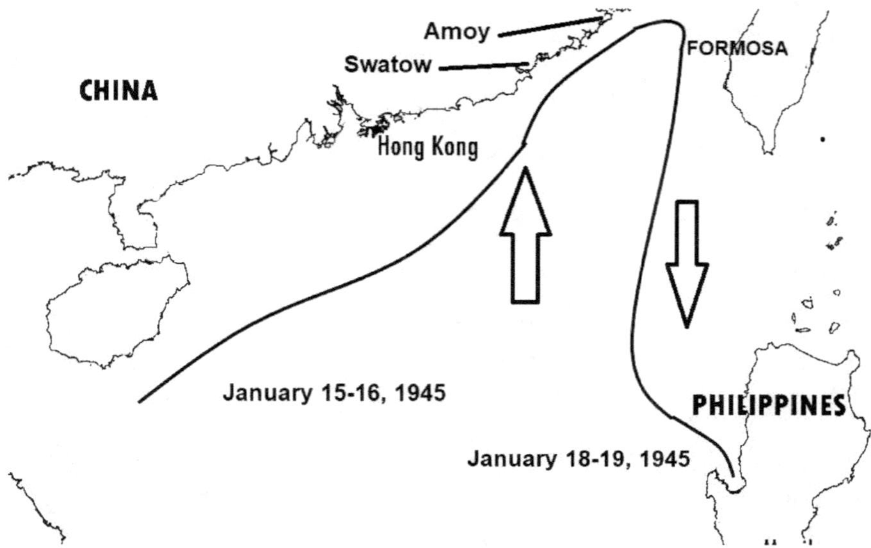

Strikes continued to the sixteenth. GQ was called on the sixteenth, but the air raid failed to produce any Jap planes. Turned out the screen fighters had cleared them all before they reached the ship.

Laws picked up three crew members from a downed Avenger torpedo bomber off the coast of Formosa and then made way for Lingayen Gulf to cover more landings on the eighteenth. The weather turned bad on the eighteenth. *Laws* abandoned attempts to deliver the three crew members to their carrier when she almost capsized. A fifty-two-degree roll almost turned *Laws* on her side. The typhoon the previous month had not been as severe.

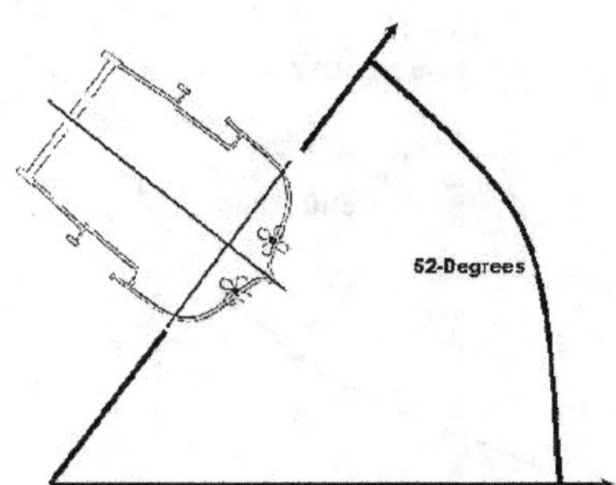

Graphic representation of a 52-degree roll
Illustration by Michael Berquist

As quickly as the storm came in, it went, and on the nineteenth, the skies cleared. Refueling started in calm seas. The reason for the roll the day before was because *Laws* was out of fuel and therefore lightweight. A deal was struck between *Laws* and the light aircraft carrier USS *Langley* (CVL-27). They would get their aviators back in exchange for two pallets of ice cream. It was a deal, except for the fact one pallet fell into the drink during the transfer. Everybody roared with laughter. The laughter stopped, and the rush was on, as reconnaissance aircraft had reported a convoy of up to sixty Jap ships spotted steaming east and about forty miles out.

On January 20 and at GQ, *Laws* went back through the Luzon Strait. Jap aircraft had been spotted but diverted when destroyers leading the group convinced them to leave. No firing took place. The sight of the ships was enough. *Laws* reached the waters around Formosa on the twenty-first, GQ 1200 to 1930 hours that day. Kamikaze attacks were stepping up in frequency, believed to be because Japan was losing the war now quickly. It was a perfect day for aircrews on both sides, calm seas and sunny skies.

During the attacks at Formosa, aircraft carrier USS *Ticonderoga* (CV-14) was hit by two Jap suicide planes.

USS Ticonderoga CV-14 Listing 10-degrees, January 21, 1945 Off the Coast of Formosa
ATTRIBUTION: This work has been identified as being free of known restrictions under copyright law, including all related and neighboring rights. This file is a work of a sailor or employee of the U.S. Navy, taken or made as part of that person's official duties. As a work of the U.S. federal government, it is in the public domain in the United States.

The carrier burned for about two hours but did not sink. Good sailor skills by her captain attributed to her survival. She would be decorated for it later. Langley, whom *Laws* had done business with the previous day, took a bomb to her flight deck but remained operative.

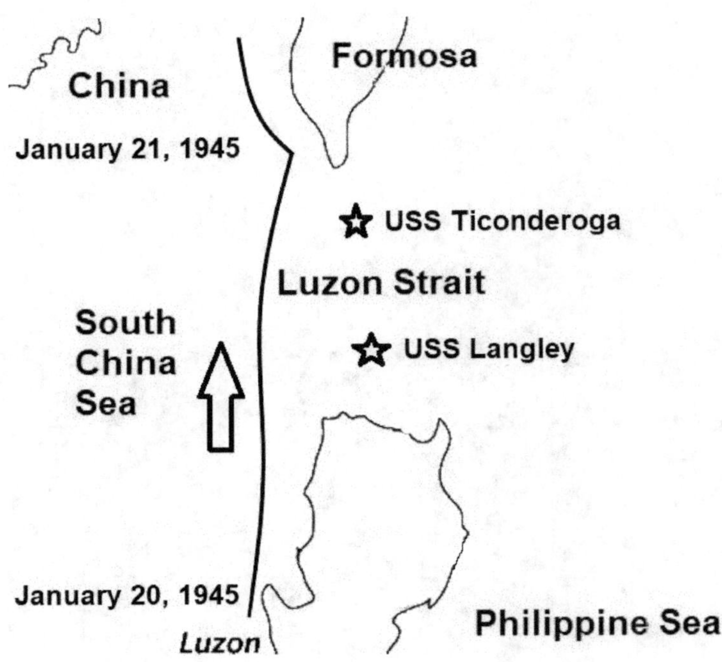

Ticonderoga left formation on the night of the twenty-first, and in the morning on the twenty-second, *Laws* refueled from battleship USS *North Carolina* (BB-55) and continued her way north past the southern Ryukyu Islands of Japan.

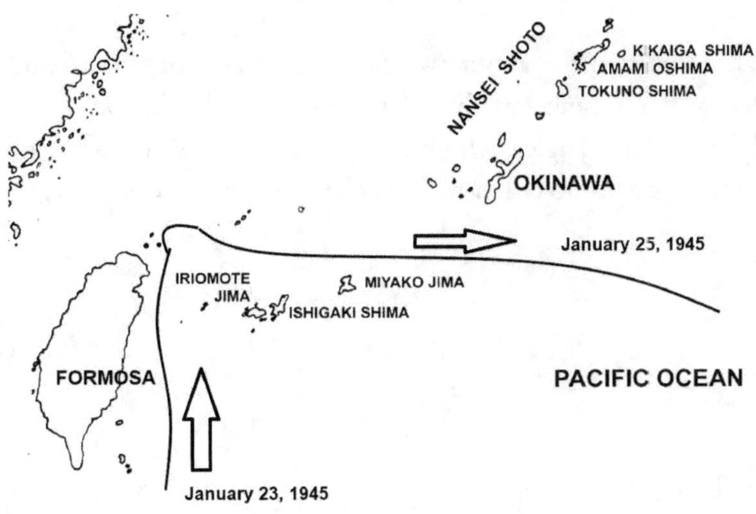

Laws was in GQ from 1130 to 1230 hours during the trip. No shots fired. Calm seas and clear skies again that day. To a cheering crew, the mail was delivered on the twenty-third.

Laws was heading back to Ulithi for a break. Along the way, they practiced surface engagement maneuvers with Task Force 34. She entered the lagoon at Ulithi on January 26.

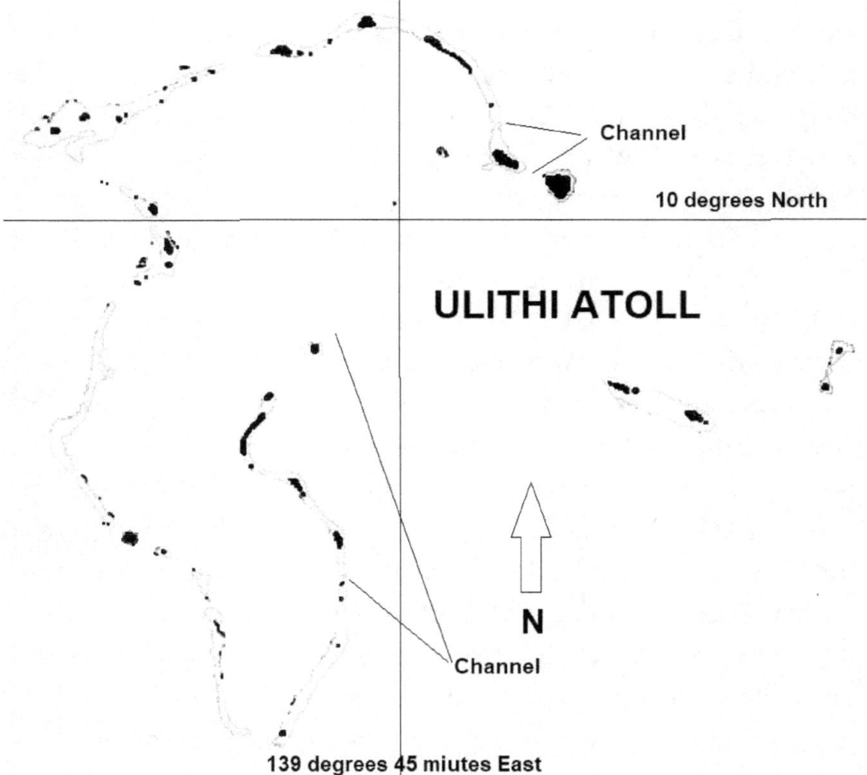

The night before, pickets at the front of the group had sunk a Jap convoy while backing off toward Iwo Jima. It was February 18. On the nineteenth, *Laws* screened aircraft carriers as they struck Iwo Jima. Kenneth wrote, "We needed Iwo Jima for an airstrip." The marines invaded Iwo Jima on February 19. *Laws* fueled and readied for air support of the invasion. *Laws* was at GQ all night on the twentieth.

On February 21, the Japs carried out a considerable air attack off Iwo Jima. During this attack, the aircraft carrier USS *Saratoga* (CV-3) suffered severe damage from four kamikaze hits. She returned stateside and was out of the war.

After another night of routine combat air patrol over Iwo Jima, the aircraft carrier USS *Enterprise* (CV-6) and her screen were detached temporarily on February 23 and steamed south. *Laws* learned she would remain in the Iwo Jima area with the task force for the near future. Kenneth wrote, "It is February 21st. Aircraft Carrier Enterprise returned to our group." On February 24, *Laws* was still with the night fighter group around Iwo Jima. Weather was still fine. Refueled from heavy cruiser USS *Baltimore* (CA-68) on the twenty-sixth. Mail was received again on the twenty-eighth. Mail was getting through regularly now. On March 4, *Laws* fueled from the heavy cruiser USS *Alaska* (CB-1). March 10 made way for a break in Ulithi, arriving there on the twelfth.

At Ulithi, Captain Wood received a medal for outstanding service. *Laws* won Battle Stars and Kenneth ribbons for the raids on mainland Japan and the Ryukyu Islands and the assault and occupation of Iwo Jima on March 16, 1945. *Laws* tied up to the destroyer tender USS *Yosemite* (AD-19) for needed repairs. Carriers and other warships from Britain were seen in the Ulithi lagoon for the first time on the eighteenth. On March 20, *Laws* departed Ulithi with the task force of fifty-five ships bound for Okinawa. *Laws* would provide fire support and patrol for the invasion that was planned to begin on April 1. Once, off the coast of Okinawa, while performing minesweeping operations, *Laws* saw British aircraft for the first time—a large garrison poised in Japan's backyard. Bombardment started in stormy weather on March 21.

Back row L-R: Kenneth Elvin Berquist, GM2c, John Jacob Scheetz, S1c, James William Climp, GM2c, William Herbert Richardson, GM2c, John George Boedigheimer, GM2c, Raul Forrest Kennedy, GM3c, Bernard Walter Sniegowski, S1c, William Edward Reggero, S1c Top photo front row L-R: Alex Gordon, GM1c, George Edwin Dunwoody, GM3c, William Rolland Dunmead, GM3c, Rudolph Michael Hoeberg, CGM(PA), Edward Martin Swillius, GM1c, Charles Nesswell Rollins, S1c

Berquist Family Photo

Back row L-R: Beecher Willard Warner, GM3c, Francis Bernard Kaine, GM1c, Leonard Earl Poirier, S1c, Robert Lee Pell, GM3c, Troy Whitteker, GM2c, John Willam Westfall, S1c, Glenn William Smith, GM3c Bottom photo front row L-R: Leslie Cyril Rountree, S1c, Bernard Joseph Rung, GM3c, Rudolph Michael Hoeberg, CGM(PA), Maurice Andrew White, GM3c, Leigh Henry Byer, GM3c
Berquist Family Photo

Standing proudly alongside the Laws Gun Director House Back row L-R: Fabian Sebastian Butovitch, S1c, Albert Garcia Gonzales, COX, Daniel Perry, WTC3c, Beecher Willard Warner, GM3c, Front row L-R: Frank Thomas Clark, Jr. WTC1c, Mark William Roper, F1c, Robert Elwood Rosentreter, F1c
Berquist Family Photo

Laws refueled from battleship USS *Maryland* (BB-46) and reported the weather was getting cold again. This was March 24. It was still winter in the northern latitudes of the Pacific. On March 25, *Laws* went on GQ at 0600 hours, screening *Maryland*, *Texas*, and *Tuscaloosa* as she approached Okinawa. Ships opened fire on the southern beachhead at 1400 hours. *Laws* bombarded on picket during the evening. No return fire from the beaches. *Laws* came to within eight thousand yards of the beach.

Laws took a Jap aerial attack as she made a run toward the beach in the morning of March 26. The plane came to within five hundred feet of *Laws'* stern. Local support was so thick the Jap plane peeled off after taking one swipe. *Laws* kept any Japs still on the beach busy with fires she started from the star shells she sent flying. The destroyer USS *Kimberly* (DD-521) was stricken by two "Vals."

A "Val" Japanese Carrier based Dive Bomber Aichi D3A
This photo is in the public domain of both the United States and Japan

Despite the anti-aircraft fire and numerous hits, one Jap plane, trailing fire and smoke, crashed into the aft gun mounts, killing four men and wounding fifty-seven. Kimberly returned to the States for repairs.

The group took the Kerama Archipelago off the southwest coast of Okinawa with little resistance on March 27.

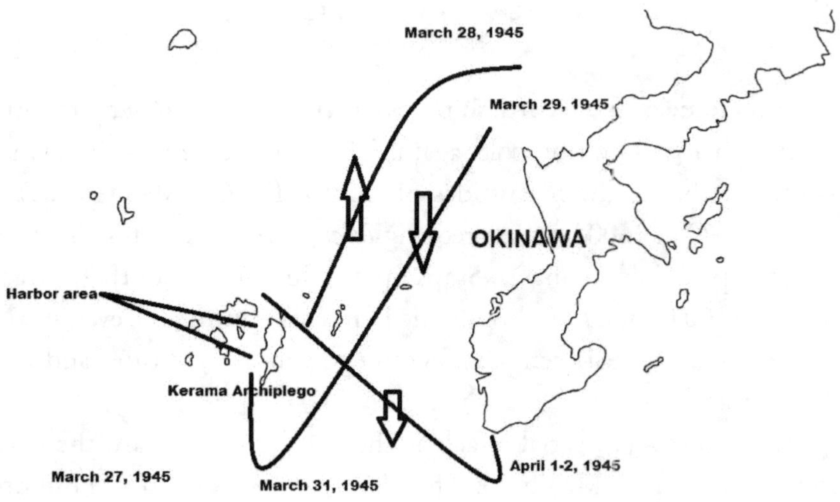

The circular shape of several islands in the archipelago made an excellent natural harbor for the landing troops. The destroyer USS *O'Brien* (DD-725) was hit by a kamikaze Jap "Val" carrying a five-hundred-pound bomb. The plane crashed into *O'Brien* amidships, exploding a magazine. Fifty men lost their lives. *O'Brien* returned to the States for repairs.

Laws was sent to the west side of Okinawa on March 28 for shore bombardment screening. Because air cover was so dense, return fire from the island was not seen. *Laws'* crew witnessed part of a great sight that day, watching underwater demolition teams preparing for troop landings on the west-central side of Okinawa. At first, the water would ripple in a circle, which grew in diameter rapidly. Then, in the middle of the circle, the water would suck down and then begin to rise, at first slowly but then quickly. It rose several hundred feet into the air, gray on the outside and black on the inside, the spray. They could see chunks of whatever blew up being tossed up in the air. Then they would feel this whack on their chests and faces, like a wave running through the air. And then came the sound. Kaboom! Anything lying or hanging loosely around them on the ship would shake. It was a sight that happened over and over again until the demo crew was done. USS *Longshaw* (DD-559) and USS *Morrison* (DD-560) were with *Laws* as support for the area. Demolition lasted for about two hours on March 29. There was no return fire from shore.

March 30 was spent supporting another underwater demolition demonstration. Everyone was tired aboard the ship that day. *Morrison* was sent southeast to chase a reported Jap sub. *Laws* went into Kerama Harbor on March 31 to refuel and take on ammo. The harbor was full of ships carrying the army and marines who were ready to be deposited on Okinawa. On April 1, *Laws* bombarded the southern beaches while the army and marines landed on the west coast of Okinawa.

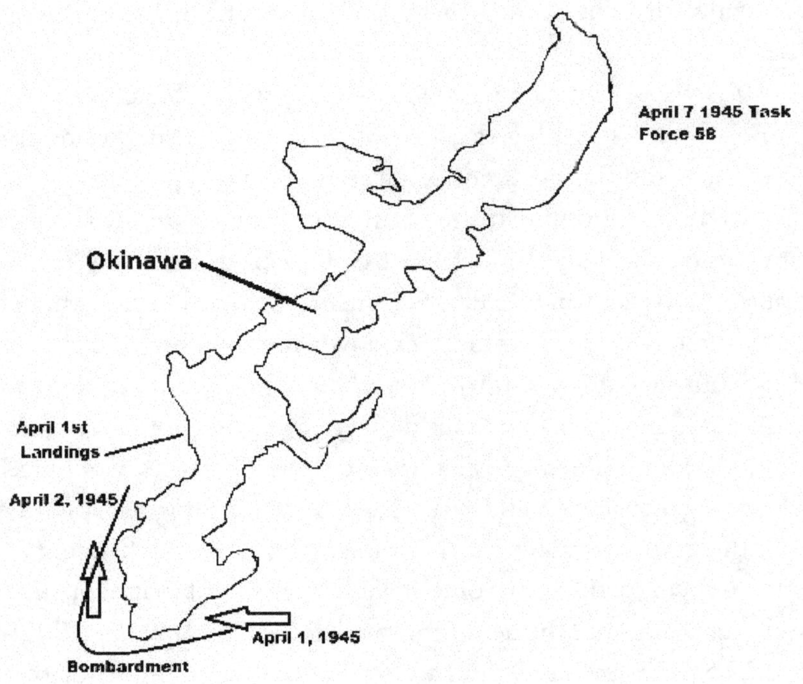

April 2 resulted in more bombardments. Kenneth wrote, "This morning a Jap plane came within 40mm AA range. Laws fired but did not get him. It was too dark, and he was apparently too far away." They bombarded all night and through the morning of April 3 and then moved to the southwestern corner of the island and shelled there. In the afternoon, *Laws* went to the vicinity of the land invasion to get radio crystals. There sure were a lot of transport craft anchored there. The weather was fine. They were still shelling on April 4, only then *Laws* had a spotting plane and, with overhead help, knocked out six large Jap trucks and three Jap landing craft. Also, a kamikaze crashed onto the main deck of battleship USS *Nevada* (BB-36) next to the number-three turret, killing several guys. The Jap knocked out both fourteen-inch guns in the turret and three 20mm anti-aircraft guns. The kamikaze attack did not sink her, and she kept fighting. *Nevada* lost two more guys the following day from the shore-based gunfire.

Laws screened the amphibious force command ship USS *Estes* (AGC-12), the battleship USS *Arkansas* (BB-33), and the heavy cruiser USS *Wichita* (CA-45) during a shelling run on April 5, 1945. During an air raid on April 12, the destroyer USS *Cassin Young* (DD-795) was hit by a suicide plane in the foremast. No one was killed, but several were injured. She retired to Kerama for repairs. The destroyer USS *Abele* (DD-733) was sunk.

The country's beloved president Franklin Delano Roosevelt died unexpectedly of a stroke while on vacation in Warm Springs, Arkansas, on Thursday, April 12, 1945. Roosevelt, who days prior had been sworn in for a fourth term as president, was gone. While the war in Europe and the Pacific raged on, the nation mourned. Harry S. Truman was sworn in as the thirty-third president of the United States the same day.

On April 19, *Laws* participated in the shelling of Naha, the largest city in Okinawa. She used so much 40 and 20 AA ammo in one day she had to return to Kerama twice in two days to resupply. *Laws* was reloading ammo every four days, minimum, now and refueling every five days. By April 27, *Laws'* score was now three sampans, two twin engines, and three single engines. She also learned on the twenty-seventh that the Japs were now using suicide boats—sampans with outboard gasoline engines—so they were fast.

Kenneth wrote, "We earned an 'atta-boy' from Captain Wood today, April 30th." *Laws* did a surprisingly respectable job with bombardment and even scored a "well done" from the captain in the evening, to the combat and gun crews. They knocked out guns, closed caves, and killed many Jap personnel with airburst shells. On May 4, they were hearing rumors about the war in Europe. Allies were pressing in from all directions in Berlin.

That morning, some of the crew found a marine floating in the water and could not tell it was a human being. What a sight! What a smell! The body must have been in the water for days because it was entirely putrefied and had little "bites" taken out of it. A couple of the guys tried picking the body up out of the water, but it would not hold together. They took his dog tags, wrapped him in a hunk of netting with some five-inch projectiles, said a quick prayer, and let him sink. It was May 6.

On May 8, Kenneth wrote that last night at 2330 hours, *Laws* received the news, "GERMANY HAS SURRENDERED." The war in Europe was over.

Laws went to Ie Shima, a little spit of an island off the northwest point of Okinawa. Destroyers USS *Evans* (DD-552) and USS *Hadley* (DD-774) were there and severely damaged. *Laws* replenished ammo from the two ships. *Evans* and *Hadley* were towed to Kerama for repairs. *Evans* returned after repairs. *Hadley* was out of the war. Also, seen for the first time on May 13 through binoculars is what was believed to be a Jap internment camp.

During the morning of May 18, destroyer, USS *Longshaw* (DD-559) in our group went up on a reef near Naha Airfield, Okinawa. The Japs opened fire on her and blew up her forward magazine. *Laws* provided covering fire, but by the afternoon, *Longshaw* was destroyed. *Longshaw* was scuttled late in the afternoon. *Laws* was about eight miles from it when it happened. Kenneth wrote, "It was misty and foggy this morning."

On May 20, the destroyer USS *Thatcher* (DD-514) was hit by a kamikaze en route to Okinawa from Kerama. A small-yet-powerful typhoon, spotted on June 1, was moving northeast. Winds were reported as high as 140 miles per hour. By June 7, it began to weaken. Typhoon Connie hit the navy's Fifth Fleet. Connie was weaker than Cobra had been a few months before, but one officer and five crew members were killed, and 150 airplanes on carriers were either lost or damaged. *Laws* sat out the typhoon in Buckner Bay, Okinawa, with *Thatcher*, who once again was hit by kamikaze. *Thatcher* was out of the war this time and departed for the States. By June 8, *Laws* had been getting close enough to the shoreline to use its 40mm and 20mm AA guns to knock out remaining Japs on the southern tip of Okinawa.

On the sixteenth of June, destroyer USS *Twiggs* (DD-591) on radar picket was hit by a low-flying Jap torpedo plane in her port side, exploding her number-two magazine. The airplane then circled and completed its kamikaze attack. The destroyer went up in flames and, within an hour, sank. Despite the hazard of exploding ammunition from the blazing ship, *Laws* helped rescue survivors, picking up seven guys from the water. Destroyer USS *Putnam* (DD-757) was nearby at the time of the attack and picked up more than one hundred. Kenneth wrote, "Today is the 16th of June. We stayed around the south tip of Okinawa until the 20th and then went to Kerama for repairs. Had a beer on some island nearby—don't know the name."

Word arrived on June 22, 1945: Okinawa had fallen to the Allied troops.

Between April 6 and June 22, 1945, *Laws* remained in the waters around Okinawa, performing screening, picket, and shelling duty. She survived two direct kamikaze attacks, went to the aid of other ships twice, plucking several sailors from the water. She dropped depth charges on subs once, supported numerous underwater demolitions, and took out three more Jap trucks and one land-based observation post. *Laws* participated in securing the small island of Tsugen Shima on the eastern edge of Buckner Bay, Okinawa, all while enduring air raids on the group every day and bogies every night. Kenneth wrote, "We are alone on patrol, in-waiting. Three times, twice at night. On permanent Ready Two status, eight hours on and four hours off for eighty straight days now." Kenneth had survived the biggest, bloodiest, and last battle of the Pacific.

On July 28, orders came to relieve destroyer USS *Callaghan* (DD-792) on radar picket. Jap planes were on the radar thirty minutes from *Callaghan*. Within minutes, word came that *Callaghan* had been hit by a suicide plane. A Yokosuka K5Y was constructed of wood and fabric, and was therefore not magnetic.

Japanese Yokosuka K5Y Biplane
This photo is in the public domian of both the United States cnd Japan

When *Callaghan*'s five-inch rounds fired the shells, internal proximity fuses encountered no metallic objects for its fuse to activate. The projectiles went sailing on by the K5Y. The plane returned to strike again on the starboard side. *Callaghan* exploded as one of the plane's bombs penetrated the after-engine room. The destroyer flooded, and the fires ignited anti-aircraft ammunition. At tremendous risk to her crew, *Laws* raced to *Callaghan*'s aid and picked up 107 men. *Callaghan* sank a little after 0230 hours.

News reached *Laws* the same day, August 6, that a uranium atomic bomb had been dropped on the Japanese city of Hiroshima. While elated with the story, the men did not know what an atomic bomb was or what the weapon could do.

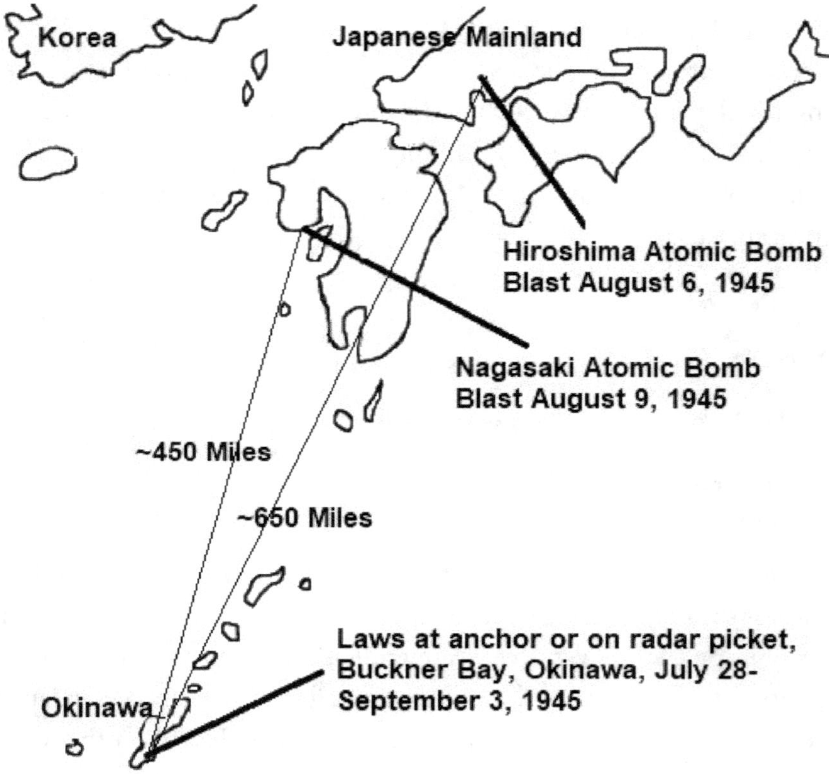

This news sank in after another nuclear bomb—a plutonium type —was dropped on Nagasaki. Three days later, photographs of the first bomb were seen. Devastation!

News arrived at 0200 hours that Japan had officially agreed to surrender terms on August 11. The news set off a gigantic celebration as gun crews began firing all sorts of flares and tracer bullets. The spontaneous celebration stopped when a call to general quarters sounded. GQ was the only way to get the men to stop. *Laws,* still at anchor in Buckner Bay, continued fighting off-air attacks on the twelfth and thirteenth. The surrender news had not reached the Japs in remote locations.

She would be detached from Squadron 12 as soon as destroyer USS *Nields* (DD-616) reached her location at Buckner Bay. The Japs signed the peace treaty on September 2.

V-J Day!! World War II Is Over!!

Laws' crew spent the better part of the day on September 3 preparing for the trip home—fueling, loading ammo, and loading food and supplies. The day included building a three-hundred-foot-long homeward-bound pennant. On the morning of September 4, she made way for Enewetak in the Marshalls.

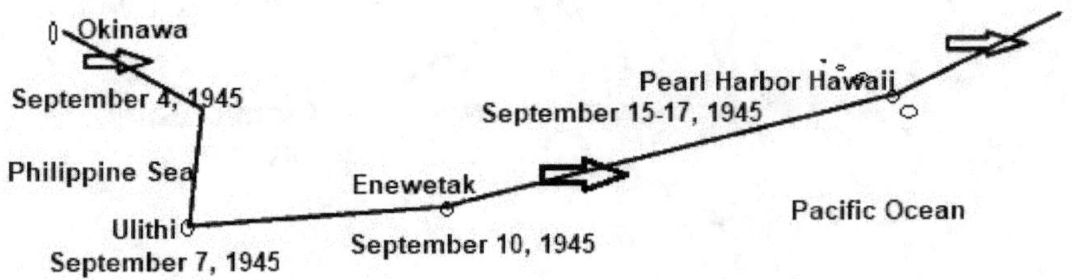

Laws, who had been a part of the entire fight from start to finish, was the last ship to leave the waters around Okinawa—first in and last out.

One of the crew suffered appendicitis on September 6, so *Laws* diverted to Ulithi instead to drop him off after an emergency appendectomy aboard ship. *Laws* arrived and departed Ulithi on the seventh and again set course for Enewetak. Nighttime cruising lights were okay to use after the eighth. The ship arrived and then departed Enewetak on the tenth. She stayed long enough to refuel. No one disembarked. Funny! On course for Pearl now. Kenneth wrote, "Arrived in Pearl Harbor on September 15th." There were ice cream sundaes for everyone. Then they refueled and resupplied at Pearl and departed for the States on September 17. Excitement aboard ship was at a fever pitch now.

On Monday morning, September 24, 1945, destroyer USS *Laws* (DD-558) pulled into Puget Sound Naval Shipyard, Bremerton, Washington. Lieutenant Commander Robert E. Sinnott, USN, relieved Commander Lester O. Wood.

Laws arrived home! But Kenneth still had navy duties to perform. The first thing he did after disembarking was call his mom and dad.X

U.S.S Laws Won 10 Battle Stars, But Never Lost A Man
—Courageous Destroyer in Yard

With 10 men from Washington state aboard, the destroyer U.S.S. Laws has returned to P.S.N.Y. after 20 months of hitting the Japs hard from Saipan to Tokyo.

In continuous command of the 2,100-ton destroyer was Comdr. Lester O. Wood, U.S.N., of Washington, D. C., who brought his ship safely to port with the enviable record of never having lost a man. The washington men aboard were:

Paul Arnold Schuler, radio technician second class, U.S.N.R.; Carlton William Taylor, fireman first class, U.S.N.R., and Lt. (jg) Charles Dudgeon Howe, Jr., U.S.-N.R., all of Seattle; Ensign William Hector MacDonald, U.S.N.R., Allen Getchell Read, seaman first class, U.S.N.R., and Robert Lee Pell, seaman first class, U.S.N.R., all of Spokane; Norman Gliddon Ross, chief radio technician, U.S.-N. R., Pullman; Charles Allan Dodd, motor machinist's mate first class, U.S.N., Tacoma; Frank Joseph Nauer, radioman third class, U.S.N.R., of Sumner, and Leonard Earl Poirier, seaman first class, U.S.N.R., of Yakima.

The Laws first drew enemy blood off Saipan, where she downed two enemy planes, and assisted in the destruction of several others. One of the Jap airmen was picked up and held aboard ship as a prisoner for eight days. None of the crew thought it strange to play checkers with this captured enemy when they weren't busy shooting more of his comrades out of the sky.

Although a major portion of her wartime career was spent in the fast moving company of task force 38 and 58, the Laws was a task force all her own off Okinawa. For more than four months she roamed the enemy-held coast line. Her guns, which supported our troops ashore with 20,000 rounds of firepower, also brought down three kamikaze attackers and caused several others to swerve into the sea. Throughout this action, the Laws seemed to lead a charmed life. Several times she narrowly escaped destruction while her squadron mates blew up close enough to shower her decks with debris. The efforts of the Law's officers and men were responsible for the rescue of more than a hundred survivors.

In all, the Laws earned 10 battle stars for action in the Marianas, Western Carolines, New Guinea, the Philippines, Iwo Jima, Okinawa, and in the waters 45 miles off the coast of Japan. Her guns have roared against the Japs on the sea and in the air, but the sentiments of her crew were best expressed on V-J Day. To them, it was "V-H (vego home) Day."

Clipping from unknown Washington State newspaper, circa September 1945
Berquist Family Possession

USS Laws DD-588 the apropos "Lucky Lady"
Sketch created by an unknown sailor aboard Laws 1943-1945

Tears ran down his mom's cheeks as she spoke to him. Kenneth learned his brother, Dick, was also on his way home. He would be there soon.

Kenneth at the Naval Shipyard, Bremerton, WA, circa October 1945
Berquist Family Photo

Kenneth with Carol Hick of California, photo dated October 11, 1945
Berquist Family Photo

Carol Hick was later identfied from the USS Laws muster log as Carrol Otis Hicks, RM2c. Kenneth turned twenty-six on October 19, 1945. It was Friday, and the weekend had arrived. The birthday celebration was "on."

In those last ten weeks after getting to Washington, Kenneth remained on duty. The treaty was signed, but news of hostilities in various areas kept coming in.

Untitled photos, unknown date and place, Top Left: Gordon, Alex, GM1c, Top Right: Boedigheimer, John George, GM2c, Bottom Left: Richardson, William Herbert, GM2c, Bottom Right: Swillius, Edward Martin, GM1c
Berquist Family Photos

Tens of thousands of Japanese soldiers stayed in China, either caught in uninhabited land between the Communists and Nationalists or fighting for one side or the other. Smaller groups continued fighting on Guadalcanal, Peleliu, and in various parts of the Philippines. It took weeks after the signing for the fighting to end for allies of the US still in the South Pacific.

On November 30, while still at the Bremerton naval yard, Kenneth declined the offer for reenlistment without hesitation. Kenneth wrote, "I declined reenlisting today. I am ready to go home." Navy recruiters would have a difficult day ahead. Kenneth headed for the train depot in Seattle with his head held high. The train and bus station in Seattle was a mass of men from all branches of the service returning to their homes. It was a hugely celebratory atmosphere. The restaurants and bars were standing room only.

Fair Weather Cars Used in Troop Train

Several cars of a troop train which arrived in St. Paul Sunday from Seattle belonged to west coast roads and are not designed for frigid temperatures, Milwaukee railroad officials said today in answering charges that 765 naval enlisted men made the trip in unheated coaches.

"The railroads are trying to do a job in six months bringing back men that took three years to do when they were sent overseas," said Hilmer M. Larson, passenger agent for the Milwaukee.

"We simply cannot get the equipment to handle it satisfactorily."

A charge of laxity was made by Lt. (jg) Robert Oates, who said one sailor suffering from pneumonia had to be taken from the train at Mobridge, S. D.

Men traveling in the last three coaches of the 17-car train threatened mutiny at Aberdeen, S. D., because of the intense cold, Oates said. The sailors also complained the train's water supply was frozen most of the time.

Larson said railroad officials had stopped the train in various places to thaw it out. The sailors were given hot coffee and made as comfortable as possible, he said.

The war department some time ago, Larson said, rescinded its order forbidding transportation of men on more than a 48-hour trip unless the troop train could be supplied with sleepers.

"But there has been such a great hue and cry to bring the boys home by Christmas the railroads are not able to supply enough such cars," he said.

"All the men were given a chance to stop over at Aberdeen and come in Monday on the Olympian, but they refused."

The sailors, all veterans of the Pacific fighting, were en route to Great Lakes, Ill., for discharge. About 100 of them were taken to the naval air station at Wold-Chamberlain field for release.

Clipping from Minneapolis Star Journal newspaper, December 10, 1945

Berquist Family Possession

At the navy separation station Wold-Chamberlain Naval Air Station next door to Minneapolis–Saint Paul Metropolitan Airport, Kenneth was honorably discharged from the navy. It was December 12, 1945.

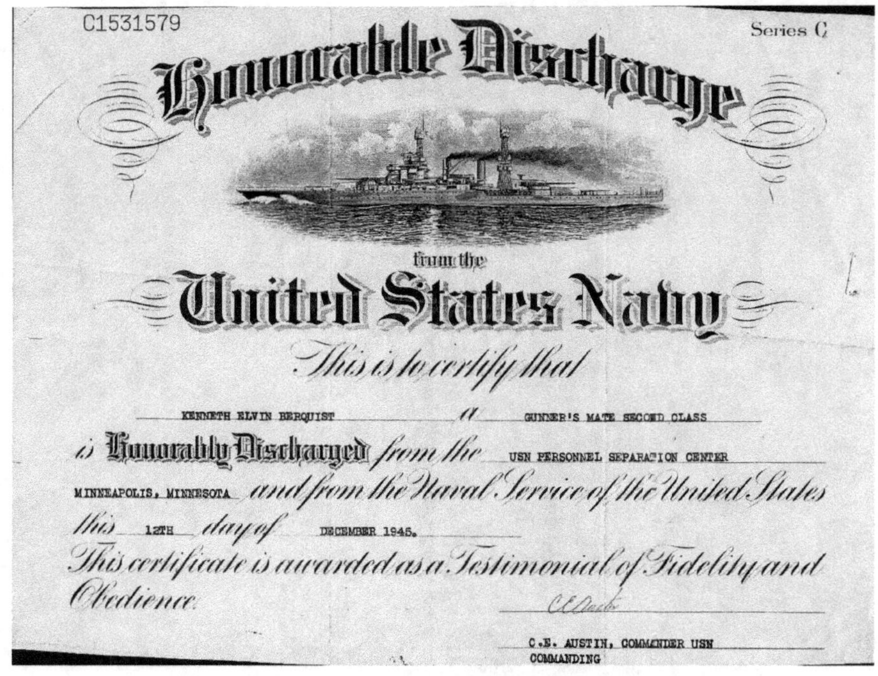

Kenneth's Honorable Discharge Certificate
Berquist Family Document

NOTICE OF SEPARATION FROM U. S. NAVAL SERVICE
NAVPERS-553 (REV. 8-45)

1. SERIAL OR FILE NO. 2. NAME (LAST) (FIRST) (MIDDLE) 3. RATE AND CLASS OR RANK AND CLASSIFICATION 4. PERMANENT ADDRESS FOR MAILING PURPOSES

5. PLACE OF SEPARATION

Co.1007
620 75 44 BERQUIST, Kenneth Elvin
Gunners's Mate 2c(T)
V-6 USNR
2024 Summer St.
Burlington,Iowa
Des Moines County

USN PerSepCen
Minneapolis,Minn.

6. CHARACTER OF SEPARATION
HONORABLE

7. ADDRESS FROM WHICH EMPLOYMENT WILL BE SOUGHT
Same as #4

8. RACE W 9. SEX M 10. MARITAL STATUS S 11. U.S. CITIZEN (YES OR NO) Yes 12. DATE AND PLACE OF BIRTH 10-19-19 Burlington, Iowa

13. REGISTERED X YES NO 14. SELECTIVE SERVICE BOARD OF REGISTRATION Des Moines, County, Iowa 15. HOME ADDRESS AT TIME OF ENTRY INTO SERVICE Same as #4

16. MEANS OF ENTRY (INDICATE BY CHECK IN APPROPRIATE BOX)
X ENLISTED INDUCTED COMMISSIONED
DATE 7-27-42 DATE DATE

17. DATE OF ENTRY INTO ACTIVE SERVICE 7-27-42
18. NET SERVICE (FOR PAY PURPOSES) (YRS., MOS., DAYS) 3-4-16
19. PLACE OF ENTRY INTO ACTIVE SERVICE Burlington, Iowa

20. QUALIFICATIONS, CERTIFICATES HELD, ETC.
See rating description booklet "Gunner's Mate second class"

21. RATINGS HELD AS,S2c,S1c,GM3c,GM2c(T)

22. FOREIGN AND/OR SEA SERVICE WORLD WAR II. X YES NO

23. SERVICE SCHOOLS COMPLETED WEEKS
--- --

24. SERVICE (VESSELS AND STATIONS SERVED ON)
USNTS Great Lakes,Ill.
AGS Sec.Base,Little Creek,Va.
USN ACC Brooklyn,N.Y.
USS Laws (DD558)

IMPORTANT: IF PREMIUM IS NOT PAID WHEN DUE OR WITHIN THIRTY-ONE DAYS THEREAFTER, INSURANCE WILL LAPSE. MAKE CHECKS OR MONEY ORDERS PAYABLE TO THE TREASURER OF THE U. S. AND FORWARD TO COLLECTOR'S SUBDIVISION, VETERAN'S ADMINISTRATION, WASHINGTON 25. D. C.

25. KIND OF INSURANCE N 26. EFFECTIVE MONTH OF ALLOTMENT DISCONTINUANCE Dec/1945 27. MO. NEXT PREMIUM DUE Jan/1946 28. AMOUNT OF PREMIUM DUE EACH MONTH 3.30 29. INTENTION OF VETERAN TO CONTINUE INS. Yes

30. TOTAL PAYMENT UPON DISCHARGE $ 56.91 31. TRAVEL OR MILEAGE ALLOWANCE INCLUDED IN TOTAL PAYMENT $ 18.60 32. INITIAL MUSTERING OUT PAY $100.00 33. NAME OF DISBURSING OFFICER F. A. NASH,JR.,LT.(jg)SC USN

34. REMARKS
---

35. SIGNATURE (BY DIRECTION OF COMMANDING OFFICER)
C. MATHIS
Lt.Cmdr.,USNR

36. NAME AND ADDRESS OF LAST EMPLOYER
Chi-Burlington & Quincy
West Burlington--RR shop
Burlington,Iowa (Mach.helper)

37. DATES OF LAST EMPL'MT.
FROM 7-41
TO 7-42

38. MAIN CIVILIAN OCCUPATION AND D. O. T. NO.
Machinist Helper

39. JOB PREFERENCE (LIST TYPE, LOCALITY, AND GENERAL AREA)
Same as #36 and 38

40. PREFERENCE FOR ADDITIONAL TRAINING (TYPE OF TRAINING)
--

41. NON-SERVICE EDU. (YRS. SUCCESSFULLY COMPLETED) GRAM.: 8 H. S.: 4 COLL.: --
42. DEGREES gen.
43. MAJOR COURSE OR FIELD --

44. VOCATIONAL OR TRADE COURSES (NATURE AND LENGTH OF COURSE)
--

45. RIGHT INDEX FINGERPRINT
46. OFF DUTY EDUCATIONAL COURSES COMPLETED
---

47. DATE OF SEPARATION 12/12/1945
48. SIGNATURE OF PERSON BEING SEPARATED Kenneth C. Berquist

jbc

Kenneth's Navy Separation Paper
Berquist Family Document

He took military transport to the train station in downtown Saint Paul and headed to Chicago on December 13. Then he took the train from Chicago to Burlington on December 14. Kenneth was home for Christmas. It was the best present his parents could have hoped for.

Battle Stars Awarded to the USS *Laws* (DD-558) (1944–1945)

- ASIATIC PACIFIC AREA SERVICE RIBBON (one star)
- PALAU, ULITHI, WOLEAI STRIKES 30 MARCH TO 01 APRIL 1944 (one star)
- NEW GUINEA OPERATIONS (HOLLANDIA LANDING) 18 TO 29 APRIL (one star)
- CAPTURE AND OCCUPATION OF SAIPAN, TINIAN, AND GUAM IN THE MARIANAS GROUP 11 JUNE TO 15 AUGUST 1944 (one star)
- CAPTURE AND OCCUPATION OF SOUTHERN PALAU ISLANDS 06 SEPTEMBER TO 14 OCTOBER 1944, STRIKES ON PHILIPPINES 09 TO 24 SEPTEMBER 1944 (one star)
- BATTLE OF LEYTE GULF 24 TO 26 OCTOBER 1944, THIRD FLEET SUPPORTING OPERATIONS FIRST OKINAWA STRIKE 10 OCTOBER 1944, NORTHERN LUZON, AND FORMOSA STRIKES 11 TO 14 OCTOBER, LUZON STRIKES 15, 17 TO 18 OCTOBER, 5 TO 6, 13 TO 14, 19 TO 25, NOVEMBER,14 TO 16 DECEMBER 1944, VISAYAS STRIKES 20 TO 21 OCTOBER, 11 NOVEMBER 1944, ORNOC BAY LANDINGS 7 TO 13 DECEMBER 1944 (one star)
- MINDORA LANDINGS 12 TO 18 DECEMBER 1944, LINGAYEN GULF LANDINGS 4 TO 18 JANUARY 1945, THIRD FLEET SUPPORTING OPERATIONS, LUZON STRIKES 06 TO 07 JANUARY 1945, FORMOSA STRIKES 3, 4, 9, 15, 21 JANUARY 1945, CHINA COAST STRIKES (HONG KONG, SAIGON, CAMRAHN BAY) (one star)
- ASSAULT AND OCCUPATION OF IWO JIMA 15 FEBRUARY TO 16 MARCH FIFTH FLEET STRIKES BY CARRIER BASED PLANES ON TOKYO 16, 17 FEBRUARY 1945 (one star)

• CAPTURE AND OCCUPATION OF OKINAWA AND NEAR ISLANDS IESHIMA AND ERAMA RETTO 24 MARCH TO 30 JULY 1945; PHILIPPINES LIBERATION RIBBON (two stars)

Kenneth Elvin Berquist, GM2c, USS Laws
Berquist Family Photo

CHAPTER 13

Back to Work

Kenneth was back from the war now. Burlington had changed since he had gone into the navy. Kenneth had changed. Friends had gotten older. They had moved on with their lives, building homes, starting families, and settling down. Celebrations were taking place in every household in town. People were ecstatic.

Christmas 1945 was like no other. The Berquists put up a tree and hung decorations on the house. Kenneth and Dick had a snowball fight or two in the yard and ate their mom's home cooking. There was nothing better than a home-cooked meal. It was the simple times that mattered most. Sleeping in a real bed could not be compared to the rack on the ship.

Crews Quarters aboard the USS Kidd DD-661 Floating Museum, Baton Rouge, Louisiana
Photo taken by Michael Berquist with permission February 2017

Taking a hot bath for as long as he wanted was another treat. After months of lukewarm/cold showers—sometimes with sea water—in thirty seconds, a long, leisurely hot bath was something to be relished. It was heaven drinking ice-cold "real" milk.

Kenneth's dad had purchased a new electric GE refrigerator with a freezer compartment while Kenneth was away. Mick kept the old icebox, "just in case." Everybody was alive, well, and happy. It was a joyous season. They all went to Christmas service together at church.

Kenneth's brother, Dick, and his wife, Lida, were also there. Dick and Lida were working on buying a small farm a few miles away. Dick wanted to grow corn and raise Black Angus. Dick had resumed working for the construction company he had worked for before the war. Dick belonged to the Pipefitters Union. Construction was booming.

Like Kenneth's sister Donna, Lida was also a hairdresser. However, Lida was also musically talented—as was her family, particularly her two sisters. She could sing and dance and play all sorts of musical instruments. The organ was her favorite though. On Friday and Saturday night, Lida could be found playing during the dinner hours at the

Moose Lodge on Mount Pleasant Street or at Bob's Stagecoach Inn in downtown Burlington.

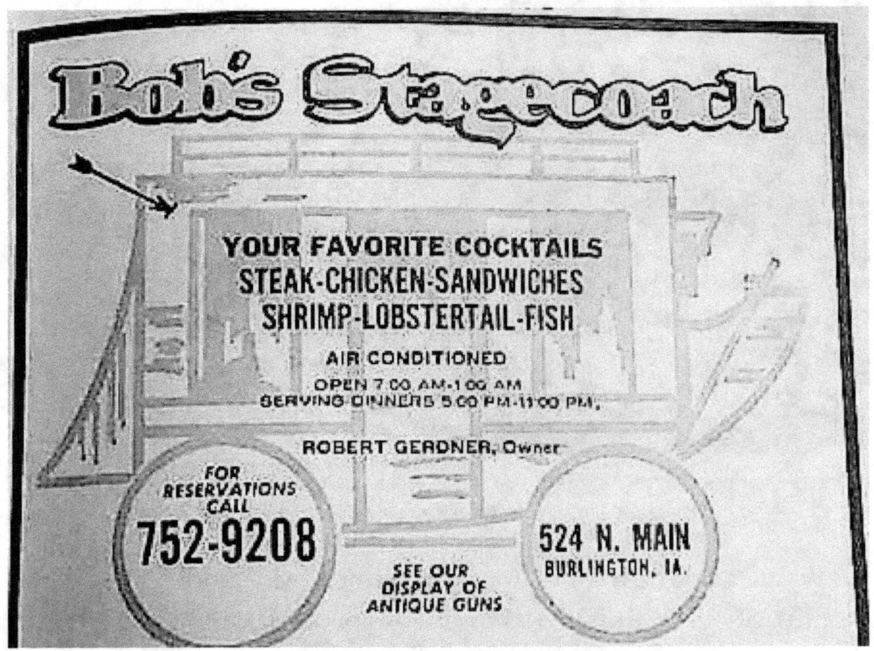

Bob's Stagecoach is no longer in business. Advertisement from 1967 Burlington Phone Directory

ATTRIBUTION: Brett Jay Metcalf and Facebook Page: Historical Photos of Burlington

Lida could have made a career out of her talent. "The Blaisedale Sisters" even had their own radio show broadcast from a station in Quincy, Illinois. But marriage, time, and circumstances changed. Lida was content doing the ladies' hair out of a studio built behind the garage at their home on Mason Road.

Dick and Lida never had kids. They had forty head of cattle instead. Both were hard workers. Dick prided himself on being able to buy a new Cadillac every two years. He loved the Coupe DeVille. Not much time had passed, and they were vacationing each winter in Las Vegas. As time went on, the vacations in Vegas turned into passing the winter months in Vegas, until finally they sold the farm and moved there when Dick retired. Dick and Lida both died in the place they loved: Las Vegas.

Kenneth's sister Donna and her husband, Dee, lived close. Donna was a hairdresser, and Dee worked for a local hospital as a buyer. Donna and Dee never had kids. They did have two yappy chihuahuas—Roxie and Cocoa. Donna and Dee moved a lot, never content with where they were. They owned several houses in Burlington, moving every three or four years, eventually moving to the Quad Cities and then to Cedar Rapids. Dee worked for an aluminum-can manufacturer in Cedar Rapids, and then he went back to work with the hospital business, which he liked the best. It was easy for Donna to pick up work as a hairdresser wherever they moved.

Like Dick and Lida, Donna and Dee liked some other place more than Iowa, and when they retired, they moved to Colorado Springs. Dee went back to work for a while in Colorado, but it was not long before he became ready to retire for good. They lived in Colorado Springs for another twenty years. And again, like Dick and Lida, Donna and Dee died in the place they loved best, in the shadow of Pike's Peak, Colorado Springs.

Kenneth's sister Elsie and her son, James, had moved back to Burlington. Elsie had divorced Charlie Stuck while still living in Los Angeles. She had been single again for a few years before moving back to Burlington. Elsie worked and lived at home with Mick and Louise. Elsie worked as a clerk for Burrough's Jewelry Store downtown. James was attending Burlington High School. Like every young man, he was restless.

James had turned sixteen years old and was looking more a young man now than the little boy Kenneth had remembered seeing two and a half years ago. It was not long before James quit high school to join the army. Elsie always thought James lacked discipline and the discipline a father would have brought had life worked out this way for her. She felt the army would be good for James, so she let him go.

James had been gone for a few years when Elsie met Richard Mack. Rich was a good and decent man. They loved each other and would spend the next twenty-five-plus years together. Elsie and Rich never had kids together. They did, however, have a crabby poodle named

Holly. In keeping with the tradition set by Dick and Donna, Elsie, too, wanted something other than Burlington. Elsie and Richard moved to Davenport, Iowa, in 1955. In 1968, they moved to Milan, Illinois. They worked together in McCullough's Department Store from 1968 to 1977. Richard sold men's clothing, and Elsie sold everything else.

Kenneth had phoned his boss at the CB&Q Shops in West Burlington and asked about getting his job back. The old boss was more than happy to help, so Kenneth could come back to work right after the New Year holiday.

Kenneth's car was right where he had left it parked in the backyard at home. Kenneth returned to work at the Shops in West Burlington on Wednesday, January 2, 1946. He had been away for three and a half years. Nothing had changed at work except for the number of workers. It was a beehive of activity. The war had brought prosperity to the railroad and Burlington. Kenneth was now getting a paid vacation every year and earning $1.56 per hour. Without skipping a beat, he was back —as a machinist's helper. Life was good.

The Chicago, Burlington and Quincy Railroad Shops, West Burlington, Iowa
ATTRIBUTION: http://www.usgwarchives.net/ia/dmoines/postcards/cbqshp.jpg

But still, his world had changed. Kenneth was four years older than when he left for the war. It was not so much the years as it was the mileage. He matured beyond his age, and it showed—in his face and in the way he carried himself. The bedroom he had shared with his brother, Richard, was still there at his parents' house. Richard had moved out of the house before the war. Kenneth felt different lying in his bed at night. It was his bed, but either he or it had changed since the summer of 1942. It was time to move on with his life.

The girl Kenneth had always cared about, Billy Karver, had married her navy man, Walter Penner, and they were living in Gary, Indiana. Mick and Lou said it had been some time since Billy was there for a visit. In fact, she had not been there since Kenneth was on leave in July 1943. Lou also thought all the Karver and Penner relatives that Billy and her mother would visit had either died or moved away. Kenneth had known for a while he had blown his chances with Billy. It was time to move on.

He found himself returned to the cyclical life of work, sleep, eat, repeat. His friends had also fallen into the same rut. Those who went to war were shunned by those who had not gone, and vice versa.

CHAPTER 14

Jane

Jane Francis Roederer was born November 21, 1927. Jane was five years old when her father, Arthur Roederer, passed away. Arthur was thirty-nine years old, and a veteran of World War I. Arthur took a good dose of mustard gas in the war. His lungs were never the same. He contracted pneumonia in 1933 and never recovered.

Jane and her three sisters (Mary, Ann, and Ruth) were left to be raised by their strict mother, Bertha Koestner-Roederer, who never remarried and died a widow on December 14, 1984.

Phillip and Amelia Roederer had left to their son Arthur the house and land at 1841 Lucas Avenue, where, in turn, Bertha raised her four daughters. The Phillip Roederer property was long and narrow and would one day be subdivided and given to the children. Arthur and Bertha's portion of the property allowed for a garden so big they grew enough vegetables to not only feed themselves but feed everyone who lived within a mile. Bertha loved her garden, spending the growing season tilling the soil.

In the fall, it was canning and baking season. It was here Jane absorbed her German-heritage values of challenging work, cleanliness, and "making do" from an early age. She always had food to eat, and all her clothes were hand sewn and made at home by her mother

Jane Francis Roederer, circa Autumn 1943, Photo taken alongside
the house on Lucas Avenue
Berquist Family Photo

Jane and her sisters went to Oak Street Junior High School.

Oak Street Junior High School, 903 Oak Street, Burlington IA, currently being used as a middle school in the Des Moines County public school system
Berquist Family Photo

The five of them lived on Lucas Avenue until Jane entered high school (ninth grade) in 1943.

The Roederer Home, 1841 Lucas Avenue, Burlington, Iowa, date unknown--it is curious to note that U.S. Highway 34 replaced the railroad tracks in the foreground of the photo--the house was taken down for the highway
Berquist Family Photo

Bertha sold the house and the land behind the house to a farmer who had adjoining property.

On this property, Bertha's in-laws, Phillip and Amelia, also owned a house located at 1841 Mount Pleasant Street. Bertha's brother-in-law, Herb Roederer, had stayed on living in the house after Phillip and Amelia passed away in 1931. Jane's Uncle Herb was married now and owned a tavern down the street.

Roederer's, 1100 Chalfant Street, Burlington, Iowa, Mary & Herb Roederer's Tavern
Berquist Family Photo

As it worked out, Mary and Herb Roederer purchased the house next to the tavern, so Bertha and the four girls could move into the home on Mount Pleasant Street. The house and lot would be less upkeep for Bertha. She would still have a garden, but not as big. In 1943, the five of them moved to 1841 Mount Pleasant Street.

Bertha owned a significant swath of land denoted by the rectangular box on the map.

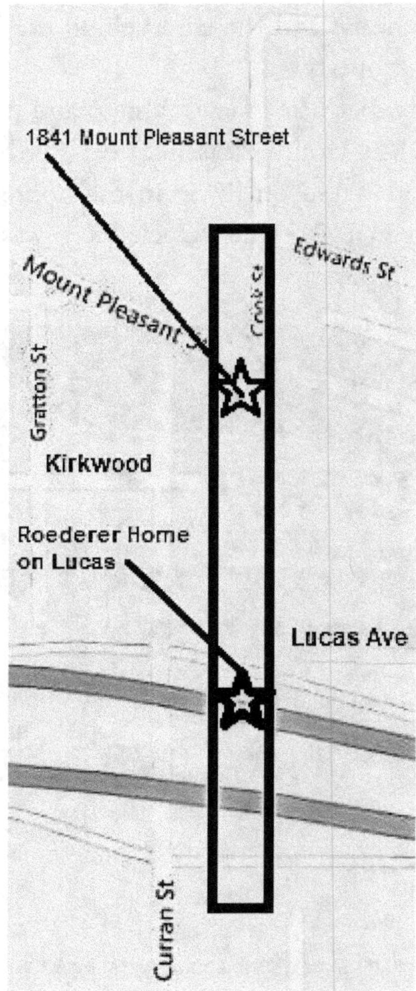

The property was subdivided and sold off in pieces through the 1950s, accounting for nine or so homesites, a beautiful wooded ravine, and the construction of the highway.

Jane, and her youngest sister Ruth, each received by bequest one homesite. Both took their inheritance from their mother right away. Jane would eventually buy two more of her mother's lots in the 1950s. After holding her lot for forty years, Ruth sold her property at the edge of the wooded ravine, making a significant amount of cash. Jane learned the value of real estate ownership from her mother. She would put this knowledge to clever use for the rest of her life.

Jane's older sisters, Mary and Ann, both took cash instead of land as part of the agreement when writing up Bertha's last will and testament. This decision was the right decision for them at the time, as they would both rather quickly have thirteen children between the two of them. Money now was better than land later.

Jane graduated from St. Paul's Catholic High School in 1946. Her sisters Mary, Ann, and Ruth also went to St. Paul's.

Saint Paul's Catholic Church, 508 N. 4th Street, Burlington, Iowa
*ATTRIBUTION: Ian Poellet (https://commons.wikimedia.org/wiki/
File:St_Paul_Catholic_Church_-_Burlington_Iowa.jpg), „St Paul Catholic
Church - Burlington Iowa"*

Located in the historic Heritage Hill District and listed on the National Register of Historic Places, St. Paul's School was also there but has been subsequently torn down.

While in high school, Jane worked at the Curly Inn Salon in downtown Burlington.

Former location of The Curly Inn, 214 North 4th Street, Burlington, Iowa
Photo taken by Michael Berquist 2013

Bertha's sister Ruth Koestner Anderson owned the Curly Inn. Ruth was one of Bertha's younger siblings. Ruth was married to Ralph Anderson. The salon was a short walk after school or a bus ride from there after work. Jane was a shampoo girl when she started and worked for tips. Jane was trained for her duties at the salon by the older experienced girls working there. As time passed and under supervision, she was allowed to assist the licensed operators. While working on the job at the salon, Jane obtained her beauty operator license.

Jane loved her Aunt Ruth, but her favorite operator and the one who would become a lifelong friend was Donna. Donna was popular, pretty, and had lots of regular customers. Donna was twelve years older. Jane looked up to Donna like a big sister.

Jane had been working at the salon for a year when the summer of 1946 arrived early.

Jane Francis Roederer, circa 1946
Berquist Family Photo

The heat usually reserved for June, July, and August started in March that year. The seasons had leaped from winter to summer, entirely skipping spring. The weather brought many people to the downtown air-conditioned businesses. Even if they did not need to buy anything, shopping inside suddenly became popular. People jammed the drug-store soda fountains and movie theaters.

The war had been over for eight months, and everyone was in an elated state of euphoria. The returned soldiers, sailors, aviators, and marines in Burlington enjoyed celebrity-like status. Cars and pedestrians flooded the downtown streets and sidewalks.

In March, at a college in a small town west of St. Louis and at the invitation of President Truman, former Prime Minister Winston Churchill gave a speech about unfolding events occurring in Eastern Europe. The Russian government was stretching and, in some cases, violating agreements concerning the division of lands taken during the war. Churchill stated, "An iron curtain" had gone up from the Baltic to the Adriatic, conjoining several Eastern European countries with the Soviet Union. Stalin claimed the actions were taken as a protective measure against another invasion. Churchill asked for tighter US alliance to subjugate the Soviets' unfettered militaristic expansion.

On a Saturday afternoon in April, the heat drove Kenneth into the downtown area. Before the war, Kenneth had learned from his dad the value of soda fountain treats on a sweltering day. Downtown on Jefferson Street, drugstores and soda fountains flourished. F.W. Woolworth's, S.S. Kresge's five-and-dime, Rexall Drugs, and a myriad of other family-owned outlets could provide in a matter of minutes the heat-quenching relief sought. Kenneth's favorite was Sutter's drug store.

The counter at the soda fountain was strategically oriented to provide excellent viewing angles across both streets and over toward Schramm's department store. Schramm's was a draw for girls out shopping. The comings and goings could be watched from the soda fountain counter at Sutter's with great ease.

Sutter Drug Store, 311 North 3rd Street at Jefferson, Burlington, Iowa, circa mid-1940s
Photo courtesy Jane Sutter Brandt

The soda fountain was the perfect hangout for a single guy looking to flirt with a girl. Kenneth preferred to do this by himself. His friends were not exactly the best to have along as a "cheering squad." Kenneth was shy, and he did not need any encouragement from his chucklehead friend Bob Doyle. It was too easy to be embarrassed.

On this specific Saturday, Kenneth found himself dropping in to the Curly Inn to visit his sister Donna. It only took Kenneth a matter of seconds upon entering the salon to notice Jane Roederer. Tongue-tied, he spoke briefly with Donna, telling her he would "be across the street at Sutter's" if she wanted to "come over and have lunch" with him.

Two more Saturdays would go by with Kenneth sitting on a stool at Sutter's, hoping for a chance glance of Jane walking to work, catching the bus, or going into Schramm's on her break or an accidental meeting on the sidewalk, and saying hello. By the third Saturday, Kenneth could not stand it any longer, and he ventured into Curly's again to see Donna and to ask her to introduce him to Jane.

Jane had noticed Kenneth on this first Saturday as well, immediately flying over to Donna, inquiring about her handsome visitor. Donna had not said anything to Kenneth about Jane's interest, as Donna viewed the attention as a young girl's infatuation with her brother, who was an older man. Kenneth was twenty-six, and Jane was eighteen.

But now with both expressing interest, Donna was not able to help herself playing matchmaker. Kenneth invited Jane to have lunch with him at Sutter's. He went across the street and arranged a place to sit.

Jane remained behind in the salon and would join him in a few minutes when her break came. Little did either one of them know, the chance visit three weeks before would be a life-changing event for both. Was it love at first sight? Jane would later confess she knew Kenneth would be the man she would marry.

With ants in his pants, Kenneth sat waiting nervously for Jane to arrive. Back in the salon was the flurry of a woman hurriedly working to ready herself for an unexpected lunch date. Did she look okay? Thank God, she'd worn a nice dress to work that day. How did her hair look? Donna assured Jane she looked fine and sent her off in a whirl to have lunch with her brother.

Kenneth stood and helped her with her chair. Within moments of sitting down, the feelings quieted. The nerves went away. And the conversation flowed like they had known each other for years. They laughed and enjoyed the stories each told of their lives. They compared lists of "likes" and "dislikes." Jane's thirty-minute lunch break went by in a blink. After lunch, the two agreed to a more traditional formal date the following Friday night. They went their separate ways, each dancing on cloud nine.

Kenneth washed his car after work on Thursday night. Friday, May 3, 1946, finally arrived. This would be the first time he would go out with Jane. Kenneth started bragging at work about having a date in the evening. The guys at work had a hundred questions to ask him. Some were inappropriate and made Kenneth smile and walk away. Other inquiries seemed usual. What was her name? How old was she? Where did she go to school?

He remained tight-lipped about her name and where they were going. He said he remembered seeing a movie in New York with Gene Tierney called *China Doll*. He said he thought Jane looked like Gene Tierney.

Jane Roederer, circa 1947
Berquist Family Photo

Gene Tierney Photo--Commonly found in the public domain
ATTRIBUTION: The Red List
/wiki-2-24-525-526-653-view-1940s-profile-gene-tierney.html

Kenneth arrived home around 4:30. He had stopped at the filling station on the way home and gassed up. The car was flat empty, and it cost four dollars to fill up! He was sweaty, nasty, and dirty, and desperately needed a bath. He needed a shave. Elsie was at the house when he arrived home, so Kenneth asked her what she thought he should wear on his first date with Jane. "Where are you going?" was her first question. Kenneth had thought about it all week. They would go to the movies and then have dinner at the Arion Club. If she felt like it, they would go dancing.

All of this sounded fine to Elsie. Now, what to wear. They agreed upon a pair of beige gabardine pleated trousers and a comfortable short-sleeved cotton dress shirt, both perfectly pressed. Elsie wanted to see him dressed for a last go-over before he left, only to be sure he looked good. The movie was a Susan Hayward show about a navy guy solving a murder mystery, *Deadline at Dawn*. Elsie thought the movie would be okay.

CHAPTER 15

Jane Gets Ready

On the other side of town, Jane was getting ready for her date with Kenneth. Her sisters were helping, but Jane's mother, Bertha, would have the last say about what Jane wore and how she looked. Jane had not been on a real date before. Her interactions with boys before this had been doing activities together with mixed groups of classmates.

Mary walked down the hallway toward Jane's bedroom. Mary was the oldest sister, and like a second mother to the girls. The closer Mary approached, the louder giggles grew. Mary tapped on the door and stepped in with a smile. The sisters were all together again.

The girls were surprised to see Mary at the house on a Friday evening. She usually came over during the weekend to catch up. When Ann, the second oldest, asked about Mary being there, Mary winked and said, "Mom told me Jane had a date tonight."

Mary and Ann turned their attention to Jane, who was standing in the center of the room in her slip and stockings. Even with her hair up in rollers, she was a beautiful young lady. Jane was one month away from high school graduation and going on her first real date. She felt so grown up and wanted everything to be perfect for her date with Kenneth. She had already decided this was going to be the man she would marry. Jane fussed with the seams on her stockings, telling the girls she was a little nervous. Ann had been dating Herb Hauser for some time and assured Jane she would be fine, and then led her over to her bed, where several dresses had been laid out. "Have you decided which dress you will wear?" Mary asked.

Ruth rolled her eyes and groaned. "Does it look like she's figured it out?" Ruth was the youngest of the girls and a tomboy at heart. Ruth had been lying on her bed with her feet up on the antique white headboard, listening to the older girls fussing over Jane. Ruth did not care about looking pretty in dresses and certainly did not care about dating boys. Ruth quickly pulled her school jumper from over her head, and now the jumper lay in a pile on the floor. The old overalls Ruth pulled on had one buckle dangling undone and the other twisted and hanging off her shoulder. "What's the big deal anyway?" She sighed and rolled over in time to get a bunched-up dress tossed in her face by Jane.

Jane had been leaning toward wearing her powder-blue dress. As she held it up in front of her, Mary and Ann both nodded in agreement. Mary thought it a perfect choice, and Ann agreed, the dress complemented Jane's dark hair and blue eyes. Jane had spotted the fabric for the dress in the window of Woolworth's and had immediately fallen in love with it. The fabric, and the dress that resulted from a McCall's pattern, was more expensive than outfits the Roederer girls usually wore but worth every bit of Jane's hard-earned beauty-parlor money.

The dress was a departure from the schoolgirl-style dresses she had been wearing. The bodice of the dress was fitted with darts up the front and back and attached to a more sophisticated, slimmer-style skirt, which fell slightly below her knees. If Kenneth took her dancing tonight, it would have enough of a flair to flow gracefully during their spins. The crisp collar was fuller than the one on her school uniform, and it had tiny pearls clustered in a delicate rose pattern at each perfect point. Jane loved the ultra-thin rolled-satin-ribbon finished edging on the collar, as well as on the cuffs of the short sleeves. Yes, this was the perfect choice for her first date with Kenneth.

Jane slipped the dress over her head and carefully buttoned the five small pearl beads down the front. The matching fabric belt had the same thin rolled satin ribbon along both edges. The tiny pearl rose cluster carried from the collar to the belt sitting at the closure edge, where an invisible inside clasp finished the look. Jane added her stylish touch by sliding the belt slightly to her right, so the pearl rose cluster was off center. She then slipped into her pumps and clasped the ankle straps. Both Mary and Ann squealed with delight as Jane flowed across the room, pretending she was dancing in Kenneth's arms.

Ruth rolled off the bed and stood with her hands on her hips. She was utterly disgusted with all the girly primping and squeals. "All this for a date, sheesh. You won't ever see me making such a fuss over a guy."

Jane assured her one day she would be going through the same thing and they would all be there to help her get ready for her first date. Under her breath, Mary replied, "Let's hope so," and everyone except Ruth giggled. Another typical rolling of the eyes and Ruth left the room with a slam of the door.

Jane sat on the bench in front of her vanity, watching her sisters work the rollers out of her dark hair. Once her locks were free, she slowly ran her fingers from roots to the tips, ending with a gentle toss of her head. Jane reached for her brush, but Mary was quicker, grabbing the lavender pearl handle and pulling it away. Mary then spritzed the brush with perfume and offered it to Jane. Introduced to the market the previous year, White Shoulders perfume was perfect timing for the sisters to purchase as a birthday gift for Jane. They had been so excited to give their sister this heady new scent with the aroma of gardenia, lilac, and jasmine with a hint of amber and musk. Jane brushed her hair with long, slow strokes infusing the mesmerizing aroma until it shone, and she was satisfied it was perfect.

Mary pulled open the second drawer on the bureau and slid out a white sweater. "It's going to be chilly tonight, so take this to slip over your shoulders."

Downstairs, Bertha had been busy in the kitchen, putting together dinner and adding final additions to her soup that would simmer on the stove over the weekend. Her hearty soups were always at the ready when the family was hungry, or relatives stopped in for a visit. Overhead, she could hear every footstep on the old wooden floor in the girl's bedroom. Hearing the movement and her daughter's laughter had her curious, and she could not stay in the kitchen another moment. As she made her way up the creaking old wooden steps, she reached into her apron pocket and squeezed the little bundle she had been carrying with her all afternoon.

Jane had finished applying her creamy new shade of red lipstick and was jokingly tossing a smooch to her sister Ann when Bertha stepped into the room. Jane was glowing with excitement, her eyes sparkling and her smile dazzling. Bertha was momentarily speechless with the sight of this beautiful young woman, no longer her little girl. "Oh, Jane, you look beautiful, honey," she was finally able to articulate.

Jane could not have looked better for her date. No one in the room could have disputed it, but not one of the girls said a thing when Bertha went over to Jane and began straightening her collar, brushing her hair back to one side and finishing by smoothing her skirt. Their mother's loving touch and final approval meant everything to the girls.

As Jane reached for her sweater, Bertha slipped her hand into her apron pocket and pulled out a small red-velvet pouch. Jane saw the flash of red and heard the gentle clicking of the contents. She let the sweater lie and walked back to her mother, who was loosening the gold cord holding the pouch closed. Bertha turned the pouch upside down and poured the treasure into Jane's open hands. Mary and Ann moved closer, knowing what was unfolding but being drawn in by their memories.

As Bertha took back the string of precious pearls, Jane was slowly turning and stopped when she saw her reflection in the mirror. Her mother was behind her now, reaching around her, placing the family heirloom on her chest, then gently tugging it up around her neck, and finally closing the diamond-rimmed pearl clasp. Mary and Ann exchanged knowing smiles and remembered the first time their mother had placed those pearls on each of them.

Tapping Jane's shoulder, Bertha told Jane, "Now don't forget to be polite." The girls broke out in laughter, with Bertha joining in. Ann held up her hand to quiet them, "Was that a knock? I heard a knock."

Ruth confirmed Ann's suspicion, soon shouting up the stairs that "Jane's boyfriend" was at the door.

Jane grabbed her sweater and purse and wasted no time in getting out the door. Kenneth was walking up the sidewalk toward the front door as Jane came flying out. The near-collision caught both by surprise. They laughed. Only a few days had passed since being together for the first time at the drug store. Six days had flown by. Kenneth turned to introduce himself to Bertha, who was standing on the front stoop watching, but she beat him to the punch, extending her hand, introducing herself in one breath, saying, "Jane should be home by eleven."

Kenneth smiled, acknowledging he'd heard her as he opened the passenger door on the car and helped Jane to settle comfortably in the seat. Under her voice, Bertha said, "A gentleman." East on Mount Pleasant Street they went, toward downtown.

CHAPTER 16

A New Journey Begins

Kenneth was embarrassed when he picked up Jane for their first date, and he was still driving the ol' '41 Chevy Special Deluxe he bought before the war. But, preoccupied with their first and subsequent dates, Jane paid no heed to the car. The one time she may have noticed was when the old car had a flat tire and she helped Kenneth by holding the lug nuts as he changed out the flat with the spare. Luckily, the spare had air.

From their first date on, Jane and Kenneth were exclusive. Kenneth's family loved Jane right from the start. Mick and Lou were happy Kenneth had found such a lovely girl. Donna loved Jane, of course. It did not take long for Dick and Elsie to love her as well. While protective, Jane's mom and sisters did not take long to love Kenneth either. There were many family dinners together on weekends. Families took turns having everyone over. It was one big happy family.

If there were any reservations about the match, it was with Jane's mom, Bertha. It was not a small reservation. The issue was with Kenneth's religion. The Roederer-Koestner families were Catholic, and the Berquist-Schmicker families were Lutheran. While Mick and Lou had no such religious requirement for their children, Bertha did. Bertha expected her grandchildren to be raised Catholic in a churchgoing Catholic household. The Catholic-Lutheran combination was going to be the obstacle in their path going forward, no detour around this one. Jane knew how her mother felt about this religious difference. Jane knew something would have to change for the disputes to be solved.

One of the other significant milestones to pass was to consider how their friends and acquaintances interacted when together. Jane and Kenneth double dated often, so this harmony of friends having a good relationship with one another was important to both. It would have been hard to find anyone who did not like funnyman Bob Doyle. A couple of Jane's friends thought Kenny Snyder was cute. Dick Fry was in a committed relationship already. The four of them had been out together on a double date several times.

Kenneth and Jane went on weekly dates through May 1946. The first big party they went to as a couple was Jane's high school graduation and celebration. Jane graduated on May 31, 1946.

Jane Roederer, Ruth Roederer, Dan Riffel, Mary Roederer-Riffel, and Ann Roederer, circa 1946
Berquist Family Photo

Mary Roederer was married to Dan Riffel on June 26, 1946. Kenneth was Jane's date for the wedding.

Dan was a realtor, and he was enjoying the real estate market boom brought about by the end of the war. Dan came from a large family in

Dodgeville, Iowa, and had been established in the Burlington real estate business before and after the war. The Riffels bought their first new house only a few blocks away from mother Bertha.

Mary and Dan Riffel's first house, 2313 Burlington Avenue, Burlington, Iowa. Mary and Dan lived here from 1946 until 1958.
Berquist Family Photo

The remainder of the 1940s was going to go by in a flash. Time was starting to move at a new determinant pace. Life and love had their schedule to keep. The two years immediately following Kenneth and Jane's first date was filled with parties. All the celebrations served to acquaint Jane and Kenneth with each other's family. Four siblings with their spouses in each family equaled lots of birthdays.

The first big celebration happened on Friday evening May 31, 1946. Jane graduated from high school. The commencement took place at St. Paul's and, afterward at home, the congratulations began. Kenneth had a shocking surprise on this night as well. In the crowd at the Roederer house was Jane's Uncle Paul Koestner. Both men were so surprised to see each other. Kenneth and Paul had gone to high school together. Paul was Bertha's little brother and, as such, Jane's uncle. Paul and Kenneth knew each other from Burlington High School but never hung around with one another. This would change in time, with the two becoming fast friends.

Jane went to work full time for Northwestern Bell Telephone Company as a switchboard operator immediately after high school graduation.

Northwestern Bell Telephone Company switchboard in Burlington Iowa, circa late 1940's
ATTRIBUTION: Virginia Bresser Jurss (woman in white sleeveless blouse standing in the background), West Bend, Wisconsin, Reminisce Magazine June/July 2010, and http://www.ms1940mccall.com/ 2010_06_01_archive.html

Jane loved working, and now she would earn a regular hourly wage. The difficulties of the pay at the Curly Inn would be behind her. The telephone company building was kitty-corner to Jane's church. She felt comfortable being close to her old high school neighborhood.

The Fourth of July was never a disappointment downtown on the riverfront by the auditorium. The night sky filled with lights and the surface of the river sparkled in red, white, and blue. Music filled the air as cars jockeyed for best viewing position. The auditorium was the place to be and be seen this Fourth of July.

There was much celebrating in August 1946. Donna turned thirty-two on the eighth, and Jane always wanted to be a part of celebrating with Donna, her close and dear friend. Dee made sure to get everyone together for a picnic lunch in Crapo Park on Sunday the eleventh to celebrate Donna's birthday. The entire Berquist clan came out to the park for fried chicken with all the fixings and a beautiful cake Jane had volunteered to make. Elsie brought her new boyfriend to the party. Rich hit it off with everyone right away. Rich became well liked by the family from the first day.

Weekly dates continued through the summer months. Going to the movies was the most popular leisure-time activity. There were dances at the Clark Field House and the auditorium. The two of them went downtown to sit under the stars on the lawn of the auditorium to watch the fireworks display on July 4. Kenneth was always a gentleman, making sure Jane was comfortable wherever they went. The public pool at the park was only open for the three fast months of summer. They went swimming regularly on Saturday afternoons and then caught a movie downtown in the evening.

On special occasions, they would have dinner at the Arion Club, leave to see a movie, and then come back to the Arion to dance. The Arion was an important restaurant downtown, which began as the Brown Derby in 1936. Jane would get all giddy about going there. It was a great date place, with drinks, dinner, and dancing all in one place. Arion was a classical Greek performer who sang and played the lyre, so it is a fitting name for a place of music and entertainment. It was half bar and half restaurant. Upstairs in the Arion Club, notable performers who had put on shows at the Memorial Auditorium a block away would perform late into the night. If Jimmy Dorsey's band were playing in the auditorium, you could bet a few of his guys would show up at the Arion after their show to blow off a little steam after their performance. These ad hoc performances were never planned. Playing happened spontaneously. And then seeing it in the paper the next day, anyone who had missed it would groan with envy.

The other thing they liked to do was get together with Dick and Lida. On an irregular Friday/Saturday-night basis, Lida could be found playing the organ and singing at either Bob's Stagecoach Inn downtown on Main Street or the Moose Lodge on Mount Pleasant Street. Lida provided musical entertainment during the dinner hours. Often, Lida's sisters would be there singing with her.

In usual highfalutin style, Dick and Lida celebrated the last of their twenties together with friends and family gathered around at the Moose.

The Moose Lodge, Mount Pleasant Street, Burlington, Iowa
Photo taken by Michael Berquist May 7, 2019

Dick and Lida knew how to party, and the Moose threw a heck of a party for its veteran members. They split the birth dates and chose Saturday, August 24 for the big party. Dick surprised everyone that night when he announced to all he was in the process of purchasing farmland on Rural Route One Mason Road. He planned to build a little ranch-style house for Lida and himself and raise Black Angus. They would grow a few acres of feed corn. No one saw this typical Dick and Lida–style announcement coming.

Often, Kenneth and Jane simply drove around, went to the various parks, bought root beers and hot dogs at the A&W, and parked somewhere to watch the sunset. September brought about a respite in parties and celebrations. It was okay because they were happy being with each other. The lazy hot days of summer were ending, and they could cuddle wrapped in a blanket, looking up at the night's sky. Both knew it was undeniable from the start they would be together for the rest of their lives.

October brought about parties for both families. Elsie celebrated thirty-five years on the twelfth. The Berquists had a small get-together in her honor. Jane attended the quiet celebration. However, this quietness was interrupted a few days later by Kenneth's twenty-seventh birthday. It was his first birthday since coming home from the Pacific, and he was so grateful to be among his loved ones. It was all he wanted. With his new love by his side, he was bursting with happiness. Never one to be enthusiastic about being singled out, Ruth celebrated her Sweet Sixteen on Halloween night with friends gathered around. Bertha baked a big, beautiful cake, and they dunked for apples. The neighbors could hear the screaming and laughter down the street.

Jane turned nineteen on Thursday, November 21, and she celebrated on Sunday the twenty-fourth with her mom putting on a huge dinner for the family. Everyone was there. After supper in the early evening, Kenneth asked Jane to marry him. The proposal came as a shock, and she asked for a few days to think it over. Her number-one thought went to the fact they had only been dating for a little over six months and she thought it was fast. Everyone had to go back to work in the morning, and Jane told Kenneth she would have an answer for him on Thanksgiving.

Jane spent the next three days talking the proposal over with her sisters and mom. Mary, Ann, and Ruth were all so happy for Jane. Ann, busy with planning a birthday party for her new boyfriend, Herb, broke away numerous times to console and counsel Jane as she worked her way through this perplexing dilemma. Her mom, Bertha, was not so thrilled, telling Jane the only way she would permit the marriage would be if Kenneth converted. Jane was worried this stipulation would cause her to lose the love of her life. She cried every night Thanksgiving week.

Kenneth's hopes were dashed after Thanksgiving dinner, when Jane said she would "think about" his proposal. She could not/would not marry outside her Catholic faith. Her mother, Bertha, would never permit this to happen. They spent the next two weeks apart. Jane feared to tell Kenneth his proposal would only be accepted if he converted to Catholicism. It was a problematic, squirmy time for her, dodging answers and steering conversation to other topics.

Kenneth's parents, Mick and Lou, were equally mystified as to why Jane had declined the marriage proposal. Mick and Lou loved Jane and were looking forward to having her become part of their family. Kenneth's brother and sister, Dick and Elsie, could not believe it. It was his sister Donna who had introduced them in the first place, and she was the most shocked.

After several days of gentle prying, Donna finally pried it out of Jane. Jane told Donna she could not marry a Lutheran. "Why the big secret?" Donna asked. Jane explained her predicament to Donna, who, replying with a chuckle, said, "Is that all?" Donna explained to Jane, Kenneth was so in love with her he would do anything to be married to her. "It can all be fixed. Tell him," Donna said.

With the weight removed and a gulp of courage, Jane told Kenneth the reason she could not marry him. Kenneth knew he could not let Jane slip through his fingers. "I love you, Jane. I cannot imagine my life without you. I'll become a Catholic," he said. Their reunion continued with tears, laughter, hugs, and kissing. Their path together was clear.

Christmas and New Year's Eve 1946 filled Kenneth and Jane with a renewed spirit of love and understanding. The future was clearing. Donna, Dee, Kenneth, and Jane kicked up their heels at a New Year's dance and birthday celebration for Dee at the Memorial Auditorium. It was a magical end to 1946.

Kenneth's conversion to Catholicism began when he met Jane's parish priest at St. Paul's Catholic Church after Mass on Sunday, January 5, 1947. Jane would accept Kenneth's marriage proposal the day he completed his conversion. Jane introduced Kenneth to Father T.J. Lew, and Kenneth's Rite of Reception into the Catholic faith had begun.

CHAPTER 17

Conversion

Pope Pius XII improved the conversion process. While Mass would continue in Latin until 1962, the prayers and the education provided to catechumens would be in English. It would be years before Kenneth was able to recite prayers in Latin during church services. Pope Pius did not change the rigor of the process. The Rite of Christian Initiation for Adults (RCIA) would remain rigorous.

At his first introduction to Father Lew, Kenneth was scheduled for a
private meeting the coming week.

Father Lew had baptized Jane when she was a baby, and he had been to the Roederer household for many celebrations over the years. Father Lew had taught occasional catechism classes to all the Roederer girls at one time or another at St. Paul's.

Father Lew was also tickled by Jane's timing with the request. The Lenten season and the opportunity for conversions would soon be upon them, assuring the two the process would finish before summer arrived.

Kenneth and Father Lew hit it off wonderfully right from the start. Father Lew had prayed for Jane and Kenneth. He was happy for the couple, knowing Kenneth to be a man of his word. The purpose of the first meeting was to discover Kenneth's desire and intentions for becoming a Catholic. While he did come from an Evangelical Lutheran family, attendance at church services was not mandatory. When he was young, Mick and Lou managed to get the four siblings to church occasionally: Christmas, Easter, and a few more times during the year. They were not regular churchgoers. Kenneth did manage to attend Catholic services with a few of his friends during the war. He was not entirely oblivious to the faith. He did not understand what was going on during Mass.

Mick and Lou had their children baptized at their church in an informal and undocumented ceremony. There was no physical proof baptism had occurred. Kenneth only knew of his baptism as an infant because he was told by his parents that they'd had him baptized. Unfortunately, merely knowing was not enough, and Father Lew explained Kenneth would need baptism again, and this additional event would lengthen the process ever so slightly. Kenneth understood the reason for the second christening.

Kenneth would meet weekly with Father Lew at the church rectory for about an hour over the next six weeks. Life outside of the conversion process went on as usual. Kenneth's mom turned fifty-seven on January 17. They had a quiet little birthday party for her at the house. Jane was, of course, inquisitive as to what Kenneth and Father Lew were talking about, and Kenneth would reply, "Sports." It was basketball season. Jane would simply smile. Father Lew had been to Sunday dinner with

Kenneth's family. Lew liked what he saw and experienced, and believed Mick and Lou had raised a loving family.

Kenneth's dad turned sixty on February 15, so they had a combination birthday-wedding anniversary party for Mick and Lou's thirty-seventh anniversary on Saturday, February 22.

The next event took place at Mass on Sunday, February 23, 1947. Kenneth had been attending Mass with Jane, her mom, and her sisters for seven weeks now. The Lenten season began on the nineteenth, Ash Wednesday. That day, during Mass, Kenneth was introduced to the church congregation in a ceremony called "Rite of Election." He would begin a period of Lenten fasting and a period called "scrutiny." Kenneth was overwhelmed by the welcoming acceptance and encouragement of the churchgoers.

Dick and Lida celebrated their fifth wedding anniversary by taking the whole family out to dinner at the Moose Lodge on Saturday night, March 1. Dick and Lida were regular fixtures at the Moose Lodge, so the party was loud and busy quickly. Kenneth and Jane bowed out early, taking Mick and Lou home early in the night. They had church in the morning, plus Lent had started.

Dan Riffel threw his wife, Mary, a surprise twenty-third birthday party on Saturday, March 22, at Crapo Park. Everyone was hiding out in the ice-skating warming shack when the two of them walked up. Mary could not have been more surprised. Mary did not like surprises. Everyone thought it was cute when she slapped Dan on the shoulder and scolded him for the prank.

Over the next two weeks, Father Lew would guide Kenneth through a period of self-searching and repentance. Father Lew was kind and gentle, but their meetings became emotional with Kenneth laying open his life until then and talking about the war. Kenneth was committed to seeing it through. A week of healing would follow concerns raised during this time and later strengthen Kenneth's good qualities. The Lenten season and Kenneth's education of the Catholic faith were quickly ending.

On April 5, at Easter Vigil Mass on Holy Saturday, Kenneth recited by memory, and in English, the Lord's Prayer and the Apostles' Creed before the church congregation. Jane was so proud of him.

Easter Sunday, April 6, 1947, had arrived, and at Mass, Father Lew announced to the congregation that Kenneth had passed through the period of scrutiny and the Rite of Election and would be welcomed into the faith soon. Jane's mother, Bertha, was now convinced, congratulating Kenneth with all the enthusiasm she could muster. Lenten fasting was over. Jane's mother, Bertha, put on a celebration lunch with both families at home. The conversion process was still not complete, as the fifty-day period of Pentecost, also part of the process, was now upon Kenneth.

Scheduling would become complicated. Pentecost Sunday would mark the completion of Kenneth's conversion. He still had some steps to complete. Timing rotated around Des Moines Catholic Diocese Bishop Gerald T. Bergan. The bishop would start traveling on March 23 to the 125 parishes in his diocese. The purpose was the administration of confirmation to the catechumens. Not all churches had catechumens to confirm, but there were a few. The bishop had to complete all confirmations by May 25. Kenneth would also need to decide upon his godparents and confirmation sponsor. These three would all be Catholic. After much discussion, Jane's Aunt Clara and Uncle Carl Stolze would be Kenneth's godparents. Clara was Bertha's sister. Kenneth asked Carl also to be his confirmation sponsor.

Donna and Dee celebrated their seventh wedding anniversary with a small get-together at Mick and Lou's. Jane and Donna were good friends, so Jane would not miss this party for anything. Donna's wedding anniversary on April 19 fell on Saturday this year. The timing was perfect for the small celebration.

Father Lew was reassigned to St. Patrick's parish a few blocks away during this time. Many parishioners at St. Paul's loved Father Lew, including the Roederer family. They were immensely loyal to him and followed him to his small new parish.

Kenneth completed what he'd started at St. Patrick's.

Saint Patrick's Catholic Church, Currently the Hibernia Rental Hall, 1204 Washington Street, Burlington, Iowa

ATTRIBUTION: http://weddingsiniowa.blogspot.com/2013/05/preferred-vendor-historic-hibernia-hall.html

Kenneth was baptized on Thursday, May 8, 1947, by Father Lew with his godparents Clara and Carl standing next to him.

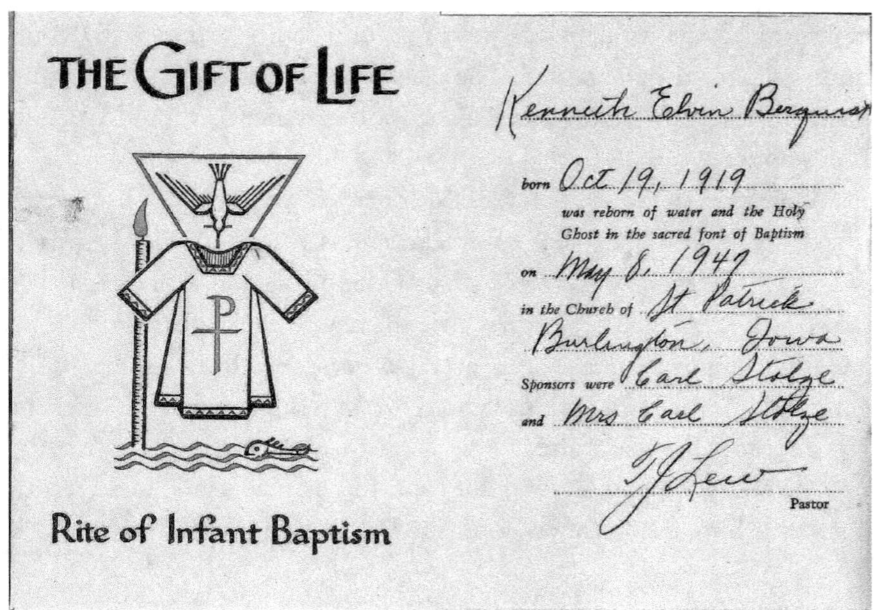

Herb Hauser planned a quiet twenty-first-birthday celebration for Jane's sister Ann on Friday night, May 9. Ann and Herb had grown close over the previous months. Jane thought Herb would be popping the big question any day now.

During the meetings with Father Lew over the past weeks, Kenneth had on several occasions discussed actions sinful within the doctrine of the church. But, since Kenneth was not yet a Catholic, Father Lew was unable to offer absolution and penance.

Now with baptism behind him and communion and confirmation looming, it was important Kenneth complete his first formal confession. Kenneth completed his first confession on Friday, May 16. Kenneth took Holy Communion for the first time, with Jane by his side, at Sunday Mass on the eighteenth.

After church services, Jane and Kenneth drove over to his parents' house on Summer Street for lunch. On the drive over, they saw a huge explosion. As they drove farther south on Summer Street, they saw what appeared to them as Perkins Elementary School on fire. Seconds later, they could hear the sirens of police cars and the fire department rushing into the area. It was then the local radio station KBUR announced a plane had crashed. The plane was part of an air show taking place at the airport. The airport was a short distance south of Mick and Lou's house.

When they arrived, they were both relieved to know the house was intact except for one piece of cracked glass in an upstairs bedroom window. The crash was a large part of the discussion over lunch that day. It was not until the next day that the newspaper reported two boys and the pilot were dead, and several others were hurt—some badly. Several homes around Perkins School had sustained damage. The event was discussed for weeks after.

The following Sunday, with his soon-to-be uncle, Carl Stolze, standing beside him, Kenneth was confirmed by Bishop Bergan.

Kenneth's Catholic Confirmation Scapular
Berquist Family Possession

Pentecost Sunday, May 25, 1947, and the fifty-day period had come and gone. Kenneth was a Catholic. Jane accepted his marriage proposal. They asked Father Lew to marry them. The twenty could not have been a better gift for Bertha's fiftieth birthday. Kenneth and Jane set the date: June 5, 1948. They would have a one-year engagement.

Father Lew introduces Kenneth to the congregation as a Catholic.

The Catholic Conversion process follows a strict schedule coinciding with the Easter season each year:
Rite of Reception, Sunday, January 5
Jane introduces Kenneth to her parish priest.
Father Lew "receives" Kenneth as a catechumen.
First meeting with Father Lew, Thurs., January 9
Second meeting, Thurs., January 16
Third meeting, Thurs., January 23
Fourth meeting, Thurs., January 30
Fifth meeting, Thurs., February 6
Sixth meeting, Thurs., February 13
Lent Begins
Ash Wednesday, February 19
Rite of Election (the scrutinies)
First Sunday in Lent, Sunday, February 23
Second Sunday in Lent, Sunday, March 2
A week of self-search and repentance
Third Sunday in Lent, Sunday, March 9
Two weeks of healing weak qualities
Fourth Sunday in Lent, Sunday, March 16
Fifth Sunday in Lent, Sunday, March 23
Two weeks of strengthening good qualities
Sixth Sunday in Lent, Sunday, March 30
Holy Week
Good Friday, April 4
Holy Saturday (Easter Vigil Mass), April 5
Recites: the Lord's Prayer and the Apostles' Creed
Easter Sunday, April 6
The fifty-day period leading to Pentecost Sunday begins.
Baptism, Thurs., May 8
Confession of mortal sins, Friday, May 16
First Communion (Eucharist), Sunday, May 18
Confirmation on Pentecost (Bishop Bergan), Sunday, May 25

CHAPTER 18

One-Year Engagement

Parties and preparation filled the next twelve months, with so many get-togethers. Bertha Roederer would be marrying yet another daughter, and Mick and Lou Berquist would be gaining the daughter-in-law they loved.

Kenneth bought a new car in 1947.

Kenneth's 1947 Ford Coupe parked in front of
Jane's house at the intersection of Cook
Street and 1841 Mount Pleasant Street
Burlington, Iowa
Berquist Family Photo

He had been back to work at the Shops for a year now and had his feet back on the ground. It was his first-ever "new" car. He paid $1,425 for the 1947 Ford Coupe and was proud he had earned every penny to pay for it in cash. It was not the convertible he had dreamed of, but it had an eight-cylinder engine, and it was fast. The next car would be a convertible.

In a series of announcements beginning on June 3, 1947, two hundred years of British rule over India and Pakistan ended. Parliament passed measures to declare Pakistan a separate nation from India on August 14, 1947. The following day, August 15, India became a sovereign nation. Conflicts between Hindus, Sikhs, and Muslims broke out across the region.

Churchill's Iron Curtain was now being referred to as a Cold War—a euphemism for the chilly relations being felt with former allies —with Russia.

Mary and Dan Riffel celebrated their first wedding anniversary on June 26, 1947. They threw a small, intimate, family-only dinner party at their house on Burlington Avenue. Everyone who came over to the party was kidding them about when they were going to give Bertha a first grandchild. Everyone had a wonderful time with all the laughter and teasing.

Summer, fall, and the beginning of winter would bring about yet another series of celebrations. Birthdays, anniversaries, and "secret" engagements would abound. Every event was cause for a get-together. Each party brought families closer together. Each event drew Kenneth and Jane closer. The events of the world would pass by almost unnoticed as their world was spinning into an ever-tightening orbit.

Kenneth and Jane spent yet another Fourth of July cuddling under the stars on the lawn of the Memorial Auditorium downtown. The fireworks seemed to be getting bigger and longer in duration each year. It was a spectacular show, again followed by a dance in the auditorium, where they met up with their friends and danced the night away.

August brought about a raft of birthday parties: Donna on the eighth, Rich on the thirteenth, Dick on the twenty-second, and then Lida on the twenty-seventh. Dick and Lida's big announcement this time was, they were going to spend the month of December with friends in Las Vegas. They had gone out to Vegas on a couple of weekend junkets over the prior few months and loved it so much they decided to escape part of the winter coming up and spend a month there. It was a surprise, but not a surprise, to everyone. Still more birthdays.

October brought about birthday celebrations for Elsie (thirty-five), Kenneth (twenty-eight), and Ruth (seventeen). November brought Jane's twentieth birthday and Herb Hauser's twenty-first birthday. The holidays were upon them again.

Mick and Lou put on the Thanksgiving Day festivities. Lou, Elsie, and Donna made every effort to impress and put on a lavish Thanksgiving Day meal. The men sat in the living room and listened to the Chicago Bears–Detroit Lions game on the radio. The Bears won thirty-four to fourteen.

Kenneth and Jane spent Christmas Day at Bertha's house. Jane's sisters, Dan Riffel, and Herb Hauser were there as well as several of Jane's aunts and uncles. It was a full house and a lot of fun, with everyone exchanging and opening gifts. In the brisk night air of the evening, Kenneth and Jane took a stroll to walk off the huge dinner. They held hands and laughed, hugged, kissed, and smiled as they talked about this Christmas being their last Christmas as single people. They mulled over their dreams for a life together. They agreed to skip the New Year's festivities the following week and be alone together somewhere, someplace, and talk. They were in love and so happy.

Nineteen forty-eight started out with Kenneth's mom's birthday on January 17. Lou turned fifty-seven that day. It was not necessarily a milestone birthday, but with the engagement and all, any event served as a reason for the family to get together. Lou's birthday was no exception. Jane baked Lou a birthday cake, and a small dinner-party celebration ensued at his parents' house. Kenneth loved seeing his mom happy, smiling and laughing.

February was busier, with Mick's sixtieth birthday on the fifteenth and then, a week later, Mick and Lou's wedding anniversary on the twenty-third. It was their thirty-seventh wedding anniversary. Another week later, on the twenty-sixth was Dick and Lida's wedding anniversary. They all met at the Moose Lodge for dinner. Mary Roederer Riffel had her twenty-third birthday on March 27. Mary and Dan hosted a birthday dinner at their house the night before, on Friday night, as everybody was going to be busy the next day.

On Saturday March 27, 1948, Kenneth's parents threw Jane one of two bridal showers. Their home at 2024 Summer Street burst with family and friends. It was the way Lou liked it, full of love and happiness. Lou, Donna, and Elsie had been baking for two weeks prior. Traditional Swedish and German specialties were spread out on the twelve-foot dining-room table.

Jane met some of Kenneth's aunts and uncles from both sides, who had traveled from as far away as California to attend the celebration: Agnes Bergquist, Helga Bergquist, Norma Sallander, Frieda Schneider, Irma Schmicker, Mamie Schmicker, Bertha Schmicker, and Uncle Art Schmicker. Kenneth's aunts and uncles were all elderly, and traveling was difficult. None would miss the youngest of Mick and Lou's brood getting married. Mick and Lou were so proud to be welcoming Jane to their family.

Saturday, April 10, 1948, Mary and Dan Riffel hosted a dinner party for Kenneth and Jane at their home. Kenneth and Jane had already decided to ask Mary and Dan to be their maid of honor and best man. At the small, intimate, family-only dinner party, Kenneth and Jane popped the question to their hosts. Mary and Dan accepted the request with a huge round of laughter and hugs.

> May 1, 1948
>
> Mrs. Arthur A. Roederer, 1841 Mt.
> Pleasant St., Announces the engag-
> ment and approaching marriage of
> her daughter, Jane, to Kenneth E.
> Berquist, son of Mr. and Mrs. Elvin
> Berquist, 2024 Summer St.
> The wedding will take place Saturday,
> June 5th, at 10 o'clock in the morn-
> ing in St. Patricks Catholic Church.

Jane's mother, Bertha, had this notice placed in the newspaper on May 1, 1948
Berquist Family Possession

Kenneth and Jane helped celebrate Donna Berquist Moore and Dee Moore's seventh wedding anniversary on April 19 at the Arion Club with dinner. It was a quiet celebration. The four of them had a wonderful time.

Jane's sister Ann's birthday on May 8 was an exception to the calm and quiet rule. It was Ann's twenty-first birthday, a milestone birthday. There was lots of celebrating that night. Ann was now engaged to Herb Hauser Jr. Ann and Herb were going to remain tight-lipped about their engagement until after Jane and Kenneth were married the next month. Then they would spring the news on everyone at a time that was more appropriate. For now, they were happy leaving the spotlight to Jane and Kenneth.

Feeling one shower was not enough, Jane's aunt and uncle, Clara and Carl Stolze, threw one more wedding shower. This one was more of a traditional wedding shower, with only the girls invited. On Saturday afternoon, May 15, 1948, at 808 Barret Street, the party began. They played games, enjoyed fruit punch, ate itty-bitty sandwiches, and opened presents. Aunt Clara made sure Carol had her ears plugged for most of the naughty talk.

Uncle Carl Stolze had spoken to and prearranged with Kenneth to show up uninvited at the end of the party and steal his bride-to-be away. Carl could make sure the party would end this way so he could have some peace in his house before it was dark outside. The girls all screamed when Carl escorted Kenneth to the backyard patio. Jane smiled and flew into his arms.

The world news went by again unnoticed. After years of fighting between the Jewish and the Arab League, the State of Israel was proclaimed in May. British oversight was withdrawn on the fifteenth.

Jane's mom, Bertha, turned fifty-one on May 26. Bertha insisted on no fuss. Bertha did not care for the light of celebration shining on her. A kiss on the cheek, a warm hug, and whisper of, "Happy Birthday, Mother," was all she wanted. Besides, to Bertha, it seemed there was a party for someone, somewhere, every week, and she was getting partied out.

In June, the Allied nation airlifts into Berlin, Germany, effectively defeated the Soviet blockade between East and West Berlin. The defeat of the embargo was a huge political victory for the Truman administration.

CHAPTER 19

Marriage—1948

Despite the fact both had only moved twice in their young lives, they shared the itch to keep going forward. A few days before their marriage, Jane and Kenneth signed a lease for an apartment at 1315½ Jefferson Street.

Kenneth and Jane's first house 1315-1/2 Jefferson Street, Burlington, Iowa (a second floor apartment)
Berquist Family Photo from the 1960s

The one-bedroom apartment was upstairs in a duplex. The place was small and cramped, but the location was closer to where they worked, and they could—if they wanted—walk to church on Sunday. The apartment was about the same distance to their parents' homes.

Ken borrowed a truck from a guy he worked with, and it took all of one day for the two of them to set up household. It was June 1, 1948.

Friday, June 4, 1948, Mary and Herb Roederer, Jane's aunt and uncle, threw a wedding rehearsal and out-of-town-guest dinner party. Herb and Mary had the food catered into their tavern on Mount Pleasant Street. Everyone was forced to act in moderation, as the morning and wedding day was only twelve hours away.

Saturday, June 5, 1948, was the wedding day. The wedding Mass officiated by Father Thomas Lew, who by this time was considered a part of the Roederer family, came off without a hitch. The wedding party, including the wedding couple, looked spectacular. St. Patrick's had not had such a glorious wedding in decades. Jane's Uncle Herb gave her away. Herb Roederer was her father's brother. Father Lew worked in a joke about Kenneth converting to Catholicism and then noted how many baptisms he had to look forward to in the coming years. Father Lew looked at Jane's sister Ruth. Ruth smiled politely and then smirked when he looked away. The wedding guests sitting in the pews chuckled at Ruth's reaction.

The wedding guests were invited downtown to the Arion Club for a luncheon from 12:00 to 2:00. Lunch was followed by a reception on the lawn at Jane's home on Mount Pleasant Street.

The Wedding Party. (L.to R. Back Row) E. Dee Moore, Donna Berquist-Moore, Kenneth Berquist, Jane Roederer-Berquist, Herb Roederer, Mary Roederer-Riffel, Dan Riffel, (Front Row) Paul Koestner, Ruth Roederer, Carol Stolze, Ann Roederer-Hauser, Herb Hauser, Jr.
Berquist Family Photo

It was a bright and sunny day. It was a perfect day. The hot temperatures had not arrived yet. The gravel alley next to Bertha's house was end-to-end with parked cars. It was the ideal place for the reception. Bertha's flower gardens had burst with colors, and the fragrance of fresh flowers was in the air.

The bridesmaids; Donna Berquist Moore, Ruth Roederer,
Matron-of-Honor Mary Roederer Riffel, Junior Bridesmaid Carol
Stolze, and Ann Roederer Hauser
Berquist Family Photo

The cars passing by on Mount Pleasant Street in front of the house blew their horns and honked at the sight of the wedding party and all the guests gathered on the lawn. Everyone was in a celebratory mood.

Kenneth and Jane departed for a New York honeymoon the following day, Sunday, June 6, 1948.

They would drive there and spend a few days being tourists and retracing some of Kenneth's steps while he was there with the navy. The highlight of the honeymoon would be a trip upstate to Niagara Falls.

Jane and Kenneth on their honeymoon. New York City, June 1948. Jane was a sport, but wished they had a more flattering bride figure for this hammy pose
Berquist Family Photo

Kenneth and Jane were both virgins when they were married. Jane would later recall Kenneth was unbelievably scared about sex when they were married. Jane said Kenneth kept repeating over and over he was afraid he was going to hurt her if he had sex with her. Kenneth was worried she would get pregnant. It was at this point Jane said Kenneth confided in her the story of his sister Elsie giving birth on the kitchen table. The subject and the circumstances of the birth were a close-kept Berquist-family secret. Kenneth's parents' admonishment about sex and premarital sex was so ingrained he had trouble consummating the marriage. Jane said it was not until a few days after they had been married and with her deep understanding, sympathy, and encouragement that Kenneth was finally able to have sex with her. This was a source of great embarrassment to Kenneth and an event never spoken of again. Jane said she thought Kenneth had never gotten over Elsie's pregnancy, labor, and childbirth. Jane would not get pregnant for eight years.

Driving through Chicago on the way home, Ken drove Jane through the Great Lakes Naval Base and showed her around a few of the places he recalled from being there. Niagara Falls was the best time. They took the boat sightseeing trip out into the river and experienced the spray of the falls. They were soaked. Niagara Falls was honeymoon central in the 1940s. The local establishments catered to war-veteran honeymooners, making sure they had a memorable trip. They did.

Ken and Jane arrived back home on Sunday, June 13, in time for both to return to their jobs the next morning.

They had moved their belongings into the duplex at 1315½ Jefferson Street the week before the wedding. On their way into town, they stopped at their folks' homes to check in.

Jane's sister Ann and her fiancé, Herbert Hauser Jr., announced their engagement to their respective families the week after Ken and Jane were married. Jane squealed with glee upon returning from her honeymoon and learning the news.

Jane's mom placed a wedding announcement in the Burlington *Hawk Eye* newspaper during the honeymoon week. Bertha bought twelve copies of the newspaper so she would have enough newspaper clippings of the wedding announcement to share with relatives.

WED SATURDAY — The marriage of Miss Jane Mary Frances Roederer, daughter of Mrs. Arthur Roederer, 1841 Mt. Pleasant, and the late Arthur Roederer, to Kenneth E. Berquist, son of Mr. and Mrs. Elvin Berquist, 2024 Summer, took place at 10 a. m. Saturday, June 5, at St. Patrick's Catholic church. Rev. Thomas J. Lew read the double ring ceremony and offered nuptial low mass.

Before the ceremony, Richard Knoll sang "On This Day", "Mother, Dear, O Pray for Me", "Ave Maria", "Panis Angelicus" and "Oh Lord, I Am Not Worthy", accompanied by William Tegtmeyer, organist.

A dinner was served at noon to the immediate families at the Arion club, and a reception was held at the home of the bride's mother from 2 to 4 p. m.

The bride, a graduate of St. Paul high school, has been employed at the Northwestern Bell Telephone Co. for the past 2 years.

The bridegroom is a graduate of Burlington high school. He spent 4 years in the navy and is now employed at the West Burlington shops.

For a wedding trip to New York City, the bride wore a pink gabardine suit with pink and white accessories and a white orchid corsage.

Pre-nuptial parties for the bride included a shower given by Mrs. E. H. Berquist; a dinner by Mrs. Dan Riffel; a shower given by Mrs. C. H. Stolze; and a dinner given by Mr. and Mrs. H. J. Roederer for the bridal party and out-of-town guests Friday evening.

Wedding announcement top half

Given in marriage by her uncle, Herbert J. Roederer, the bride wore a white satin wedding gown with a fitted bodice. Her full skirt extended into a long train edged with Chantilly lace. A fingertip veil of double illusion net edged in Chantilly lace was held in place by a tiara of pearlized orange blossoms. She carried a cascade arrangement of white gladioli buds centered with a white orchid and a prayer book which was carried by her mother and grandmother on their wedding days.

Mrs. Dan J. Riffel, sister of the bride, was matron of honor. Mrs. Dee Moore, sister of the bridegroom, Miss Anne Roederer and Miss Ruth Roederer, both sisters of the bride, were bridesmaids. Carol Stolze was junior bridesmaid. They wore identical styled gowns of imported organdy in pink, blue, yellow, green and white, respectfully, with matching lace mitts. Their cascade bouquets and halos of daisies were in contrasting colors.

Dan J. Riffel was best man, and Dee Moore, Herb Hauser, Jr., and Paul A. Koestner were ushers.

Mrs. Roederer was attired in navy blue sheer, with which she wore white accessories, and a corsage of white daisies. Mrs. Berquist wore a navy print dress with white accessories and a corsage of white daisies.

Wedding announcement bottom half

And then Ken and Jane went home to their own place for the first time. They had a ton of wedding presents to unwrap and a ton of thank-you notes to write. They would have a few late nights writing and thanking all the friends and relatives for their generosity.

CHAPTER 20

July 1948–December 1949

When Ken and Jane arrived back in Burlington from their honeymoon, they went home together for the first time to their Jefferson Street apartment. Ken carried Jane across the threshold. Jane hit her head on the door frame, and the two fell through the doorway, landing gingerly on the floor, laughing uproariously. They were home. Laughter would fill the rest of their lives.

Their dreams and their plans were always the same. They dreamt of their first house, a place that would belong to them. They started writing a list of what they wanted in their next home. After a few weeks at the apartment, the one item that bubbled to the top of the list was "no steps," or at the least a minimum number of steps.

Driving west on Jefferson Street coming out of downtown Burlington, you would be going uphill as soon as you crossed Central Avenue, straight uphill. The apartment was at the crest of the hill. Parking was on the street, and then you would climb twenty-five steps from the street to the front door. Entering the front door of the building, thirteen additional steps to reach the apartment door on the second floor presented themselves. Ken and Jane would often laugh about being at such a high altitude they could see Chicago in the distance. Bags of groceries were always dreaded. Carrying bags up thirty-eight steps grew old after the second trip.

Ken and Jane took Mary and Dan Riffel out to the Arion restaurant for Saturday dinner on June 26, 1948, to celebrate Mary and Dan's second wedding anniversary. Ken and Jane also wanted to thank them properly for participating in the wedding as maid of honor and best man. It was a quiet, relaxing dinner unlike anything from the previous few weeks.

On July 4, everyone decided to go to the public pool at Crapo Park to cool off a bit from the scorching summer, which had now arrived in Burlington.

Jane at the public pool, July 1948
Berquist Family Photo

After the park and the pool, everyone retreated to freshen up before regrouping downtown to watch the fireworks display. The fireworks were always a big draw on Independence Day in Burlington. It was

Sunday night, but many of the drug stores stayed open a little later that night to help quench the thirsts of the masses descending on the Memorial Auditorium lawn and parking lot along the river. It was a festive atmosphere.

There were four birthdays and three parties in August. Donna turned thirty-four on the eighth. Richard Mack turned thirty on the thirteenth. Dick turned thirty-one on the twenty-second. Lida turned thirty-one on the twenty-seventh. Dee Moore threw a little dinner party for Donna. Richard and Elsie celebrated at Mick and Lou's house. They had invited family to join them so they could get to know Richard a little bit better. Dick and Lida celebrated their birthdays together downtown at Bob's Stagecoach Restaurant on Friday the twenty-seventh. Lida was playing the organ that night.

September was always a welcome month with only one birthday to celebrate; Dan Riffel's, on September 4. Mary Riffel planned a small quiet immediate family only get-together, as Dan preferred to avoid the fuss. There were no parties or anniversaries in September. It was a quiet month. It was nice having a month off. Toward the middle and end of the month, shoppers downtown were raving about being able to watch WLS from Chicago on TVs displayed for sale in the windows of Woolworth's, Kresge's, and Sears. They packed in three deep to catch a glimpse of the flickering ten-inch black-and-white screens.

The rest of the year, October through December, was packed with activities. Elsie celebrated her thirty-seventh birthday on October 12. Jane threw Ken a birthday party on October 19. Jane loved saying, "my husband." It was Ken's last HOORAH for his twenties—he turned twenty-nine. At the end of October, Ruth celebrated her milestone eighteenth birthday. Jane also had a milestone birthday and her golden birthday, turning twenty-one on November 21. Herb Hauser turned twenty-two on November 24. It was suddenly Thanksgiving again. There was much to be thankful for in all the families. Christmas 1948 arrived.

Ken and Jane, First Christmas as Mr. and Mrs. December 1948, photo
taken at their apartment 1315½ Jefferson Street
Berquist Family Photo

Donna and Dee celebrated Dee's thirtieth birthday alone on the twenty-ninth. Perfect timing for New Year's Eve this year, it was on Friday night. As far as the news went, there was absolutely nothing going on anywhere in the world, which interested the residents of Burlington. The quiet birthday Dee had enjoyed a couple of nights ago was held in contrast to all the noise and celebration going on at the Memorial Auditorium. Jane and Ken, along with Ken's sisters, his brother, and their spouses cut a rug to the big band at the auditorium. They rallied in 1949 and danced until one in the morning. Nineteen forty-eight was a year to remember.

The year after Ken and Jane were married, the Machinists Union ratified the forty-hour workweek. The surge in union employment after the war had calmed down, with membership settling in at half a million members strong. The IAM enjoyed the influence.

In April, an organization calling itself NATO (North Atlantic Treaty Organization) started. Twelve countries had united for the objective of providing security against the strengthening Soviet Union.

Ann and Herb were married on May 4, 1949. Herb had already moved to Moline, Illinois, a few weeks before. He was working for Herman Nelson/American Air Filter Company in Moline.

Ann and Herb purchased their first house on Twelfth Avenue, living only a short distance from Herb's work. Jane, Ruth, and Mary were anxious to drive up to Moline to see their sister's new home.

Ann and Herb Hauser's home, 1123 12th Avenue, Moline, Illinois May 1949 - Dec 1950
Photo taken by Ruth Roederer sometime in the late 1950s after the Hauser's had already moved from the house

Jim Hill was the only offspring on Ken's side of the family. Nieces and nephews on Jane's side would abound for Ken. Being a big kid at heart himself, Ken loved children. Jane's sisters, Mary and Ann, would provide thirteen offspring over the course of the next fourteen years. Ken would be bouncing babies on his knees for many years.

Mary and Dan Riffel provided the first. Jim was born on July 8, 1949. Ken was thrilled holding his new nephew, Jim Riffel, for the first time. Ken and Jane were ecstatic their maid of honor and best man had a baby boy. It was such a blessing. Jim Riffel would be the center of attraction for the next few months, and he would be the source of much tomfoolery in the coming years.

Ken and Jane purchased their first new car together in September, a convertible. Kenneth had dreams of the day he would own his first convertible, a 1949 Oldsmobile 88. She was a beauty.

Ken posing with his new 1949 Olds 88 Convertible in front of the Jefferson Street apartment building, circa fall 1949
Berquist Family Photo

Ken and his new 1949 Oldsmobile 88 Convertible, location unknown
Berquist Family Photo

In October, the Communist leader of China declared the creation of the People's Republic. The declaration ended thousands of years of Imperial Dynastic rule. Communism was quickly spreading around the world. The announcement only served to create fear war was inevitable in the future.

The New York Yankees defeated the Brooklyn Dodgers in five games to win the 1949 World Series on October 9.

Ken celebrated his thirtieth birthday on October 19. Jane turned twenty-two on November 21. The decade ended quietly for Ken and Jane. The world was round for the Berquist, Roederer, Riffel, and Hauser families. Everyone was content.

CHAPTER 21

The 1950s

The 1950s kicked off ten years of growing prosperity and general happiness, both in Burlington and amongst the Berquist and Roederer families. Ken's union wages had increased to $1.82 per hour. He was grateful for the added job security the union provided.

Ann and Herb welcomed daughter Nancy to their family on February 24, 1950. It quickly became apparent the house was going to bulge, as five months after Nancy was born, Ann was pregnant again. In December, they sold the little house on Twelfth Avenue and bought a bigger home on Fourteenth Street.

Ann and Herb Hauser's second home. 1906 14th Street, Moline, Illinois Dec 1950 – September 1953. Photo taken by Herb Hauser in the 1980s
Berquist Family Photos

Ken and Jane could not wait for summer to arrive to meet baby Nancy. The first bright weekend in March, they drove up to Moline to meet their new niece. They stayed over on Saturday night and drove back to Burlington the next day.

Ken's sister Elsie and Richard Mack married on June 25, 1950. Elsie's son, James, now twenty years old, slipped away from the army and his life in California long enough to attend and participate in his mother's wedding. Richard and James liked each other, and Elsie could not have been happier having her two men together. Elsie, now forty, had a previous tough twenty years. She was looking forward to her new life with the love she felt was always entitled. Richard was smitten. It was clear he was in love with Elsie. The future would be bright for both.

Coincidental to Elsie and Richard's wedding, the Korean War started on the same date. James received a telegram informing him of his rescinded leave and orders to report to Camp Roberts in California. James would eventually land in Camp Irwin a few weeks later and then South Korea.

Six months pregnant, Ann and Herb moved into the new house. Three months later, they welcomed daughter Susan to their quickly growing family. It was March 23, 1951.

Every spring, after the roads had cleared from the winter snow and ice, the migration of families took place in Southeast Iowa. The annual pilgrimage to Burlington and the city park of choice took place. A trend started, family reunions. These sometimes-impromptu family gatherings occurred every year until it grew difficult for far-flung family members to get together regularly. The first summer, 1949, Jim Riffel was the center of attention. The next summer, Nancy Hauser joined Jim at the family gathering. The following summer, 1951, Susan Hauser joined Nancy and Jim. Each year, like clockwork, the families gathered, and the adults passed babies around. Ken loved his first nephew, Jim. But the little girls, Nancy and Sue, took his heart.

A few days before the end of the year, the country of Libya, which had been under Italian authority since the end of the war, was given its independence as a free territory.

Ken and Jane traded in their 1949 Oldsmobile for a 1951 Oldsmobile, the same model in a convertible again. They loved the convertible.

Ken's 1951 Oldsmobile 88 Convertible, Left-to-Right: Jane's Uncle, Phillip Roederer, Jr., Jane, Ken, Dan Riffel, Jane's cousin, Patricia Phillips, Mary Riffel, and Jane's cousin, Rosemary Phillips. The house in background belongs to Jane's Aunt Mary & Uncle Herb Roederer, 1110 Chalfant Street, Burlington. The house is right next door to the tavern Mary & Herb owned at the time.
Berquist Family Photo

Nineteen fifty-two was a banner year for kids. Mary and Dan Riffel welcomed Sam to their family on February 13. Mary and Dan asked Ken and Jane to be Sam's godparents. Then, three months later, Ann and Herb, welcomed Mary Pamela on May 5. Ken had another girl with whom to play "peekaboo."

King George VI died in February, simultaneously bringing an end to the Queen Mother's reign over the dominion. Their daughter Elizabeth II was coronated at the age of twenty-five as Queen of England.

On cue, Ann was pregnant again eight months later. Time to buy a bigger house. They cut this one a little closer. Ann was in her delivery month when the Hausers moved to East Moline.

During the winter of 1952, Jane and Ken drove down to Fort Myers, Florida, to visit and stay with Jane's Aunt Gert and Uncle Harry Koestner.

Ken with Jane's Aunt Gert Koestner, Fort Myers, Florida 1952
Berquist Family Photo

Jane and Ken on vacation at Harry and Gert Koestner's trailer park in Fort Myers, Florida
1952, Ken's 1951 Oldsmobile in the background
Berquist Family Photo

Gert and Harry were snowbirds. While in Fort Myers, Harry and Ken went fishing. They came home with two beautiful snook for dinner.

Soviet Premier Joseph Stalin died in March 1953. His death brought about a drawdown of hostilities in Korea, ending US and China involvement in the Korean peninsula by July.

The building lot that Jane's mother had given her as part of Bertha's last will and testament preparation, located at 1013 Cook Street, was about to be used for good reason. It was the last lot on the street and on the far north end of the property Bertha owned. The lot had farms to the west and north. Jane and Ken dreamed of the day when they could build their first home on this lot. They started saving from the beginning.

They lived at the Jefferson Street apartment for four years and began building a tiny home on Cook Street in 1952.

On the back, Jane wrote, "(Uncle) Harry (Koestner), (Uncle) Ralph (Anderson), (Aunt) Gert (Koestner), Grandma Koestner and Ken at our first homesite 1952"
Berquist Family Photo

Jane described the new house as being the size of a two-car garage. At twenty-two feet by twenty-four feet, it was a two-car garage. Over the years, the roof has been replaced a few times, as has the siding.

Nevertheless, the house Ken and Jane built stands today at 1013 Cook Street in Burlington. The front of the house—not on Cook Street—faced an adjoining building lot to the south. The back of the house faced the extension of Edwards Street west, which was more of an alley than it was a street. The alley ended in a business parking lot.

Ken walking across the lawn at 1013 Cook Street, Burlington, Iowa, circa 1953
Berquist Family Photo

Ken and Jane moved into their new house on Cook Street in April 1953. News reached Burlington at the end of May that Sir Edmund Hillary, with his Nepalese sherpa guide, had summited Mount Everest, the tallest peak in the world. Bart Hauser was born on September 3, 1953. Bart did not wait for the move. He was ready to join the world. It was a hectic month, but the move to East Moline and the delivery came off without a hitch.

Ann and Herb Hauser's home, 2628 6th Street, East Moline, Illinois, September 1953 – July 1969 photo taken by Herb Hauser on the day the Hausers' moved to Waterloo, Iowa
Berquist Family Photo

Herb Hauser went to work for John Deere in East Moline.

Manufacturers stopped building television sets during the war, throwing their resources instead toward the war effort. The stores in Burlington started advertising and selling television sets in Burlington with a fair amount of regularity in 1949.

Sales of TVs in Burlington did not get going until the National Broadcasting Company (NBC) started broadcasts from Davenport, Iowa, as WOC-TV in October 1949. The Central Broadcasting System (CBS) was a quick follower in July 1950, broadcasting from Rock Island, Illinois, as WHBF-TV. By now, TV seemed to be gaining a following, as there were now two TV stations to watch. Those in Burlington were accepting of the idea TV was here to stay, and for those who could afford to buy a TV, it was a luxury item. TV owners were the draw in their respective neighborhoods. If someone had a TV, all the kids in the area knew.

Three years later (1953), the American Broadcasting Company started sending a signal from the KHQA-TV station in Hannibal, Missouri. The popularity of TV had more than doubled in the three years, driving the cost down for a black-and-white set. Jane and Ken bought their first TV in 1953. They had three stations to watch.

Life had gone wonderfully for Ken and Jane during a busy 1953, so they decided to kick up their heels on New Year's Eve at the Arion Club downtown.

Jane and Ken, New Years Eve, 1953
Berquist Family Photo

It would also be a belated celebration of their fifth wedding anniversary.

In a military coup d'état, Abdel Nasser ousted the Egyptian monarchy, placing Muhammad Naguib as the first president of the country in February 1954.

Mary and Dan Riffel welcomed their third son, Ron, to the world on April 30, 1954. Like the family thought Ann and Herb Hauser had set the trend with three girls, Mary and Dan had the same thing happen to them with three boys. The Hauser trend broke when Bart was born.

Ken was an enthusiastic fan of St. Louis Cardinals baseball team.

**Ken's St. Louis Cardinals Bumper Sticker,
which never got applied to a bumper, circa
1955**
Berquist Family Possession

When the spring baseball season opened in 1954, it was not a big deal for Ken to hop in the car early on a Saturday morning and drive to St. Louis for an afternoon game. St. Louis was about five hours and 220 miles south on Highway 61. Bob Doyle, Kenny Snyder, Dick Fry, and occasionally Cousin Cliff Martin would go with Ken to the baseball game. The group would then drive back to Burlington afterward, arriving home in the later part of the evening.

Ken and his friends took the train into Chicago to see the Bears play a few times, but only in the early fall when the weather was tolerable. Ken was a Green Bay Packers fan, and he loved to watch the Packers beat up the Bears.

An almost-sixty-year-old law allowing states to have segregated schools was voted unconstitutional by the Supreme Court on May 17, 1954. Desegregation was a hard pill for Southern states to swallow.

The families descended on the Hauser household in East Moline, Illinois, for Christmas 1954.

Adults; Ken Berquist, Herb Hauser, Dan Riffel, Jane Berquist, Ruth Roederer, Bertha Roederer, Mary Riffel, Kids; Mary Pam Hauser, Susan Hauser, Sam Riffel, Nancy Hauser, Jim Riffel, Bart Hauser, Ron Riffel—8 months Photo taken by Ann Hauser Christmas 1954
Berquist Family Photo

By 1955, it was starting to become impossible to celebrate every life event that happened to every member of the Roederer and Berquist family. It was apparent: adults did not count anymore. It was the kids who mattered the most. Agreed, if you were over the age of twenty-one, a verbal "Happy Birthday" or "Happy Anniversary" would be about all you could expect. There would be some exceptions.

At work, Ken's career could not be going better. He was now earning $2.33 per hour, plus he now had health and welfare benefits. No more worries about getting sick or having to go to the hospital. The real goodness of these benefits would present themselves in another year or two. Ken was also getting more involved with the local chapter of the Machinists Union. He had been voted in by the membership to be on the local board. It was a proud moment for him.

In mid-June, Ken and Jane had been waiting for official confirmation from the doctor. It was confirmed. Jane was pregnant. After seven kids and number eight scheduled to arrive sometime in September, the Roederer kin mostly yawned at the announcement. On the other hand, the Berquist family was ecstatic. It was the first grandchild for Mick and Lou. Ken and Jane were the happiest though. They had prayed and hoped for a child for eight years. After trying for such a long time, they never thought it was going to happen. Words were not enough to express their joy.

In the 1930s, Disney was a household name. Ken had been watching Mickey Mouse cartoons in the movie theaters since he was ten years old and had seen every Walt Disney movie since 1937. Some he had seen more than once. Walt Disney opened a theme park called Disneyland in Los Angeles, California, on July 17, 1955. The opening made the nightly TV news across the United States. Ken and Jane watched the news reports in amazement. They hoped to go someday.

Ann and Herb Hauser called on Wednesday morning to let everyone know son Mark had been born the night before on September 27. Ann and Herb were happy they had gotten the bigger house. Everyone met Mark at Christmas in 1955. The Riffels hosted the family gathering this year.

Racial unrest hit the nightly news big on December 1 when a black woman sitting in the segregated section of a city bus refused to give up her seat to a white passenger. The Little Rock, Arkansas, police arrested her. Ken and Jane had not heard of Montgomery, Alabama, before, and now every night it seemed like it was all they heard about for the next year. To Ken and Jane, it was disgusting the way people were treating each other. To them, it felt like Burlington was a million miles away from the violence in the South.

Michael Berquist was born Wednesday, January 25, 1956, at 6:47 a.m. in Mercy Hospital in downtown Burlington.

Mercy Hospital, 610 North 4th Street, Burlington. Iowa
ATTRIBUTION: cardcow.com

Jane had gone into labor in the afternoon of the twenty-fourth and had to call Kenneth at work to get him home early to take her to the hospital. Overnight temperatures had dropped to twelve degrees, and by the morning, temperatures had only climbed to fifteen. The humidity was a little high, and the low areas were blanketed in fog. The snow, which had fallen on the twenty-first, was still on the ground, as temperatures had not been above freezing for days. Burlington was deep into winter. It was a long labor, about fifteen hours, but Michael's birth was uneventful.

After allowing Jane time to rest, a parade of happy new grandparents, aunts, and uncles started to arrive after work in the later part of the afternoon. Bertha, Mick, and Lou came first, followed closely by Dick and Lida, Mary and Dan, and Ruth. Father Vogel from St. Patrick's even stopped by. It would be a few days before Elsie and Rich, and Donna and Dee would get to Burlington to see their new little nephew.

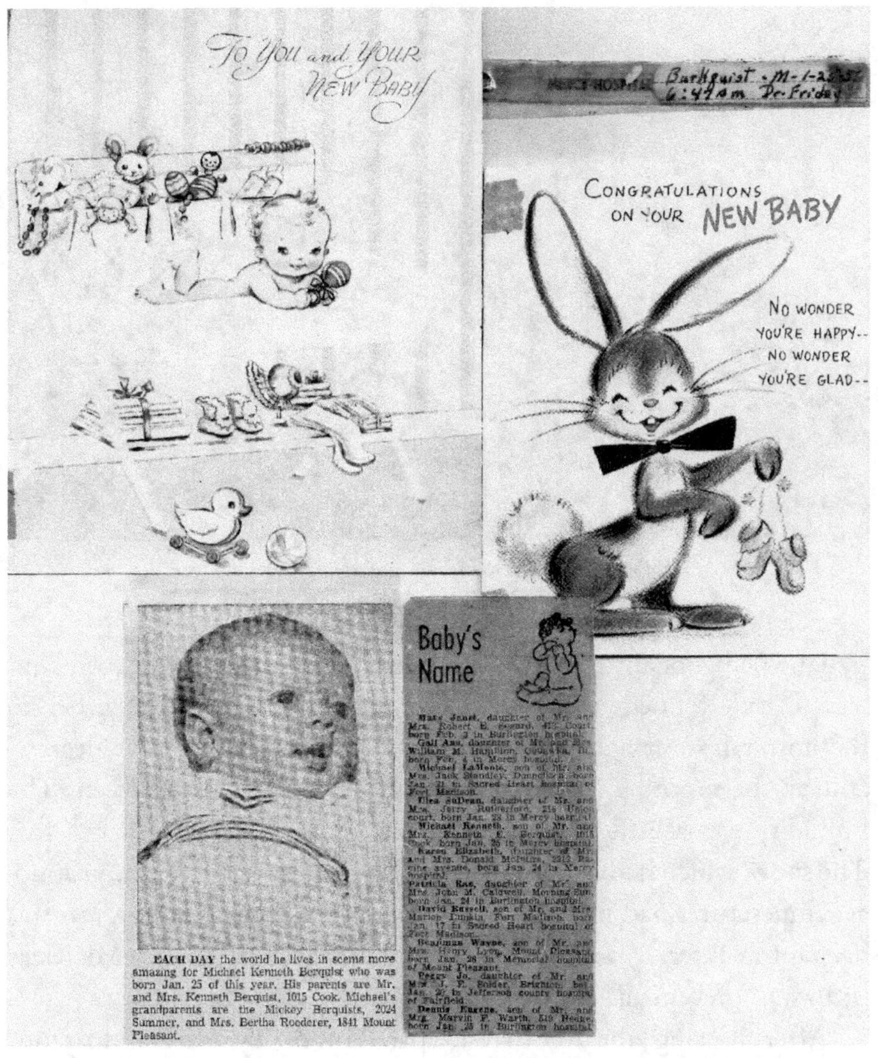

New baby cards from happy Aunts and Uncles, Michael's hospital wrist band, newspaper clippings from Hawk Eye newspaper, 1956
Berquist Family Possessions

Jane and Ken had to take Michael back to the hospital a few days after his birth to have his circumcision fixed. Ken and Jane cried over the feeling of helplessness from hearing Michael screaming when the doctor clipped him again. It was all over in seconds.

Herb Roederer was Arthur Roederer's brother and was Bertha's brother-in-law. Herb was Jane's uncle. Herb married Mary Elizabeth

Vorwerk, and they lived in Burlington. They owned Roederer's tavern, which still stands today. Herb and Mary never had children. Herb and Mary are Michael Berquist's godparents. Michael was baptized at St. Patrick's Catholic Church within a few days of his birth.

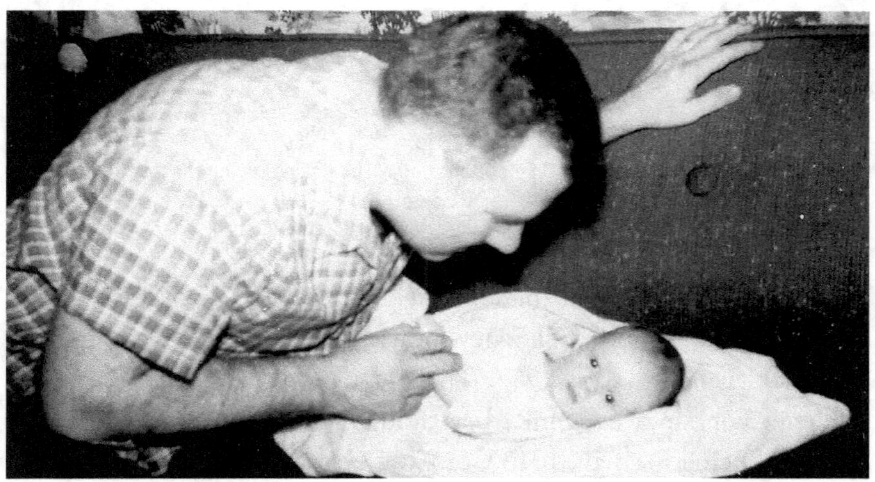

Ken and Michael at home, 1013 Cook Street, Burlington, Iowa, circa 1956
Berquist Family Photo

Actress Grace Kelly married Prince Rainier III of Monaco on April 19, 1956. Millions of television viewers watched the event live from their homes around the world. It was the Cinderella story every little girl acted out in childhood. Women swooned.

News reporters called it "the wedding of the century." [5]

In July, President Abdel Nasser of Egypt took control of the Suez Canal back from French-British governments with whom Egypt had been arguing the past few months.

Jane and Ken gave up the convertible in 1956, buying the more family practical Buick Special two-door hardtop.

Jane and Ken's 1956 Buick Special 2-door hardtop at the dealership on the day they brought it home
Berquist Family Photo

Ken and Jane bought the lot next door at 1015 Cook Street from Bertha and started building a new house in March 1957. Jane became pregnant again in April 1957. The pregnancy seemed like a miracle to them. For the next home, they thought they would try something different. Being so small, 1013 Cook was easy to build, as it was a stick-constructed home. This time, they were going to use Capp Homes.

Capp Homes Advertising Booklet, circa 1957
Photo from a Capp Homes advertising booklet in the public domain

In 1957, Capp Homes presented a new concept in home construction called "precut." The parts to build the house were dropped on the lot by truck/trailer. You merely waded through the stacks, picked out the wall you needed, and started nailing them together. It was fast, and it was efficient.

1015 Cook Street, Burlington, Iowa--at the right-hand edge of the photo 1013 Cook Street can be seen, circa 1958
Berquist Family Photo

The Berquist family moved in during August. The house at 1015 Cook Street had a full basement, which Michael and Mary eventually claimed for themselves. Tricycles, wagons, and dollies with strollers parked neatly along the wall. Jane decorated one basement wall with hand-drawn and colored Disney characters. Mickey Mouse could be seen peeking around the corner when you came down the basement stairs.

There was also a breezeway separating the house from the garage. The breezeway was Jane's territory. Besides being a "breeze" "way," it also served as an extension of the refrigerator. It was cold in the winter and cooler storage in the summer. Jane also started her spring vegetable garden in the breezeway. Racks of potted vegetables abounded in March/April each year. They would be transplanted in the garden in the backyard come spring. Jane inherited a green thumb from her mother.

Ken would turn the soil over in the garden with a spade after harvesting each fall. Space, which was once a garden, would now be a tiny ice-skating rink for the winter. Ken loved to ice skate, and nothing gave him more pleasure than teaching the kids how to skate. Each year, a new ice skating rink was constructed.

On September 4, 1957, nine black students attempted to enter Central High School in Little Rock, Arkansas. Despite the 1954 desegregation laws, the students were turned away by the Arkansas National Guard on orders of Arkansas's governor. During the next three weeks, violence in Little Rock made the nightly TV news. President Eisenhower intervened, ordering the army from Fort Campbell, Kentucky, to escort the nine black students at the school. In the same order, Eisenhower federalized the entire Arkansas National Guard removing control of Arkansas's governor. The military remained on campus for the school year.

The Cold War between the US and Soviet Russia expanded dramatically on October 4, 1957, when the Soviet Union launched the first artificial satellite, Sputnik 1, into low Earth orbit. Russia's surprise announcement of the launch garnered the desired propaganda punch they sought. Sputnik's radio signal, "beep-beep-beep," was quickly detected by ham-radio operators around the world and sent a chilling wave across the United States. The second launch on November 3, of Sputnik 2, shattered the American perception of US technological superiority. The two back-to-back events started the Space Race.

Jon Riffel was born to Mary and Dan Riffel on October 31, 1957—the fourth son. The inclination toward male sex shifted to the Riffels now, with the family wondering if the boy trend would ever end. Time would tell. Ruth Roederer was the most thrilled with Jon's birth. Jon and Ruth shared the same birth date, October 31, Halloween. Household space was now getting tight with the Riffels at their tiny house on Burlington Street. Time to start looking for a bigger home.

The American psyche took another blow on December 6, 1957, when the US attempted its first foray into space. On live television, the Vanguard Test Vehicle Three rocket blew up two seconds after liftoff, falling back onto the launch pad, exploding in a massive fireball at Cape Canaveral, Florida. The embarrassment dialed up the urgency of the Space Race a notch.

It was an unusually warm fifty-four-degree day in Burlington. Ken raced Jane to the hospital in the rain. It did not feel at all like winter that day. Mary Carol Berquist was born on Thursday, December 19, 1957. Jane's labor and delivery was much more comfortable this time, and Mary arrived within two hours of Ken and Jane getting to Mercy Hospital. Mary was a bruiser when she was born: ten pounds and twenty-three inches.

Mary was baptized a few days later, receiving her godmother's first name "Carol" as her middle name. Jane had always loved her younger cousin Carol Stolze and wanted to honor Carol by sharing her name with Mary. Carol was asked to be Mary's godmother.

In an alternate explanation, giving Mary the middle name Carol had the added benefit of distinguishing Mary Berquist from the umpteen other Marys already in the family. When someone said, "Mary Carol," there was no doubt they were talking about Mary Berquist.

Ken and Mary Carol Berquist, at home, 1015 Cook Street, Burlington, Iowa, circa 1958
Berquist Family Photo

Christmas 1957 had arrived, Ken and Jane's first Christmas in their new home with their brand-new baby girl. They could not have been more content.

Mary turned into a tall, beautiful woman as she grew up. She is a smart, talented, sweet, and funny woman, who took on all the best qualities of her parents and grandparents.

Mary Carol Berquist, high school graduation
portrait, 1976
Berquist Family Photo

America started to catch up with Russia and the Space Race with the launch of the four-stage Juno rocket from Cape Canaveral, Florida, on January 31, 1958. The booster rocket carried Explorer 1, the first American satellite to orbit Earth.

Ken rarely saw his nephew Jim Hill through the 1950s. The last time they saw each other was at Elsie and Rich's wedding in 1950. Jim was always traveling with the army, stationed at various bases throughout the States. It was not until the late 1950s when Jim and his wife, Sumi Yamashita, moved to Burlington and started having babies. First Tod, and then Doland, and then Donna.

By the time Mary and Dan Riffel's oldest son, Jim, had turned ten, they had moved into a bigger home on Gunnison Avenue; south of where they were currently living. The timing for the move could not have been better, as Mary Riffel would be pregnant again in a few months.

Mary and Dan Riffel's House, 101 South Gunnison Avenue, Burlington, photo taken by Dan Riffel sometime in mid-1970s
Berquist Family Photo

Ken had two weaknesses. Root beer was the first. He had acquired the taste from his father. Mick bought Hires syrup at the pharmacy soda fountains downtown for many years and made his root beer at home from an old recipe. It was the taste Ken had grown up with. So Ken's own family would also grow up with love for root beer. It was a treat frequently available in the house, fresh root beer by the gallon. Nothing was better than seeing Ken coming home from work with his finger hooked through the loop of a gallon jug of A&W Root Beer.

One gallon A&W Root Beer bottle--typical appearance of 1950-1960
bottle

Photo from the public domain

It meant root beer floats were on the menu for dessert after supper. Weekends would signal the time to return to Otis's A&W drive-in on Roosevelt with the empty bottles to retrieve the deposit and buy another bottle of the tasty elixir for the coming week.

Ken discovered A&W Root Beer in Oakland, California, in 1943 and then again after the war while waiting out his last few days in the navy in Bremerton, Washington. He brought this new taste for the treat back to Burlington with him.

Otis' A&W Drive-In advertisement from 1967 Burlington Phone Directory
ATTRIBUTION: Brett Jay Metcalf - Historical Photos of Burlington

Ken's second weakness—Van's pork tenderloin sandwiches. Ken shared his taste for Van's with Jim Riffel first. Jim was hooked and passed the obsession on to his brothers over the following years. Van's Lunch Box was only a couple of blocks away from the apartment at 1315½ Jefferson, so resisting Van's temptation was a little bit harder for Ken.

Van's advertisement from 1967 Burlington Phone Directory
ATTRIBUTION: Brett Jay Metcalf - Historical Photos of Burlington

Ken's seventh nephew, Steve Hauser, was born on September 27, 1958. The Hauser home was splitting at the seams, with three girls and three boys. Ken and Jane had fun with their nieces and nephews. Ken loved dancing with Nancy, Sue, and Mary Pam as they took turns standing on Uncle Ken's feet, twirling around the living room. Sister dancing paid off again. Uncle Ken loved roughhousing with his nephews. Not too much longer and his son, Michael, would be added to the heap of roughed-up boys.

Ken and Michael washing the 1956 Buick on the Cook Street driveway, circa 1958
Berquist Family Photo

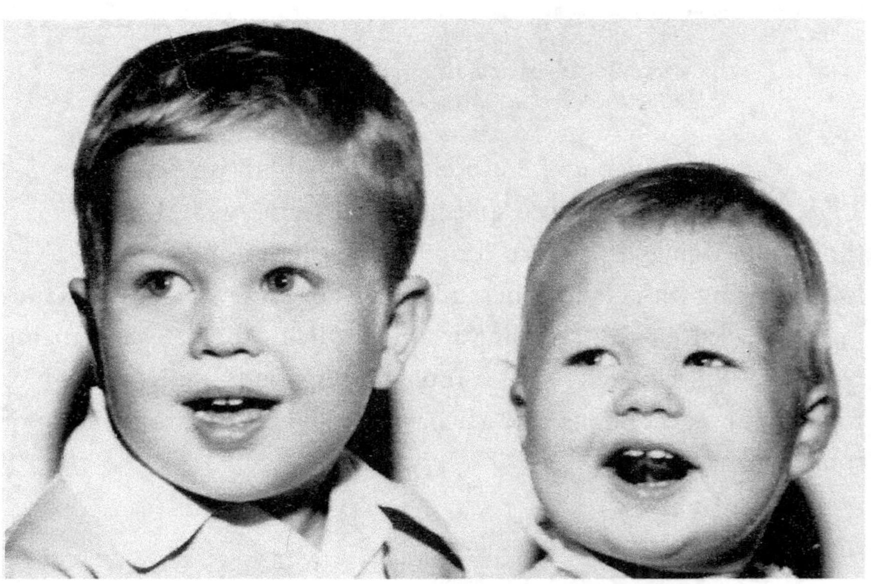

Michael and Mary Carol Berquist, Christmas 1958
Berquist Family Photo

New Year's Day 1959 brought news from Cuba. Fidel Castro had
successfully overthrown the US-backed Batista regime. By the eighth

of the month, Castro had moved into Havana to the cheers of crowds lining the roads. Castro had a puppet government in place and then himself sworn in as prime minister on the sixteenth of February. A Soviet Communist–backed government only ninety miles from US shores was in place within the year.

On the other side of the world, a Tibetan Buddhist year-long uprising occurring because of Chinese repression drove the fourteenth Dalai Lama and thousands of Buddhist refugees into exile in India.

The Riffel boy trend ended on May 28, 1959, with the birth of Julie. Mary and Dan could not have been happier welcoming a baby girl to their family finally. Julie would be Bertha's birthday present that year. Bertha had quietly celebrated her sixty-third birthday two days before Julie's birth. Julie was a belated birthday present for Bertha. And it had been a couple of years since Ken had a new girl to toss in the air. Julie would grow up with the protection of four older brothers.

Ken celebrated his birthday on Tuesday, October 19, 1959. He was forty years old.

The decade ended with the name Senator John Kennedy on everyone's lips. Was he running for president, or not? Despite his denials, the cat was quickly slipping out of the bag by the end of the year. Kennedy made appearances in Iowa City and Des Moines in mid-November. He sealed the deal with the Iowa voters when he attended an Iowa versus Notre Dame football game in Iowa City on Saturday, November 21.

With a smile on his face, Kennedy delicately handled the Catholic institution's one-point win over the Hawkeyes on Iowa turf, saying he "cheered for Iowa but prayed for Notre Dame." [6]

Christmas 1959--Ken surrounded by the kids. The youngest of the group Steve Hauser (2 yrs.) and Julie Riffel (19 months) on Ken's lap. Ken's son and daughter Michael (4 yrs.) and Mary (3 yrs.) to Ken's left. The rest of the bunch clockwise from the 8:00 position; Jon Riffel (3 yrs.), Mark Hauser (5 yrs.), Ron Riffel (6 yrs.), Susan Hauser (9 yrs.), Jim Riffel (11 yrs.), Nancy Hauser (10 yrs.), Sam Riffel (8 yrs.), Mary Pam Hauser (8 yrs.), and Bart Hauser (7 yrs.) Coming soon; Paul Hauser and Jill Riffel
Berquist Family Photo

CHAPTER 22

The 1960s

Ken was elected president of his local chapter of the Machinists Union in the early part of 1960. He had been working in other capacities with the union for the past few years. He was paid six dollars per month as president. In the rare case when he had to travel away from home on union business, he would be paid his regular hourly wage. He was also paid fifteen dollars per day for living expenses and received seven cents per mile when he drove his car. Jane was proud of the union president. Ken and Jane voted for John Kennedy in the election on January 2. Kennedy's inauguration was on TV on January 20. He became the thirty-fifth president of the United States. It turned out to be a close election, with Kennedy defeating Richard Nixon by the narrowest popular-vote margin in the twentieth century. Kennedy was forty-three years old.

At the end of February, Ken and Jane threw a huge party at their house to celebrate Mick and Lou's fiftieth wedding anniversary. The Berquist and Schmicker families and many friends attended. There must have been forty people at the house over the course of the day. The party, the dinner, and the decorations were a tremendous success. Jane was a great party planner and hostess.

(L. to R.) Kenneth Berquist, Elsie Berquist Mack, Mick Berquist, Louise Berquist, Donna
Berquist Moore, Dick Berquist, Michael (5) and Mary (3) in front, photo taken in the
basement of 1013 Cook Street
Berquist Family Photo

The news did not come out for a few days, but a US spy plane
was shot down over Russia in May 1960. Russia captured the pilot. In
a top-secret mission, the pilot took high-altitude photos over Russia.
The Soviet Union started bragging about the event. Eisenhower did not
have a choice about the news slipping out. Beginning in May, the story
popped up on the nightly news every few days.

Ken started out his day on Wednesday morning October 19 with
a surprise. Jane had secretly baked Ken his favorite coffee cake for his
birthday breakfast. Like usual, he had quietly slipped out of bed and
proceeded to get dressed and ready for work. Ken did not want to be
late, as his carpool picked him up at the same time every workday, at
6:30 a.m. He was the last to be picked up for the fifteen-minute drive
out to the Shops in West Burlington. He had a couple of minutes to
leave a note on the kitchen counter. Ken turned forty-one years old
that day.

Sweetheart Jane
    Don't forget to call your
Mother when you get up.
    Your coffee cake was delicious
Honey thanks for making it. If you
can save me 3 pieces for tomorrow
    I sure do love you for all the
things you do for me Honey. You are the
greatest.
                I love you very much.
        Don't work to hard today, Ken

Ken, Jane, Michael and Mary Carol, Christmas 1960
Berquist Family Photo

Ken adored the kids. They would ice skate at Crapo Park in the winter. Michael and Mary were still learning how to skate. The Riffel boys gave Ken a run for his money on the ice. Ken loved every one of them. He loved hearing the kids yelling, "Uncle Ken, Uncle Ken!" He enjoyed playing ball with the boys in the field, and he loved dancing with the little girls at the parties.

When spring 1961 came, Ken would put on the Easter Bunny costume Jane and Ruth had made and let the kids chase him all around the yard as he dropped Easter eggs for them.

Back row L. to R. Julie Riffel, Jim Riffel, Sam Riffel. Front row L. to R. Michael Berquist, Jon Riffel, Mary Carol Berquist, Ron Riffel Ken Berquist in the Easter Bunny costume. Photo taken in the side yard at Bertha's house on Mount Pleasant Street, Burlington Easter Sunday, April 2, 1961
Berquist Family Photo

A secret operation until April 21, when news leaked out, a US-backed paramilitary invasion of Cuba had taken place and failed terribly on the twentieth. Surviving military from an invasion force of over 1,400 men had surrendered and been taken as prisoners by the Castro regime.

The ultimate symbol of the Cold War was under construction in the German Democratic Republic (GDR) (East Germany) beginning in August 1961. As part of World War II agreements, the Soviet Union and the four Allied powers divided Germany into East and West. Bonn had become the de facto capital city of the Federal Republic of

Germany (FRG) (West Germany). The Soviet-backed GDR built a wall in their capital city of Berlin, encircling and cutting off the entire western section of the city. This action had a two-pronged punch. First, the encircling wall trapped all French, British, and American citizens living there. Second, the barrier prevented East and West Berliners from traveling freely east to west within the city. Families became separated by the location of their residence or where they worked. It was a nightmare.

Ken celebrated his birthday on Thursday, October 19, 1961. He was forty-two years old. The news talked briefly in February 1962 about the Soviets releasing from prison the spy-plane pilot they captured in 1960. The pilot was exchanged for a Soviet spy held in custody in the United States.

Ken and Jane started on the next home-building quest. The "itch" would interrupt life again. They bought another lot from Bertha. Like 1013 Cook Street, this new lot was at the end of a dead-end street. This lot had an abundance of land associated with it. The back of the lot was a picturesque, heavily wooded ravine. In the front, there was an open flat field, which looked directly at the back of Bertha's home on Mount Pleasant Street. To the east, there was another big, flat field with a small —seven or eight—apple tree orchard of sorts growing along one side.

You could access the lot by driving south on the gravel alley next to Bertha's house at 1841 Mount Pleasant Street, or from the west via Kirkwood at Curran Street. Kirkwood dead-ended right in the front yard, where you could turn north on the gravel alley and head back out to Mount Pleasant Street. It was a private, secluded location. A slight hiccup presented itself first. A buyer for 1015 Cook Street came out of nowhere and wanted the house quickly.

Jane and Ken were forced to find temporary living quarters while construction of the basement foundation on Kirkwood was underway. They took a small row house in Flint Hills Manor. It was not their first choice, but they had to make a quick decision and move to sell the current house.

Paul Hauser was born on July 2, 1962, in time for the annual family reunion picnic in Burlington. Ann and Herb were so proud to be introducing to the family the last of the Hauser offspring. Paul was an itty-bitty baby at his first reunion. Ken could hardly let him go when it was his turn to hold his new nephew.

The nightly government and political news coverage on TV grew dim in October. The US had spy-plane photos showing a nuclear buildup was taking place in Cuba. This news was shattering to the security all Americans felt, being so far distanced from Europe and the Soviet Union. Kennedy was on the news every day, providing assurances to the US citizens he was working for a peaceful outcome to the situation. Kennedy put in place a naval blockade around Cuba, preventing anything from going to or leaving the island nation. The blockade went up on October 16, 1962, and the TV news for the next thirteen days had people sitting on the edge of their chairs, praying. Everyone was sure we were on the brink of nuclear war.

School-aged children in Burlington who had practiced "duck and cover" drills on and off for the past few years were now practicing again. One month, it was a fire drill. The next month, it was a nuclear attack drill. The sound of the alarm was different for each type of drill, so the kids learned what was expected of them quickly. Following instructions from the nuns, Michael practiced these exercises at St. Patrick's School starting in the 1962–63 school year

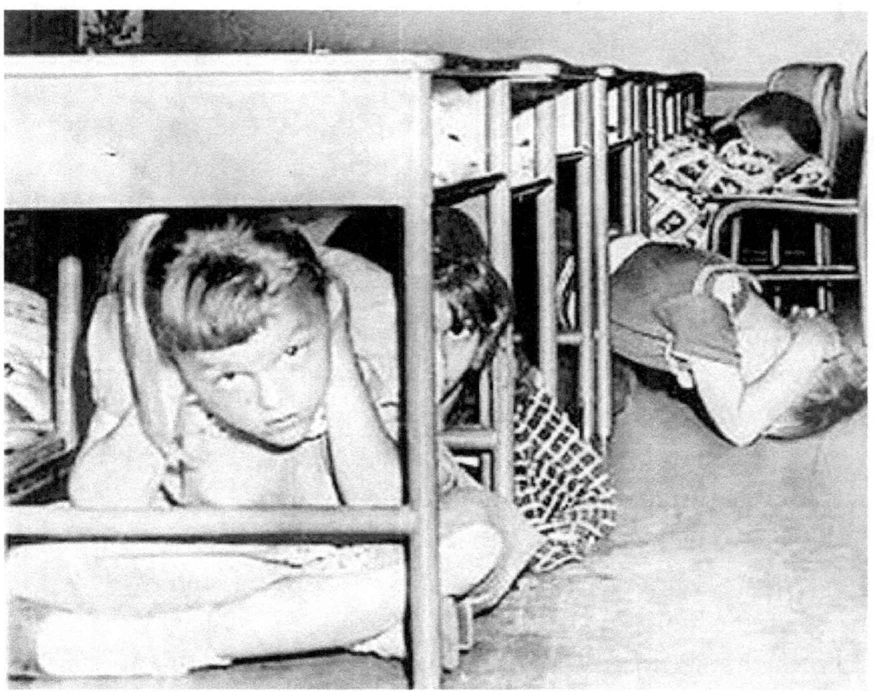

Duck and Cover Drill School children hiding under their desks during a nuclear attack drill
ATTRIBUTION: http://www.museumofyesterday.org/government_gallery/index.htm

The nightly news reported the Communists had withdrawn offensive weapons from Cuba. The naval blockade lifted on November 21. Fidel Castro and Nikita Khrushchev were allied. Kennedy claimed victory but had made some recompense from the failed Cuba invasion months before.

When the Berquist family moved to the Manor, which it had become known as, for several years, the development was only eighteen years old. The area and the block homes remained in livable condition, not great. Some people lived there for the exact reason the Manor was intended—transient, short term, in and out. Others had taken up residence permanently. Flint Hills Manor was built in the 1940s by the federal government as temporary housing for workers coming into the area during World War II. The opening of the army ammunition plant in West Burlington was thought to bring hundreds of workers seeking a place to stay for the short term. And it did. The development was always intended to fill a niche for low-income housing for a transient population.

Ken's nephew Jim Hill and his wife, Sumi, and their kids, Tod, Doland, and Donna, lived at the Manor. Jim was still in the army and traveled to both coasts regularly as part of his job. So moving to the Manor resulted in Kenneth and Jane becoming closer to Jim Hill's family, at least temporarily. This closeness was both good and bad. A few times over the next two years, Ken was called on the phone (usually in the middle of the night) to run over to the Hill household and get Jim Hill cooled down from one of his drunken, belligerent outbursts. Ken would help, but the results would only last a few days before Jim would be back at it with Sumi and his kids.

One Saturday afternoon, Ken received a phone call from Sumi saying Jim was on a rampage and she was scared for herself and the kids. Jim had torn the house up. By the time Ken and Jane reached Jim's house, Sumi had locked herself and the kids in the bathroom. While Ken distracted Jim somewhere inside the house, Jane and a neighbor helped Sumi and the three kids climb out a narrow, high bathroom window. Jim was furious, but everyone was safe. Sumi and the kids went back into the house. Jim left in his car, disappearing for a month. No one knows where he went.

Many years later, Flint Hills Manor became a haven for criminals and trapped many elderly folks in a predicament from which they could not ascend. Flint Hills had spiraled into an unrecoverable blight. The subdivision was a highly visible residential area along Roosevelt Avenue, which only served to perpetuate an opposite view of what Burlington wanted to portray to the passerby. Burlington was a safe place to live and raise a family. Using eminent domain to acquire the 170 homes situated east of Roosevelt Avenue, the site was razed in 2007 by the City of Burlington.

Flint Hills Manor - Burlington, Iowa
Top Photo: Courtesy https://www.facebook.com/treephd/photos/
a.537598839603098.23306124.173021719394147/611451338884514/?type=3&theater, circa 1967
Bottom Photo: Courtesy Darell Truitt, circa 1950 Both photos have been edited to remove personal
information

As they lived in the Manor, Ken and Jane built another Capp Home on Kirkwood Street. They had such good luck with the construction of the first Capp Home that they chose to go with Capp again. The yard sloped dramatically toward the ravine in the backyard, which was ideally suited for a walk-out basement. There was a brick paved patio outside the basement walk out. There was a redwood deck off the family room, which led down to the brick patio. There was a formal living room and dining room, a large eat-in galley-shaped kitchen, three bedrooms, and one bathroom.

The house had all the modern conveniences of the time, including a powered house-ventilation system, which sucked the warm air out of the house through a powered louvered vent in the hallway. It was not central air conditioning, but it was sure close.

A note written by Ken to Jane sometime during the construction of the house on Kirkwood Street illustrates their dogged determination to build the house, and their love.

Honey

So I can work as soon as I get home. Why don't you go down to Brueck and get tank of gas so I can sweat those other joints together.

Ask John if I should put something under drain in tub. putty or something. Also I'll need a couple of 45 elbows from tub to stack.

get this so I can work as soon as I get home

Be careful

I love you

Ken celebrated his forty-third birthday on October 19, 1962. Ken and Jane would entertain family in their new home for the first time during the holidays in 1962.

Ken and Jane built 1841 Kirkwood Avenue, Burlington, Iowa Jane held on to Kirkwood as a rental property/investment through the mid-1970s finally selling at a substantial profit
Berquist Family Photo

Ken had a heart attack in February 1963. He was experiencing breathing problems, started sweating, turned a shade of gray, and complained about indigestion. Jane drove him to the hospital, where the doctors gave him nitroglycerin to dilate his arteries. The pain suddenly stopped. It was not indigestion. Bed rest was prescribed, and no strenuous work or activities for several weeks. Ken missed several weeks of work.

After Jane and Ken were married, summer movie-going always included Friday-night trips to the drive-in beginning in 1949.

The Burlington Drive-In Theater, 406 East Agency Road, West Burlington, Iowa, razed September 1994

ATTRIBUTION: http://cinematreasures.org/theaters/44386/photos/113909

When Michael and Mary Carol came along in 1956–57, drive-in theater trips would eventually become a family outing. Michael loved riding the little train in the play area under the big screen before the movie started. The kids in the back seat wearing pajamas lasted halfway through the first show and would have to be picked up and carried into the house. There was nothing more "all-American" than a family at the drive-in theater. The first movie would always be something children liked: *Hatari!* in 1962; *The Nutty Professor* and *The Sword in the Stone* in 1963; and *Mary Poppins* and *The Incredible Mr. Limpet* in 1964. The kids would be fast asleep before the movie that Ken and Jane wanted to see got started.

Advertising Flyer for the Burlington Drive-In Theater, circa 1963
Myron N. Blank, Central States Theater Company, Des Moines, Iowa 1949-1994

At the end of June, Ken and Jane took Michael to see the movie *PT 109* at the Capitol Theater downtown. Going to the movie was an important event for Michael for a lot of reasons. First, this was not a cartoon. It was a real adult movie. Second, Mary Carol was not there. Michael had his parents to himself. Mary was at Gram's house. And finally, it was a nighttime movie downtown. Michael had only been to the drive-in and daytime movies on Saturday.

Ken told Michael, "I want you to see this." Michael was unsure why his dad said this to him. The movie was about Jack Kennedy's World War II navy experiences.

PT 109 Theater Movie Poster, circa 1963
ATTRIBUTION: http://movies.pics/movie/pt_109_1963

Did Ken tell Michael this because it was a Kennedy movie, or were there other reasons? What was Ken trying to convey to his son? Was it how he felt about what he had done in the war? Michael was seven years old.

It was not long after Donna Hill was born in 1963 that the Hill Family was once again being relocated, this time to Newport News, Virginia. It was the last time Kenneth would see his nephew Jim Hill.

Ken and Jane admired President Kennedy. Did they respect him because he was Catholic? Kennedy was a navy war veteran. Or was it because Kennedy supported the unions? Ken's household was a Catholic-veteran-union home.

Ken had gone back to work after having lunch. Jane had picked Mary Carol up from morning kindergarten and was having something to eat at home. Michael was back in his classroom, having run off excess energy in the schoolyard.

Ken was the first to find out. Radios at work blared out the news for all to hear. Kennedy had been shot, and then shortly after the announcement, the president was dead. The Shops closed early. It was Friday, November 22, 1963. With employees scrambling to their cars to get home to their families, the Shops were a ghost town by 2:00 p.m.

The nuns at St. Patrick's had also heard the news at about the same time as Ken. Between the weeping and tears, the nuns had to get the buses rolling and announcements out to the school that they were closing right away. With tears streaming down her face, Sister Maria burst into Michael's second-grade classroom and made the announcement John Kennedy was dead.

Michael climbed on the bus with all the other screaming, and some crying, kids and went home. Ken had been dropped off from work. He scooped Michael up after he got off the bus, and into the new house on Kirkwood they went.

No cartoons for Michael on Saturday-morning TV. All they had was news coverage of the president. Jane's thirty-sixth birthday celebration planned for today was overshadowed by the events. Ken, Jane, and their kids went to church a lot over the next few days. Jane and Ken loved John Kennedy. The Berquists were Democrats.

The defining moment for Ken came on Sunday morning. Ken and Michael were sitting on the couch, watching the news coverage of Lee Harvey Oswald at the Dallas police station. Never in the infancy of television had coverage of murder been captured for all to see. Ken's raw emotion, jumping off the couch, pointing at the TV, and yelling, "They shot him! They shot him!" remained with Ken for months. Ken and Michael watched Jack Ruby shoot Oswald live on TV. It was a madhouse. Ken was flabbergasted. Michael was sent outside to play.

Jack Ruby shooting Lee Harvey Oswald live on national TV, Sunday, November 24, 1963
ATTRIBUTION: Photo in the public domain

Monday, November 25 was the day of the funeral. President John-son had declared a day of national mourning. All the businesses closed. It was Thanksgiving week. Ken and Jane watched the funeral on TV from home. The cadence of the drums, the gait of horse hoofs on the pavement, and the utter silence of the crowds lining the Washington,

DC, streets still echo in memories. On Friday, November 29, *Life* magazine published still-frame images in black-and-white of an amateur film taken during the assassination. It was horrific for all who saw the photos.

Jill Riffel was born on November 30, 1963. Mary and Dan were so happy to have another girl in the family. Jill was Ken's last-born niece. It was Jill's misfortune to have been born a week after the darkest time in the history of the nation. Current events overshadowed Jill's birth. By the time the next family reunion rolled around, Jill would be the center of attention from a family who loved her beyond imagination. Jill's sister Julie and her cousin Mary Carol made sure she had all the little-girl female attention she could take.

Michael's eighth birthday was January 25, 1964. Ken was excited about this birthday, as age eight allowed Michael to play Little League Baseball. Ken was excited to be a part of his son's baseball experience. Ken signed Michael up for the VFW-sponsored team. First practice would happen in the spring.

In April, baseball started with the usual tryouts, skills assessments, and training. Michael would play right field. Ken was there and beaming with pride every step of the way. During the workweek, Ken would take Michael to practice at the baseball fields by Flint Hills Manor. And on nights with no practice, Ken would work with Michael in the backyard—playing catch and teaching the fundamentals of batting and fielding. Games were played on Friday nights or Saturdays.

Ken and Michael in the backyard of 1841 Kirkwood Avenue,
Burlington, Iowa, little baseball practice, May 1964
Berquist Family Photo

Ken took Michael to a Burlington Bees night game in May 1964. Ken loved going to Community Field on Mount Pleasant Street and watching a baseball game. Ken also liked to go to his old alma mater, Burlington High School basketball games at Clark Field House. Ken loved baseball most and was lifelong supporter of his school team.

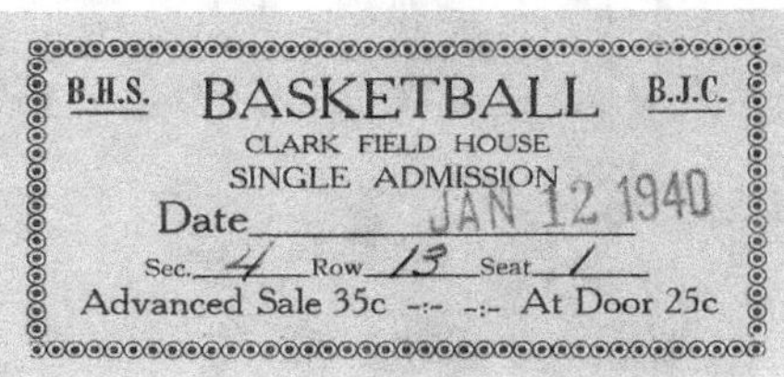

**Leftover High School Basketball Ticket from
1940**
Berquist Family Possession

Ken had been going to Community Field since the year after returning from the navy. The Bees were a Midwest Minor League team, which fed players to the Los Angeles Angels. Going to a Bees game was as close as you could get to a big-league team without leaving Burlington.

Ken had been to many Bees games between 1947 and 1964, with his friends on a few occasions and with his nephew Jim Hill a few times. Now it was time to introduce his son, Michael, to Bees baseball.

In June, Ken and Jane went to Ken's twenty-five-year high school reunion. Ken did not want to go, and he dragged his feet on sending his information to the reunion committee, missing the cutoff date. Ken was not the only one who missed the deadline. In an addendum, slow-pokes were mentioned on the last page of the program booklet.

The Hotel Burlington, 206 North 3rd Street, Burlington, Iowa
Attribution: Ian Poellet (https://commons.wikimedia.org/wiki/File:Hotel_Burlington_-_Burlington_Iowa.jpg),
„Hotel Burlington - Burlington Iowa", https://creativecommons.org/licenses/by-sa/3.0/legalcode

It was a big dressy affair taking place at the Hotel Burlington downtown.

Ken's 25th High School Reunion booklet--a "who's who from the class of 1939"
Berquist Family Possession

P R O G R A M

THE 1939 – 1964 BURLINGTON HIGH SCHOOL CLASS REUNION
Hotel Burlington -- Mezzanine Floor
July 18, 1964
* * * *

Registration . . . . 10:00 A.M.

Cocktail Hour . . . . 5:30 P.M.

Buffet Dinner . . . . 7:00 P.M.

MENU

Swiss Steak---Fried Chicken

Oven Browned Potatoes-----Candied Sweet Potatoes

French Green Beans----Frozen Peas/Mushrooms

Tossed Salad - Jello Salad - Cottage Cheese

Relish Tray

Orange and Plain Rolls

Apple Pie/Cheese

Coffee

Master of Ceremonies . . . . .R.J. (Jim)Cowles

DANCE 9:00 P.M.
Freddie Scherer

The hotel was known for extravagance, luxury, and outstanding food and entertainment. By the time they arrived and were settled in, the evening turned out to be a lot of fun. Ken had not seen many of his classmates since graduation. Even in small Burlington, you could lose touch with friends.

Dinner was spectacular, and they danced until midnight. When it was all said and done, Ken was grateful Jane had pushed to go because he had a fabulous time.

The rest of summer flew by. Mary and Michael on summer vacation from school and the Little League Baseball season was ending for the year.

Ken would get dropped by his work carpool at the top of the alley on Mount Pleasant each day. He would walk down the almost-four-hundred-foot gravel alley each night only to be greeted by his kids running up the lane toward him. He would sweep Mary Carol up off her feet and onto his shoulders. Mary would scream with delight. He would take Michael by the hand and continue to the front door of the house, talking about what they did in school that day.

Ken turned forty-five on October 19, 1964. Jane slept in late on her birthday morning, Saturday, November 21, and found this note waiting for her on the kitchen table.

To the most wonderful wife in the world.
Happy Birthday Sweetheart!
I love you very much.
Honey
  Please buy something for yourself down town this morning dress or shoes or what ever you want some place where you can charge it though.
          I love you
            XX ♡ ♡

please forgive for not buying you anything—

It was a little love note from Ken to Jane on her thirty-eighth birthday. Ken had gone over to his mom and dad's house early in the morning to clean up the yard a little bit before winter arrived there.

Mary turned seven on December 19, 1964. Julie Riffel came over for Barbie-doll cake.

Mary Carol Berquist birthday party December 19, 1964 Left to Right: Louise Berquist, Mary, Michael, Jane, Kenneth, Julie Riffel, Bertha Roederer, Mick Berquist, and Aunt Bertha Roederer
Berquist Family Photo

President Johnson carried on the tradition of strong support of the labor unions. Ken's wages increased during 1964, to $3.10 per hour.

CHAPTER 23

1965

After Dad recovered from his first heart attack, it was clear he was not the same man. Over the course of the next two years, Dad went from a sturdy, healthy, athletic frame to something of a drawn appearance.

Ken (45), Jane (38), Mary Carol (7), Michael (9) at home 1841 Kirkwood Street, Burlington, circa 1965
Berquist Family Photos

These two photos taken of us in mid-1965 clearly show Dad was holding something inside. His mind was elsewhere. Dad could easily "ham it up" for a photograph, but not that day. Whatever was on his mind that day kept him from smiling.

Dad started to think about fall college football, months before it started. He picked up a schedule at the Knights of Columbus Hall. He carried it with him in his wallet.

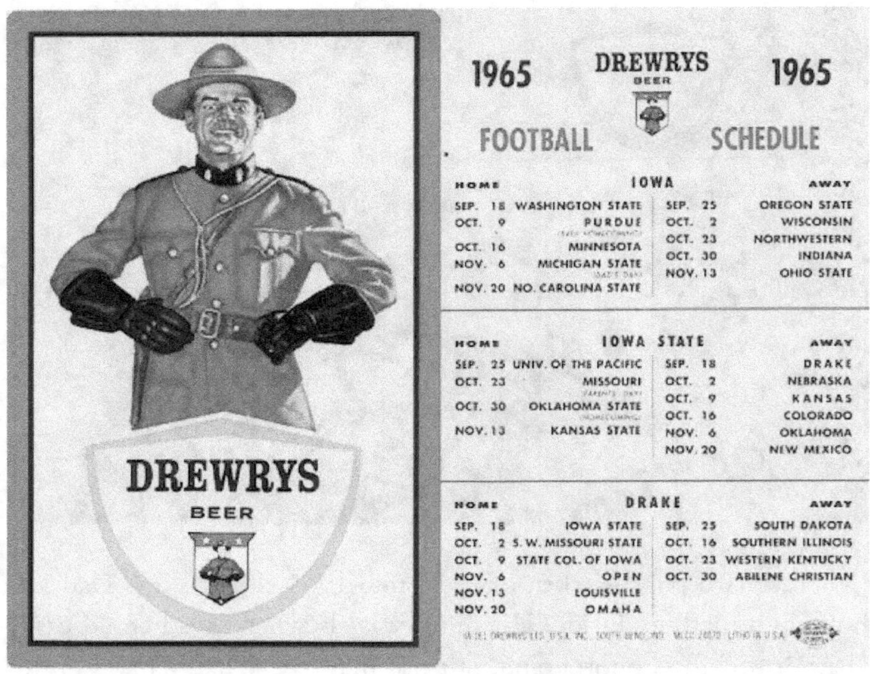

HOME	IOWA		AWAY
SEP. 18 WASHINGTON STATE	SEP. 25		OREGON STATE
OCT. 9 PURDUE	OCT. 2		WISCONSIN
OCT. 16 MINNESOTA	OCT. 23		NORTHWESTERN
NOV. 6 MICHIGAN STATE	OCT. 30		INDIANA
NOV. 20 NO. CAROLINA STATE	NOV. 13		OHIO STATE

HOME	IOWA STATE		AWAY
SEP. 25 UNIV. OF THE PACIFIC	SEP. 18		DRAKE
OCT. 23 MISSOURI	OCT. 2		NEBRASKA
OCT. 30 OKLAHOMA STATE	OCT. 9		KANSAS
NOV. 13 KANSAS STATE	OCT. 16		COLORADO
	NOV. 6		OKLAHOMA
	NOV. 20		NEW MEXICO

HOME	DRAKE		AWAY
SEP. 18 IOWA STATE	SEP. 25		SOUTH DAKOTA
OCT. 2 S. W. MISSOURI STATE	OCT. 16		SOUTHERN ILLINOIS
OCT. 9 STATE COL. OF IOWA	OCT. 23		WESTERN KENTUCKY
NOV. 6 OPEN	OCT. 30		ABILENE CHRISTIAN
NOV. 13 LOUISVILLE			
NOV. 20 OMAHA			

Drewry's Beer promotional give-away, Iowa college's 1965 football game schedule
Berquist Family Possession

Dad was also a big Green Bay Packers fan. On occasion, he would root for the Chicago Bears, but it depended on who the Bears were playing. Dad's mother passed away on July 5, 1965. This only added to what was already distracting him.

Grandma Lou was seventy-five years old. She and Grandpa Mick had been married since February 23, 1910. Grandma Lou had for the year prior been suffering from some gastrointestinal ailment, which kept her from leaving the house for extended periods of time. She grew incontinent over time, having difficulty keeping solid foods and liquids down. It was a miserable, undignified existence for her with people waiting on her hand and foot, helping with bathroom and eating duties, and lots of cleaning up.

Dad customized an old high-back wooden chair into a skirted commode with a large white-porcelain bedpan on a rack below. Grandma Lou spent the last few weeks of her life sitting in this chair on the front porch of their house on Summer Street with Grandpa Mick faithfully beside her until the end finally came. Dad was relieved his mother's suffering had ended, but he was devastated nonetheless with her passing.

Services for Grandma Lou took place at the United Church of Christ. She was laid to rest in Aspen Grove Cemetery in Burlington. Among her pallbearers were two of Dad's cousins' husbands: Wanda Schmicker's husband, Delbert Walker; and Eleanor Schmicker's husband, Janius Clark.

Each year, a phenomenon takes place in the Mississippi River in Burlington called the mayfly hatch. On the day it happens, the sky can turn black with clouds of mayflies that have recently hatched from the muddy bed of the river.

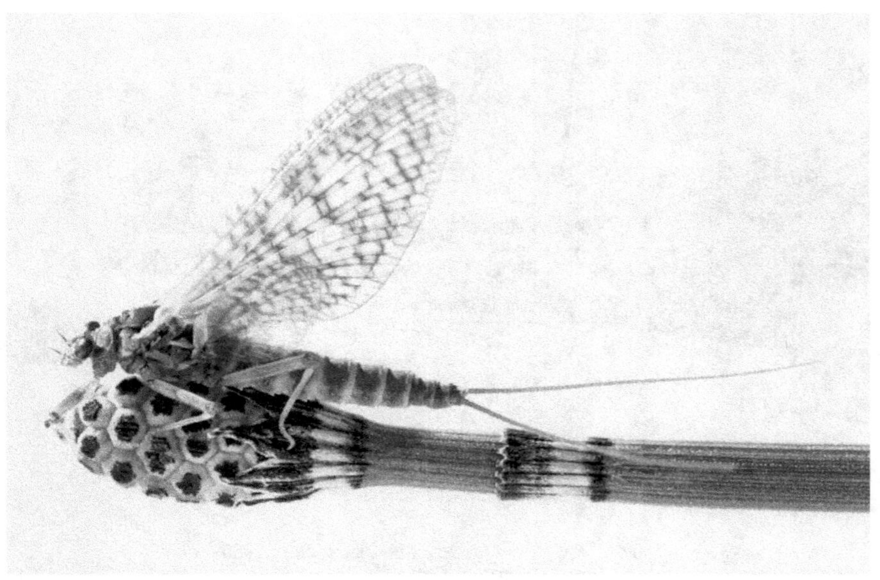

A Common Female Mayfly The physical size of the photo was reduced and positioned in landscape format to fit better on the page of this book.
Attribution: Richard Bartz, Munich. Licensed under the Creative Commons-share alike 2.5 generic license, January 2008

Taking flight, they search for the one mate who will assist them in the perpetuation of their species. In its minutes-long life span, it mates and then it dies. The plague-like proportions of dead mayflies, sometimes ankle deep, squish underfoot and can be scooped up by the shovel full for days after the hatch.

The thing is, you never know exactly when in this three-month window these little buggers will hatch. And if you are caught outdoors when the hatch takes place, take shelter quickly. Otherwise, you will be covered in mayflies. They do not bite or anything, but it is a little unnerving to have all these bugs clinging to your clothes and hair.

From the day it opened, the Dairy Queen on Roosevelt in Burlington has always been in the same location. The building has been updated and modified innumerable times, but it remains the Dairy Queen that has always been there.

Typical Dairy Queen circa late 1950s, early 1960s
ATTRIBUTION: Photo in the public domain

Dad loved hot fudge sundaes. We would go to the Dairy Queen on the way to the drive-in theater. Dad would take us there on special occasions.

This special occasion at the Dairy Queen unknowingly coincided with the mayfly hatch. Mary, Mom, and I remained in the car while Dad was at the DQ window getting our treats. A swarm of mayflies descended on the Dairy Queen. It was dark outside, but the lights of the building and parking lot illuminated their fluttering frenzied wings. They were everywhere. Poor Dad.

As luck had it, Dad made it back to the car before the swarm reached him. We knew the event would pass quickly, so we sat in the car, windows up, and began eating our DQ treats. Seconds later, Dad started to gag. We thought something was seriously wrong with him. A mayfly had made it into Dad's sundae, and he ate the better portion of it in a spoonful of his treat. He gagged and gagged and spit and spit but could not get the taste or knowing realization of what he had eaten out of his mind. It was the last good laugh we had with Dad, albeit at his expense.

Dad bought a new car in September 1965. It was a red four-door Chevy Impala hardtop with a red-vinyl interior. It had a 283-cubic-inch V8 engine with a Powerglide transmission. It was a pretty car. Mom drove this car until she gave it to me in 1972. It was my first car.

My sister Mary Carol and I are standing next to the car alongside Gram's house in this photo
taken in January 1966.
Berquist Family Photo

By 1965, Dad was earning $3.25 per hour, which translated to over $9,300.00 annually from straight and overtime pay. He was still working ten to fifteen hours of overtime each week. The overtime provided a comfortable life for his family. He was proud of what he had accomplished.

Dad had a second heart attack on Friday night, October 1, 1965. I remember this one, as he moaned in pain during the night when it occurred. Mom was at his hospital bedside twenty-four hours a day. My sister Mary and I moved in with Aunt Ruth and Gram the first night.

Dad was prescribed nitroglycerin, which he was supposed to take in an emergency after he was discharged from the hospital on the ninth, but he never had a chance to take his medication.

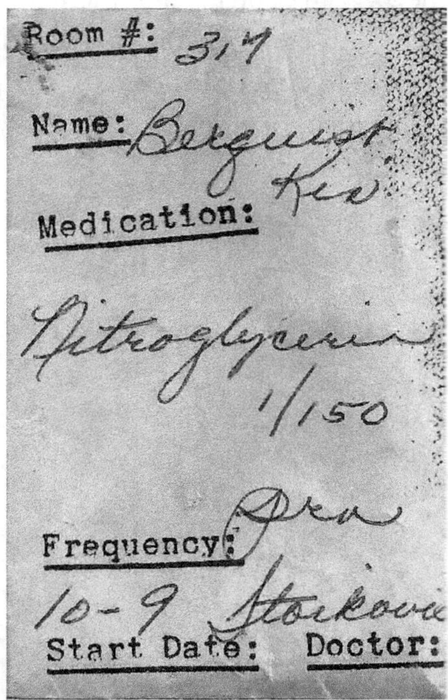

The tiny manilla paper envelop contained 150
small white nitroglycerin pills
Berquist Family Possession

On Sunday night, the four of us (Gram, Aunt Ruth, Mary, and I) were watching Walt Disney on TV when the phone rang. Aunt Ruth answered. It was Mom. The tears flowed. We knelt on the floor in the living room and prayed the Rosary. Dad was dead. Twenty-five years had concluded. He was sixteen days short of his forty-sixth birthday.

The HAWK-EYE

Burlington, Iowa

Monday, October 4, 1965

7

Kenneth Berquist

Mr. Kenneth E. Berquist, 45, 1841 Kirkwood, died at Mercy hospital Sunday at 6:30 p.m.

He was born Oct. 19, 1919, in Burlington, the son of Elvin and Louise Schmicker Berquist. He married Jane Roederer in Burlington, June 5, 1948.

Mr. Berquist was a member of St. Patrick's church, vice president of the Holy Name Society, and was a member of the Knights of Columbus, a past president of the Machinists Union and a member of the Railroad Veterans Assn. He was a veteran of World War II, serving three years in the Navy. He was a machinist in the West Burlington shops.

Survivors include his wife; two children, Michael and Mary Carol, both at home; two sisters, Mrs. Elsie Mack and Mrs. Donna Moore of Davenport; a brother, Richard, of Rt. 1; his father, of 2024 Summer; and several nieces and nephews. His mother is dead.

Services will be Wednesday at 9 a.m. (CDT) at St. Patricks church with Father Lawrence Vogel officiating. Burial will be in Sacred Heart cemetery. The body is at the Elliott-Lunning chapel where the rosary will be recited at 7:30 p.m. (CDT) on Tuesday. A memorial fund has been established for St. Patricks church.

Ken's Obituary clipping from Burlington Hawk-Eye Newspaper

Berquist Family Possession

Dad became an immortalized figure after his death by all who knew him. Like the Greek god, his figure sculpted in marble was idealized. Those who held tight to the belief of speaking no ill of the dead adhered to this idea. Please do not misunderstand me. In his absence, I have learned to love my father. But let's face it—he was a man. He was not perfect. He had flaws and faults. He endured all the embarrassing moments, of which all men are secretly ashamed. I love my father despite his human frailties.

Trying to find an adult who knew my dad well and could tell me what he was like was impossible. His misdeeds were immediately forgotten/forgiven when he died. There is no Saint Peter waiting for us at the Pearly Gates between heaven and hell. It is the people we leave behind when we die who are the deciders of our souls' fate.

Dad was sainted at his death by those he left behind. His sainthood made it extremely hard for me to write these words. I could not get anyone to tell me the unabashed truths about Dad. All I would hear was a cacophony of "He was such a nice man."

Over the course of my life, I have met children of veterans from World War II, the Korean War, and the Vietnam War who all told me the same story. They would say, "Dad doesn't (like to) talk about it." Even when pressing for an answer, they would be met with an angry scowl and a turned head. Were they ashamed? Or were they spending the remaining days of their lives trying to forget the events that made them who they are? A lot of us will never know. I count myself among those who will never exactly know who their fathers were.

Berquist Service

Services For Mr. Kenneth E. Berquist, of 1841 Kirkwood, who departed Oct. 3, will be held at St. Patrick's church at 9 a.m. (CDT) Wednesday, Fr. Lawrence Vogel officiating. Interment will be in Sacred Heart cemetery. Recitation of the rosary will be at 7:30 p.m. Tuesday, CDT. Friends who wish may contribute to a memorial fund in his memory for St. Patricks church.

Elliott-Lunning Chapel

A second services notice--clipping from Burlington Hawk-Eye Newspaper
Berquist Family Possession

Drafting this book has helped me understand Dad a little better. If he had lived as I grew into adulthood, I am quite sure I would have liked him. A Rosary was said at Elliott-Lunning Chapel on Mount Pleasant Street, in Burlington, on Tuesday, October 5, 1965.

Elliott Lunning Chapel, Mount Pleasant Street, Burlington, Iowa

The funeral Mass took place at St. Patrick's Catholic Church.

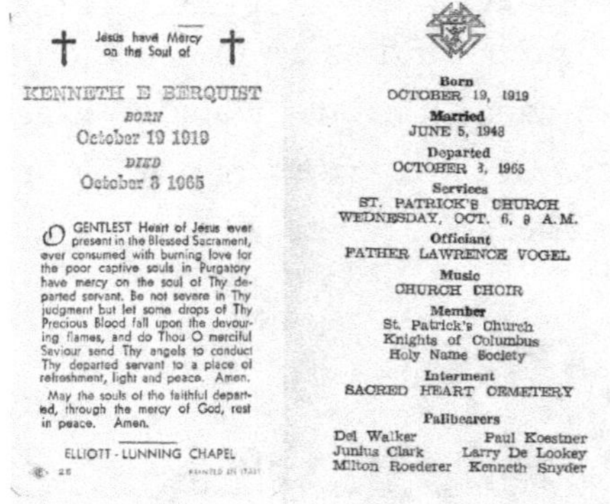

Prayer Cards distributed at the chapel and the
church
Berquist Family Possession

A Catholic funeral service, including a military rifle salute followed by the playing of "Taps," ceremonial folding, and presentation of the flag, took place at Sacred Heart Cemetery. He was laid to rest on Wednesday, October 6, 1965. Ann and Herb Hauser hosted a breakfast at the Arion Club after the graveside service.

Anne--Herb

We would be happy to have you join

us at Breakfast, immediately

following the ceremony

at the Arion Club

**Ann and Herb Hauser handed breakfast
invitations to attendees after the graveside
service at Sacred Heart Cemetery in
Burlington**
Berquist Family Possession

Mom had gotten a job with the CB&Q Railroad in West Burlington where Dad had worked since 1942 and Aunt Ruth had worked since she graduated from high school. Mom and Aunt Ruth were both transferred to the main railroad offices in Chicago in November 1965. They moved to Chicago, where they would live together for the next eight months. Mary and I lived with Gram at her house in Burlington on Mount Pleasant Street.

**The Roederer House, 1841 Mount Pleasant
Street, Burlington, Iowa, August 1966**
Berquist Family Photo

Burlington to Chicago was eight hours by train. Mom would come back to Burlington every other weekend on the train on Friday afternoon. She would return to Chicago on Sunday afternoon to resume the workweek on Monday morning. This grueling back-and-forth pace would continue until the summer of 1966. After the school year ended, all of us would move to Aurora, Illinois. Mom, with Mary and me, and Aunt Ruth with Gram left for Illinois and a new life.

I asked Mom about Dad's death many years later, and she told me she did not shed a tear the entire time. She said it was not until a few days after everything was over that it hit her. One night, sitting by herself in the living room, she held out her hand to hold Dad's hand like she had done countless times before, and he was not there. In private, she wept.

The End

ENDNOTES

[1] https://www.royalnavy.mod.uk is published under the Open Government License, and you can reproduce information from the site as long as you obey the terms of that license. Anniversary of the Navy's greatest modern triumph - defeat of the U-boat.

[2] https://en.wikipedia.org/wiki/Mid-Atlantic_gap.

[3] Crowsnest Pass Herald. 2016. "Clever Takes on the 'Something Old, New, Borrowed, Blue' Tradition," February An Old English rhyme dating back to nineteenth-century Lancashire, England.

[4] https://en.wikipedia.org/wiki/Typhoon_Cobra_(1944).

[5] Choron, Sandra; Choron, Harry (2010). *Planet Wedding: A Nuptial-pedia*. Houghton Mifflin Harcourt. p. 103. ISBN 978-0-618-74658-3.

[6] Pressbox quarterbacks, The Daily Iowan, Nov. 24, 1959, The Daily Iowan Digital Collection; Historic photos: JFK at the UI, 1959 – Digital Scholarship & Publishing Studio (uiowa.edu)

http://www.ibiblio.org/hyperwar/USN/Admin-Hist/
110.2-3rdND/3rdND-2.html

http://www.ibiblio.org/hyperwar/USN/Admin-Hist/172-Armed-
Guards/172-AG-2.html#AGC-Atlantic

http://www.ibiblio.org/hyperwar/USN/Admin-Hist/075-Ord-
nance/075-Ord11R.html

http://marshall.csu.edu.au/Marshalls/html/WWII/USN_Chro-
nology.html

https://en.wikipedia.org/wiki/Mid-Ocean_Escort_Force

http://www.destroyers.org/SMR/RegistryConfirm.htm

http://www.ussdehaven.org/typhoon_cobra.htm

http://www.usmm.org/ag/r.html

http://usslaws.blogspot.com/

http://www.hazegray.org/navhist/denver/logfeb44.htm

http://www.aviastar.org/index2.html

http://marshall.csu.edu.au/Marshalls/html/WWII_Recollections/
WilliamRoberts_USSBrackett.html

https://afatherswarstorynevertold.wordpress.com/2013/08/

http://goatlocker.org/resources/nav/trivia.htm

http://submergedtenth.tripod.com/housing/manordestruc-
tion.html#

http://www.aspengrovecemetery.com/

http://olive-drab.com/od_history_ww2_ops_bat-
tles_1943newguinea.php

http://usslawscontinued.blogspot.com/
http://www.usmm.org/casualty.html
http://www.convoyweb.org.uk/hague/index.html
http://www.ibiblio.org/hyperwar/USN/ships/danfs/APA/apa11.html
http://www.dobrinkman.net/lowndes/decklog/dindex2.htm
http://destroyerhistory.org/
http://www.archive.org/stream/navalhistoryoftr00unitrich/naval-historyoftr00unitrich_djvu.txt
http://www.armed-guard.com/honorpgs.html
http://cisupa.proquest.com/ksc_assets/catalog/11227.pdf
http://www.armed-guard.com/searchmil.html
http://www.navsource.org/archives/10/03/pdf/03011a.pdf

The first paragraph at the top of page 2 of this pdf file describes how I surmise Kenneth traveled from San Francisco to Pearl Harbor, February 26–March 3, 1944.

THE ORIGIN OF NAMES

Berquist = or Bergqvist, Swedish: name composed of the element's berg "mountain," "hill" + quist, an old spelling of kvist, "twig."

Per Olaf Bergqvist and Mathilda Jonsdotter Bergqvist immigrated from Stockholm bringing six children (four girls and two boys) ages two to twelve with them to America in 1880. One child, a son, who had passed away as an infant remained behind in Sweden. The Bergqvist's moved to a home at 1617 Market Street: at about the corner of Market and South Leebrick Streets in Burlington. The house was razed by the city in the late 1990s/early 2000s and remains an open lot on the corner now. Per and Mathilda would have six more children after they immigrated. Three more sons would die in childhood, but two other sons and another daughter would live on to adulthood. Mathilda had her hands full birthing children into her early forties. Per was a machinist who passed away at the age of forty-eight in 1891. Mathilda, a housekeeper, passed away in 1906 at the age of fifty-eight. Their son, Elvin Herbert, was parentless by the time he was nineteen. Discord, which had developed in the early years, was at the root of Elvin's decision to drop the letter "G" from his last name, thus distancing himself from arguments and misunderstandings amongst his siblings. Elvin became simply a "Berquist" early in his adulthood.

Schmicker = North German: name for a maker of whips, or a nickname for a harsh person, from Middle Low German smicke, "whip."

Occupational Surnames—more commonly found in German families than almost any other culture, these last names are based on the person's job or trade (Lukas Fischer—Lukas the Fisherman). Three suffixes that often indicate a German occupational name are -er (one who), commonly found in names such as Fischer, one who fishes; -hauer (hewer or cutter), used in names such as Baumhauer, tree chopper; and -macher (one who makes), found in names like Schumacher, one who makes shoes.

Koestner = or Köstner, German name from a Bavarian dialect word Köstner "granary administrator," "treasurer," name for someone from either of two places: Kösten near Bamberg; or Köstenberg, name for someone living on a "shelf"—ledge—in the mountains.

Roederer = or Röderer, South German: variant of Roeder. Variant of Roder. Name for someone from any of the places named Rödern, in Alsace, Rhineland, and Saxony; or Röderau in Saxony; or from any of various places in Germany and Austria called Rode.

After enlisting, Uncle Dick went to boot camp at Naval Training Center San Diego. He went aboard a Clemson-class destroyer USS *Brooks* (DD-232) toward the end of September 1942 in Seattle, Washington. The navy converted *Brooks* to a high-speed transport during this time. On December 1, 1942, *Brooks*'s classification changed to APD-10, and she moved to the South Pacific. *Brooks* served as a transport and minesweeper during the,

- Lae, New Guinea, landings (September 4–14, 1943);
- Finschhafen, New Guinea, landings (September 22, 29–30, 1943);
- Cape Gloucester, New Britain, assault (December 26, 28–29, 1943);
- Saidor, New Guinea, landings (January 2–February 17, 1944);
- Admiralty Islands landings (February 29, March 5, and March 19, 1944);
- Hollandia, New Guinea, assault (April 22–28, 1944);
- Saipan capture (June 14–22, 1944);
- Leyte occupation (November 18–December 4, 1944);
- Mindoro invasion (December 12–18, 1944); and
- Lingayen Gulf, Luzon, landings (January 3–6, 1945).

On January 6, 1945, a kamikaze crashed into *Brooks*, starting a fire. Three crew were killed, and eleven were wounded. She moved to San Pedro, California, on January 12, 1945, and was out of the war. Uncle

Dick's skills as a pipefitter came in handy. He worked at various navy bases in and around Long Beach until his discharge in November 1945.

- Colleen Pierceall, Palmetto, Florida--thank you darling for helping me and putting up with me during the five years it took me to write this--thank you for your deligent proofreading over and over again--thank you for putting your "female voice" to Chapter 15 "Jane Gets Ready", it is a much better chapter because of you
- Elaine Berquist Habiger of Farmington, Minnesota--thank you daughter for your proofreading and help with Chapter 15, it is a much better chapter because of you
- Donna Berquist Moore, RIP--I sure am glad you were such a good history keeper Auntie
- Jon Riffel, Burlington, Iowa--thank you cousin for all the leg work in Burlington
- Mary Carol Berquist Esch, Hudson, Wisconsin--thank you sister--the front and back cover of my book looks really great because of you
- Erin Esch Dennison--thanks for being such a great photographer, I've always liked this candid photo of me that you took
- Mary Pamela Hauser Olarte, Houston, Texas--thank you cousin for proofreading the "Hauser" passages with your Mom
- James Riffel, Milwaukee, Wisconsin--thank you cousin for proofreading the "Riffel" passages
- Lisa A. Kirby, PhD, McKinney, Texas--thanks for the advice during a seminar about remembering the five human senses

- Patrick Daly, Burlington, Iowa--thank you friend for letting me run things by you--thanks for your advice
- Jane Daly Seaberg, Doylestown, Pennsylvania--thank you friend for letting me run things by you--thanks for your advice
- Mark Behne, Burlington, Iowa--thank you friend for letting me run things by you--thanks for your advice
- Brett Jay Metcalf Facebook Page: Historical Photos of Burlington. Thank you.
- Sue Waltman Killeen, Inver Grove Heights, Minnesota--thank you for your encouragement early on in the process
- Doctor Philip Morales, MD, Cardiologist, Plano, Texas--thank you for your encouragement early on in the process
- Amanda Penner, Sugarland, Texas--for helping me to identify "Billy"--it was really important to the story that I find her and that you confirmed for me that she was the one I was looking for
- Mort Gaines, Fairfield, Iowa--thanks for the photos--Mort had pictures of buildings and locations that no longer exist, having the pictures helped me to tell my Dad's story
- All information about specific convoys was politely stolen from the late Arnold Hague Convoy Database with sincere and thankful gratitude to Mrs. Gill Hague. "https://www.convoy-web.org.uk/ugs/index.html"
- "A WWII Sailors Story," December 1944 through September 1945, LaMantia, Joseph, Scottsdale, Arizona, http://usslawscontinued.blogspot.com/
- For the description of "The Equator Crossing Ritual," Richardson, Keith P. (1 April 1977). "Western Folklore." 36 (2): 154 –159, "Ceremonial Certificates-Neptune Subpoena" Usni.org. Retrieved 2013-11-18.
- USS *Kidd* (DD-661) Floating Museum, 305 South River Road, Baton Rouge, Louisiana 70802. Many thanks to the tour guides working on this day who gave Colleen and I exceptional access to areas not normally on the tour. Your kindness made this story come alive for me.

- I'd like to extend my special thanks to Jane Sutter Brandt for her graciousness in allowing me the use of the Sutter name and photos in my book. Sutter's played an especially romantic role in my telling of Dad' story. The leads and advice you so readily offered are very much appreciated. Jane can be reached at: https://www.suttermedia.net
- I am especially grateful to my editor, Audra Gerber. My story is so much better because of you. It has been very easy working through you to accomplish this. Thank you for your kind words and enjoyable emails. I cannot help but think we share a similar love for our fathers. Audra can be reached at: https://www.my-creativedetail.com

A self-described nerd, Michael worked for technology manufacturers from a variety of industries for thirty-seven years. Michael earned an undergraduate degree in Business Management from the University of Saint Thomas in Saint Paul, Minnesota in 2001. Born in Iowa, he has also lived in Illinois, Minnesota, and Texas. He has settled in his favorite, living along the southwest Gulf Coast of Florida. Michael enjoys drawing and painting in his spare time. After thirty-eight years carrying a torch, Michael was reunited with his grade school sweetheart in 2006. He and Colleen have been together in love since and plan to spend their remaining years laughing, holding hands, and watching the sunset over the Gulf.